Dying Retribution

Anne Foster

ISBN: 979-8-218-69856-0

Published by Brayer-Scott Publishing.

Cover by Katie Jaspersen @ K. Jaspersen Designs

Dedication

To my little sibling that we never got to meet.

This one's for you,

Spencer

Chapter One

"Fix This"

"Fix this."

It rattled in Spencer's ears, cold and dark and deep as before. As much as he hated to admit it, he was pretty sure the bone-chilling sound would forever linger.

Haunt him. Maybe that was a better way to put it.

The words entranced him as he stared at the ground. It felt like his gaze would remain planted there for all eternity, away from his friend. He couldn't make eye contact, not when he was about to bring up everything he had buried deep inside.

Be it feeling, intuition, or something else entirely, Spencer was sure this was where his newest vision took place. The living room was set up to mirror what he saw, two dining room chairs next to each other atop a tarp. He glanced around the white-painted walls, though every time he blinked, he saw the blood that would soon splatter.

"'Fix this?'" His best friend Donovan echoed. He stood up to pace around the living room, running his fingers through his jet-black hair. "What does that mean?"

"I have no idea."

All he knew was that the unnatural, gravelly voice had returned, putting an end to its ten-year silence. A blood-soaked girl laughed in one ear, the phrase was chanted in the other, then...

That's what he was trying to remember: what happened afterward. With the girl came visions of people — people Spencer loved — dying. Sometimes, it was so vivid that he could blink and remember every gory detail. But when he needed it the most, all he could remember were the red splotches that littered the ground.

But why?

Who was a better question, but Spencer couldn't stomach it. "There was blood," he whispered. "That's all I know."

"Whose blood? Yours?"

Spencer opened his mouth to reply, but he could only manage pitiful gushes of air. It didn't take long for Donovan to catch onto that; he went back to silently pacing.

Silence. Somehow, it was comforting. It let Spencer lose himself in his thoughts, consumed in its embrace as he kept his eyes trained on the ground. He found himself keeping his arms close to his sides, the absent-minded gesture causing an ache.

A familiar one.

And he remembered that in his vision, he was tied up. Bound as he was forced to listen to agonized, heart-wrenching screams.

Spencer took a shaky breath. "Someone was with me."

"Who?"

The sight flickered in and out of Spencer's head, like a lighter starting to go out and extinguish any lead.

But the screams wouldn't stop.

"Fix this"

"Who was with you?" Donovan repeated.

Spencer closed his eyes and clenched his jaw, the painfully vague vision threatening to slip past him. "I don't know, man. I could barely see."

"Okay, let me start over. Just think as hard as you can, tell me everything that happens, whether it seems important or not. I'll remember, and we can make sense of it later."

"But what if—"

"I'm here." Donovan knelt down in a futile attempt to make eye contact. "Spence, it's okay. What did you see?"

A soft sigh escaped Spencer. He tried to force the screams to echo in his ears again, and with it, the vision.

Then he slowly opened his eyes, and the blurred sun blinded him as he looked out the window. Something about that — the way the light shone brightly and brought sharp pains screeching through his head — made everything come back. He said it all aloud, never to know if he was coherent enough for anyone other than his friend to understand.

"Fix this."

He remembered waking up in the living room, a dull pain in his neck. At first, there was just that and the pounding in his skull. But as he opened his eyes, a haze formed from the sunlight seeping in through the shattered window.

Duct tape on his face to peel at his lips, muffling every attempt at a scream. Tight, unforgiving ropes dug into his skin.

That's when the screaming started.

There was a heavy thud. Someone to the other side of him was thrown to the ground, too far in the distance for Spencer to see. He tried with everything he had in him to break away from the stupid rope and—

The attempt was useless.

Something about that person hurt; he knew he cared about them. He knew he'd do anything for them, but he genuinely had no *freaking* clue how to get over there.

A pair of cold, heavy hands rested on his shoulder, making him shiver as something whispered in his ear. The motion was so close that he could feel the small gush of air against him. It made him draw back, even if he could only manage a wince. A wince to try and get away.

Away from the cold, deep voice that *still* sent a chill down his body.

"Fix this."

The screams next to him stifled. The room muffled. His chair rocked back and forth with every useless attempt at breaking free. Spencer couldn't see much through the tears, but he could hear the racing of his heart.

And then the loudest scream of all.

The sun caught the blade of a knife.

Blood splattered on his face, mirroring the maroon-coated walls. Something fell, emitting a thud that drowned out the feral cries around him.

One last chant – Spencer knew he would remember it forever. Much like the sickening silence when the person remained there, a silent heap on the floor.

The phrase was all that remained.

"Fix this."

Chapter Two

Unspoken

The next day was sufficiently 'fine,' all things considered.

Spencer was a second-year med student, so, naturally, he spent a majority of his time buried in books. The rigors provided a much-needed distraction as he stuck to his regular routine. The back of the class was just as appealing as ever, he quietly finished his case studies, and he listened to a recorded lecture as he made his way through campus.

Now, he found himself doing one final chore for the day before he could head home. He stood in line at the dry cleaners to pick up his little sister's graduation sash, silently willing the queue to move along before his mind wandered too much.

Which, Spencer soon realized, was wishful thinking. He blinked, and before him he could see scattered remnants of the newest vision. They started long ago, after The Incident.

Or at least, that's what he and his little sister Kaylee called it.

Ten years prior, someone broke into the house with a knife while he and Kaylee were away. Their parents were there, and they weren't paying attention.

All Spencer knew was that when he and Kaylee got home that night, their house was a crime scene with more blood than paint on the walls.

"Next."

Spencer stepped forward and gave the worker a slight smile, vaguely recognizing her from high school. The color of her hair and the way she pinned it up reminded him of pumpkins and autumn leaves.

Alexis, that was it.

"Name?" she asked.

He frowned, embarrassed that he thought she'd remember. He reached into his back pocket and held out a wrinkled receipt. "Spencer Levign."

Naturally, not five minutes after dropping the sash off, he had almost lost his proof of payment. It took embarrassingly long to realize that it was just in his other pocket.

Alexis took it and punched something into the register, and like always, the brief pause made Spencer's mind wander.

He was fourteen that night. Apparently the attacker went for Mom first, nearly killing her. He went after their dad next, turned his back for just a moment, and Mom didn't hesitate.

The attacker's neck was broken. Spencer could still see him there, twisted. Mangled.

The Mangled Man.

Little did Spencer know at the time, after coming home to a bloodbath and a dead stranger on the ground, that he *would* see The Mangled Man again.

Just like the visions, 'haunt him' really was the best way to put it.

Alexis came back to Spencer through double doors, sash in hand. He hadn't seen her leave, but she returned with a half-smile on her face. "There you are."

He forced a grin in return, uneasy. "Thank you."

She nodded, and Spencer went outside. His blue car was parallel parked – albeit poorly – along the small downtown area. People passed him by, some holding hands and talking, others doing something on their phones. The small shops' exterior paint had long ago started to peel, the rustic appearance matched by signs whose letters were fading away. Spencer's eyes darted around the small town he called home, then he got in his car and locked the door.

He gave the lock a few extra clicks. It was a habit he was not proud to slip back into – the motion was ingrained in his brain, having spent the better part of ten years begging to resurface. And if memory served him, it wouldn't take long for him to start looking over his shoulder, too.

Spencer sighed and looked down at Kaylee's sash. It was his own, having been taken off and abandoned in his closet, but something stood out to him even then. In a sentiment shared by Kaylee, with its past problems washed away, it was ready for its own fresh start.

Perhaps being weirdly sentimental was a genetic trait. The two of them certainly shared it.

He reached into his back pocket and pulled out a plastic-wrapped pin, idly twirling it in his fingers. He gently took the pin out of its wrapper and looked down at the navy-blue paw print, their high school's Ridgeback logo. Its outline was black, lined with rhinestones or glitter or something that shone in Spencer's eyes. Maybe it was dumb – he could've gotten her a different sash and done away with the pin altogether.

But he would give Kaylee the world if he could.

Their mom was gone, and their dad wasn't sure if he'd show. Spencer couldn't give her their parents.

But this, he could manage.

He put the pin away and let the dark blue sash rest against his passenger seat. Then, he got out and walked along the sidewalk. He only knew about the dry cleaners because it was a couple buildings away from Larry's, the coffee shop he used to work at. Even though it was May and he hated coffee, hot chocolate was something he'd never say no to.

A familiar chime sang through the shop when he opened the door. They were little Christmas bells that his boss had him tape up after a coworker hung around back and kept customers waiting. Larry's was cozy as ever, a bit like a log cabin, with a small bookstore next to it. In high school, sometimes he would stop by after class to read there.

A familiar voice chirped, "Oh look! A brand-new customer."

Spencer smiled at the girl behind the counter. Her dark-brown, curly hair was loosely brought up in her hat, sending loose strands to cascade down her shoulders. She had a stain on her green apron from her first day of training, where she held a cup too close to the machine and coffee splattered on her. Being her trainer, he'd made sure she was okay and helped her clean it up.

But as her boyfriend at the time, he did so while laughing.

Spencer walked up to the counter and planted his hands down, purposefully making a loud thud. "Think I'm gonna venture out today."

"Lemme guess. Hot chocolate."

He exaggerated a toothy grin. "*Please.*"

"With two percent and at least half the whipped cream can."

Spencer scoffed. "I *guess*, if you're feeling stingy today."

Kirsten laughed and rolled her eyes, the light catching in them. They were big, black, and they shimmered every time he saw her. Honestly, it was something that always stuck with him.

It had been just over two years since they started talking again, six since he left her. She had a couple boyfriends since him, none too serious. He had tried the occasional dating app before moving on, and one girl in an undergrad class was nice enough, but it never was the same. Not as real, he supposed, was the way to put it. There were too many manufactured conversations and forced laughs.

Which only reminded him that he *never* had that problem with Kirsten.

She had her back to him; Spencer hadn't realized it at first. She asked over her shoulder, "Did you end up getting the new laptop or getting your old one fixed?"

He blushed, and he was glad she had turned around. She always took an interest in the most random things. "Just couldn't part with the keyboard. Its clicks are perfect."

"They make ones with the same keys."

"Well, *yeah*," Spencer replied, exaggerating his words. "But those keys aren't broken in yet."

She snorted and threw her hand over her face. Spencer's cheeks got hotter, and a bit of his brown hair moved in his eyes. He tossed it around, glimpsing at his reflection in one of the machines. When he and Kirsten were together, she'd mess with his hair – he never could get it to sit the way she could.

Kirsten turned and sat the cup down on the counter. "That would be eight even please, good sir."

"Thank you." He reached into his back pocket for his wallet. "Did you use half the whipped cream as I requested?"

"Three-quarters."

"*Nice.*"

Kirsten chuckled and put the money in the register. But her smile started to fade as she looked back up at him. "Hey, do you have a minute? I kinda needed to tell you something, and I'm about to go on break."

"Of course."

"I'm just gonna make myself a coffee real quick. Meet you over there?"

Spencer didn't need to ask what 'there' meant. "You've got it," he replied, raising the cup in the air. He walked over to the adjacent bookstore and sat on their favorite black couch.

The horror section was near his spot, and he always liked to look at the covers. Kirsten didn't usually join in; she thought the genre was too predictable. Instead, she always gravitated towards fantasy books or anything to do with romance. But Spencer scoured the shelves for the scary ones, and by the look of it, he had read all the ones they had in stock.

With distraction gone, the burn in his hands felt more prominent. It reminded him of when he and Kirsten were in high school, sitting on the couch with their coffee and hot chocolate regardless of the season. All their problems felt so overwhelming back then, but those seemingly world-ending struggles would dissipate as sure as the steam from the coffee cup: prominent at first, painful. Before fading into nothing.

Then The Mangled Man took that all away.

Kirsten sat down next to him. "See any new ones?"

"Nope." He took another sip and gestured towards the romance section. "Any rom-coms?"

"Sadly not."

"Dang. Fantasies?"

"One! Bought it this morning. If you think about it, this is basically free. I just had to make coffee to pay it off."

Spencer chuckled. She told him that exact thing every time she bought a book before or after one of her shifts. Texted him about it sometimes, too.

She uncomfortably shifted next to him. At first, he thought he had done something wrong – maybe she didn't have enough room or something. Then he realized that she stared at her coffee, deep in thought, and it wasn't as simple as giving her a bit more space.

He sighed, sensing that this conversation would be a difficult one. "What's up?"

"The school district called. They offered me a job at my old elementary school."

There was no hiding the huge smile that spread across Spencer's face. "Kirs, that's great!" He raised his arms and almost spilled his hot chocolate. It started to make him laugh, but she didn't return the gesture. "Congrats, I know how badly you wanted that one."

She sighed. "Thanks. But I also got a call from a school in California, and they offered me a job."

Spencer's smile wavered, but he managed to keep it. "Oh, well, it's good they were interested! How does a school district find out about you when you're out of state? Did they, like, see you when you were applying for your license or—"

"Maybe I should be more clear." She set her coffee down on the table in front of them. "They offered me the job that I applied for. I'm thinking about going there with Donovan and Ari."

Spencer fought to keep his smile, but he wasn't sure if it stayed. Those three were all seniors in college, set to graduate next month. Donovan and his girlfriend Arizona had big plans to move to Hollywood and make a movie together. Spencer had prepped himself to say goodbye to them, but he thought for sure that Kirsten would stay.

He looked down at his lap. "That's the one you wanna take, isn't it?"

"It is... Spence, it's not that I want to leave." She started to put her hand on his leg but hesitated and rested it on the couch instead. A selfish part of him wished she kept it where it was. "I just – I need something new. It's been this same little town all my life. Now my best friend is off to LA, and when I saw the nicest school in the district had an opening, I figured I should at least *try*.”

Spencer bit the inside of his cheek. It killed him, but he had to admit that he loved hearing about the adventures she wanted in the city. The 'big buildings,' that's what she'd always say. She wanted to see the big buildings. Spencer was happy for her and could never dispute that.

But, he couldn't *not* think back on the time when he was supposed to go with her.

Naïve thoughts like that cut Spencer deep, even then. She never found out about The Mangled Man, much like how she didn’t know that ever since The Incident, the ghost of the intruder was always around. Kirsten didn’t understand that the reason she almost died after his graduation wasn’t her choking on her food.

She didn’t know that if he didn’t choose to leave her, one day The Mangled Man would rip her away.

More than that, there was no point in admitting that he ran out that day or how hard he cried after he left her. She stopped by his house to check on him, and he said it was over. She didn’t get hurt again. Not physically, at least.

It worked, he had to remind himself.

He forced a smile. “Sounds perfect, then. I'm happy for you.”

“I just—” Her discomfort was etched in her features. She brought her hands down to her lap and looked at them, trying to hide it. Just like every time she talked about when he ended things. "I really do wanna be able to get outta here, and it seems like the perfect time, yanno?"

"Kirs, you should go. That's what you want." He forced a chuckle, and a stray tear trickled down his cheek. He hurriedly swatted it away, hoping that, somehow, she hadn't noticed. "Go see your big buildings."

She quietly laughed and twirled her coffee cup around. "You sure you'll be okay?"

The thought was nice. She always wanted what was best for him.

For a moment, the slightest part of him wanted to say no. That he made a mistake when he left, that he never wanted to hurt her. And he wanted to ask her to still go, but let him come with. Let him find a way to transfer or at least try. And if not, he could do long distance for a while.

But then the image of her in that restaurant, with The Mangled Man over her, flooded his mind. Still out there, the ghost of the man who took nearly everything. His head lay limp by his shoulders, his neck twisted and shattered beyond repair – sometimes he'd get so close, his matted blonde hair would brush against Spencer's back. It was Spencer's graduation when The Mangled Man nearly killed Kirsten.

And that memory silenced any attempt at getting her to stay with him.

Instead, he lied, "Don't worry, I'll be fine."

Chapter Three

Cries of Urgency

Spencer kicked a few rocks down the road, losing them to the night's shadows. The crickets around him sang their same songs, never shying away from their optimistic tune. Owls chimed over them in unison with the trees' branches as they swayed in the wind. The rocks crunched underneath his weight, altogether forming the chorus to the same old song he'd listen to when he needed to think.

Of everything he did to clear his mind, nighttime walks were one of Spencer's favorites. The habit was a parting gift from his mom, he supposed.

It started off as a small thing they'd do here and there, with preteen Spencer deciding to be angsty when she mentioned spending the time together. Though after The Incident, the memory of every "no" burned.

Then when he met Kirsten, he went home begging Mom to have a 'meeting' with her outside. Sometimes, Mom would have something she'd want to share, but usually, she'd let Spencer lead the way. Whether it was about what residency high school Spencer was looking into that week, the order of college classes he wanted to take, or what weird after school club he needed to try, he'd go on and on. And Mom would always listen intently, not a care in the world as she absorbed everything he had to say.

Spencer turned right at the stop sign ahead, amused by how second-nature the route was. They never really ventured away from their path, and the tradition carried through, even with her gone. The first time he went out alone, he thought he'd decide to try something different, assuming that going this way without her would hurt too much.

But that couldn't be further from the truth. When he did this, it felt like she was there alongside him, face adorned by that same smile as he rambled on.

Sometimes — well, most of the time, if he was being honest — he'd talk to her. And he swore her voice was still there.

He stayed towards the grass; Mom always wanted to be the one to walk closer to the road. He glanced over to where she should have been, and before long he could see her brown, wavy hair and her hazel eyes. Both were features that she had passed down to him, prompting everyone to tell him that he was, in exact words, 'certainly his mother's son.'

"Kirsten's moving," he whispered. "When she looked at her old school, I thought she changed her mind. I just wish we had more time, yanno?"

The crickets offered the only response.

He still liked to imagine what Mom would have said, had she been there. After a childhood of going to her for everything, he still felt lost without her. And watching her slip away was one of the hardest things he had ever done.

After The Incident, his dad was bad enough. Distant, obsessed with some random spot in the woods that he hadn't cared about beforehand. He had even set up his trailer there, claiming it was for his long-distance jobs, but Spencer knew better. But even then, Dad at least retained who he was.

Mom, on the other hand...

They never really got her back. And it only got worse. Despite no one else in the family wanting to talk about it, there seemed to be more to it than her processing what happened. She'd scream in the middle of the night; she'd whisper to herself for hours about how she couldn't do something. She'd apologize to Spencer sometimes.

Then others, she'd slam him into the wall – one time, even pushing him onto a glass table so hard he had to go to the hospital to remove shards from his skin.

She died just before his high school graduation. Spencer didn't know what happened, and his dad would never tell.

He thought back to the vision from the living room, the whole thing as vague as ever. "The Girl's back. I didn't see her, but that laugh..." He rubbed the back of his neck. "It was just like when she showed me Kirsten dying. We lost so much time."

But deep down, he knew that wasn't what scared him the most.

"Now that The Girl's here, what do I do if the ghosts come after her again?"

Mom would probably say that there was a way, he'd just have to find it.

"You're right, Ma." The trees' branches got caught in the soft breeze. He looked towards the ones on his side, away from where Mom should have been. "You always know what to say."

The waiting game hadn't worked before. The first visions were of his mom, and his dad thought he was still recovering from bearing witness to The Incident's aftermath — that the blood-stained walls messed with him, making him sleepwalk and have nightmares. He took him to the doctor to get tested for insomnia, schizophrenia, any diagnosis, really.

Then when Mom died, just like the vision promised, neither of them knew what to say. Visions of Kirsten started after, and he had hoped it was as simple as leading the ghosts away from her.

"This time, I don't even know what The Girl was trying to show me." Spencer shuddered. "*Who* she was showing me."

Whether it was Kirsten in the vision or someone else entirely, Spencer didn't know what to do.

"What do I do? I can't even see who's next."

Silence. He wasn't sure if even *she* knew the answer to that one.

"This time, she said, 'fix this.' I don't know why, she was never clear before. In the past, she told me stuff without actually telling me anything." Spencer scoffed. "She's throwing in more coherent phrases now, but her visions or whatever make way less sense. I miss the old way."

Mom would tell him that he could figure this out, just like last time. It'd just have to be done differently.

"You're right," he whispered. "You're right, Ma. 'Fix this,' she must've meant something by that, right?"

She definitely did.

Spencer nodded and looked up at the path for the first time in a while, noting that he was about halfway done with this lap. "When I get home, I'll write it down. See what she means by that."

The crickets' tune changed. It was more upbeat, somehow.

"Thank you for that. Really, I had no clue how to—"

"*Spencer.*"

He stopped in his tracks. The source came and went in an echo, but he could still hear its distant remains like it came from a tunnel. One that found its mark right inside his head.

Spencer looked around, spotting nothing. "Hello?"

The crickets stopped.

And the world was silent.

"Hello?" Spencer repeated, louder.

"Over here."

A crunch. Spencer whipped his head back around.

It stood in front of him.

In the distance, a silhouette stared at him, draped in a robe or dress. They chuckled, the sound grave and hoarse as it rattled in his head.

It chimed inside of him, not spoken, like The Girl always did. But this wasn't her.

Spencer said through his teeth, "Get outta my head."

But instead, they held their arm out, and the light from the moon reflected back at him.

Reflected against the blade of a knife.

At first, Spencer couldn't move. He watched in a daze as they held the knife like a butcher.

"Run."

Spencer took off before his scream registered. Didn't even realize it until he rounded the stop sign from earlier. His feet slammed against the gravel and behind him, he could hear a different pair follow.

So, he kept going.

And whatever he did, he didn't look back.

Spencer's heart pounded in his chest. It felt like something grabbed him and tried to pull him, his body leaning back as his feet propelled him away.

Towards home. Towards Kaylee and the place where someone was meant to be killed.

Spencer turned left, guiding the person away from her. He had no idea where he was going; all he knew was that his lungs were burning.

Something grazed his shoulder.

But he did not look back.

Through the burning of his lungs and the pain that crept up his neck, somehow, Spencer ran faster.

And the person's steps got quieter — until they went away completely.

He kept running, eyes darting in every direction. All he could see was trees and miles upon miles of branches that were darker than the night sky. The world was reduced to nothing more than a blurred mess of black as he traversed through the woods, no end in sight.

When he gathered the courage to look back, the person wasn't there anymore. Spencer slowed his pace just enough to look through his phone. He scrolled to Kaylee's name and pressed call.

"Pick up, pick up, pick up, pi—"

"Hello?"

"Get in your room. Lock the door. Turn off the lights."

"Spence, what are you talking about? What's going—"

His foot caught on a tree stump, and he fell.

The first thing he registered was the dull pain in his right hand. The next, how his fingers slipped when he touched it. He grit his teeth and looked at his bloody palm, not sure what he cut himself on.

But he stood anyway and held the phone to his ear with his good hand. "Just do it, I'll be home soon."

A few more steps brought him to a new clearing, where he looked up and saw home in the distance. He made a beeline towards his house, hugging his hand, but still gritting his teeth as every step sent shockwaves down his arm.

Spencer ran up the steps and threw the front door open, locking it behind him. He screamed in a loud, cracking voice, "Kaylee!"

Nothing.

"Kaylee!"

He sprinted up the stairs, tripping up a few steps along the way. Rounding the corner, he heard Kaylee's muffled voice through the door. He cried, "It's me! Are you okay?"

Kaylee opened it, her eyes wide. "Yeah, Spence, I'm fine."

She looked at his hand, and he followed her gaze. His dark grey shirt was covered in blood, hand still shaking. And his skin was pale. He could only imagine his face was just as white.

"What happened to you?"

But he couldn't answer her question — he could barely process it. All he knew was that she was okay, despite the person that followed him, and the visions and everything else that he was trying so hard to elude.

He stood there, arms at his sides as he looked at her.

Kaylee rushed forward and pulled him into her arms, allowing Spencer to rest his chin against the crook of her neck.

He couldn't stop shaking.

He was losing it.

When she was at her worst, Mom did this, too. She saw things, screamed, grew terrified of the world and repeated that whole process over and over again until one day, he never saw her again. And as much as he tried to hide it from Kaylee, after everything he got from Mom, he couldn't let her see that happen to him, too.

"What's happening?" Kaylee asked.

Mom would scream every cuss word known to man. He knew she couldn't help it; she had stopped being her a long time ago. The color in her eyes would go away, replaced with black. With a vast, endless nothing that made her impossible to reach, no matter how close she was.

Two empty pits where the once gleeful, lively hazel eyes used to be.

It was why he decided long ago not to cuss. Because it just reminded him of what Mom slipped into, what she hated becoming. To him, it represented what he was up against.

Kaylee repeated, firmly this time, "What is happening?"

But he didn't know what to say. She deserved better than 'I don't know.' Better than the same empty responses she had received ever since they were fourteen and eight, slowly losing their family over an 'incident' that they never could learn more about.

He'd have to get her an answer.

If she were there, and she was her normal self, Mom would have said that same thing.

So far, it was a broken promise. One that Mom had tried to keep, but ultimately couldn't.

Spencer would just have to do it *for* her.

Chapter Four

Rabbit Hole

Just as Spencer was 'certainly his mother's son,' Kaylee resembled their dad perfectly. Her hair was brown, not as dark as Spencer's, and her eyes gray. He could still remember how bright they were when she was a baby — light blue, something that they hadn't expected to change — and bald until she was around four. Spencer remembered when the first group of little strands of hair appeared on her head and how quickly Mom brought out the bows.

Now, Kaylee was eighteen. Spencer was in disbelief about that one. But she was one of the most mature people he had ever met. He'd told her over and over that he was proud of her, but his wording never really could do her justice.

After a while, Spencer drew back. Kaylee glanced at his shaky, bloodied hand, and asked, "Gonna tell me what happened?"

Spencer bit his lip. He didn't want to lie, but he certainly wasn't about to tell the whole story. "I was in the forest."

"What, why?"

"Got lost."

Kaylee squinted. "Why would you..." She hesitated, like she was calculating out how his story would work. "How? What does that have to do with your hand?"

"I'm," Spencer started, forcing out any words he could think of. "I'm hurting, Kaylee."

She nodded. "Okay, you're right. I'll get the first aid kit. See you in the kitchen."

Spencer didn't say anything else as she closed the door. In the light, he kept his eyes trained on his hand. It hurt and it was going to mess with him for a while, but it didn't look as bad as he had expected. He whispered to himself, "Spence, if this is the worst you get from whatever that was, you're fine."

His and Kaylee's rooms were upstairs. He couldn't even remember getting there; he was by the front door, then in her room. He turned, looking down at the sporadic red droplets on their beige carpet.

"Again, not too bad, all things considered."

He walked down the hall and rounded the corner. His room was at the top of the stairs, but instead of going to bed and passing out like he wanted, he trudged back down the steps. Since he was notoriously clumsy like Mom, he'd usually use the handrails. This time, though, he could only stretch his left hand out to hover over the wall. Just his luck that otherwise, he'd stain the handrail red.

Spencer walked through the entryway near the front door and hung a right to get to the kitchen, stopping himself from sneaking a glance at the living room. He approached the sink and turned the water on.

With his low pain tolerance, Spencer winced as he ran his hand under the water. Grunts escaped his lips when he added soap to the mix.

Not too long after that, Kaylee and her boyfriend Brett walked in. Brett asked, "Hey man, you alright?"

"I'm okay, thanks. Stings, but I'll be fine."

"Stop being so brave," Kaylee argued. "You could've really hurt yourself."

He bobbed his head to the side, unable to argue with that one. Even though he lost whoever followed him, he couldn't stop himself from looking out the windows. It'd be that way for a while, and that was one of the worst parts about this. After so many years, Spencer had finally thought The Mangled Man and The Girl were gone. He stopped looking over his shoulder and getting jumpy when the wind blew too hard and made the hairs on his neck move. But now, all over again, he felt something was there.

Always there.

Spencer sat down at the kitchen table and motioned towards the first-aid kit in Kaylee's hands. "Can I see that?"

Kaylee quietly handed it to him. He opened it and went for cotton balls and cleaner, gritting his teeth in anticipation. A pained hiss escaped him when he poured alcohol on the wound. He bandaged his hand carefully and stared at it, thinking about how much worse that could've been.

When he looked up, his eyes went to Kaylee. He took in how tightly she squeezed Brett's hand and winced at Spencer's every move. She rested her head on his shoulder, her brown hair contrasting with his blonde. Her cheeks were puffy, with a few stray tears trickling down.

Spencer and Brett shared a silent glance. Brett's eyes were bluer than usual, something that happened when he was upset. But he didn't seem too bothered by watching Spencer – it was Kaylee and the way he knew he couldn't do a thing to take her pain away.

Spencer asked quietly, "Can I have a minute with Kaylee?"

Brett let go of her hand and kissed her on the cheek. "I'll be upstairs." He looked at Spencer. "Glad you're okay."

"Thanks, Brett."

When Brett left, Kaylee slowly sat down next to Spencer. She wasn't looking at him. In his direction, yes, but not *at* him. She recoiled and made herself small, as if Spencer was one step from toppling over.

"I'm okay." He tried to close the first aid kit, but he couldn't grasp it right. Spencer nodded in a silent thanks when Kaylee helped him. "I'm sorry for freaking out like that. Shouldn't have panicked and called you."

"Please tell me what's going on. I'm worried that you'll run off and get yourself killed or—"

"Hey, Kaylee, I'm alright. We are so, so far from having to worry about that." He hesitated before whispering, "I thought I saw something, and I panicked. That's all."

"You're a terrible liar. Not nearly as good as our parents." She tucked her hair behind her ears. "Thought we agreed to never lie to each other."

Spencer sighed. They had, over and over again. After getting shot down by Mom and Dad after asking about The Incident, they quickly got tired of lies. Or secrets, or fibs, or whatever everyone decided to call them. As a result, the siblings made a pact to never keep secrets.

A broken promise. Spencer made a lot of mistakes in his life, but that wasn't one he made a habit of.

"I honestly don't understand what's going on," he said after a moment. "There's not much I could tell you anyway."

She looked at him this time – looked him in the eyes. "You know something and you're not telling me."

But the full truth wasn't something he was sure he could say, much less in a way that was coherent. It took him eight years to explain all of this to Donovan, and even then, there were gaps that Spencer hoped he'd never have to fill.

He told her, "Just know that everything I'm doing, I'm doing it to make sure nothing bad happens. And when I know what's going on — what happened to *Mom* — Kaylee, I swear I'll tell you."

Not that he could blame her, but Kaylee didn't necessarily seem happy with his reply. "Whatever it is that you need to do, please be careful. Can't lose you, Spence. I just can't."

He half-smiled, hating the pained expression that washed over her face. The dark circles under her eyes seemed to never go away. Spencer could still remember when she was born. He was six, and he looked into the hospital's nursery where she was getting checked out.

Dad had started to point her out, but among the babies in that room, somehow it was her. He fell in love instantly. It was like she knew he was there, because she turned her head, and Spencer swore she smiled at him.

Ever since, he knew he'd do anything to keep that smile. So, he said playfully, "Don't worry, alright? You're stuck with me forever."

"Now, now, let's not get carried away. You're not that awesome."

"Hey!" Spencer threw his arms out, pretending to be offended. "Not cool. I think *you're* alright."

"Yeah, but you can't take five steps without falling."

"You tried to burn the house down last week."

"I was hungry! I didn't know that the mac and cheese cup needed water."

"It legit *says* to put in water. There is a fill line and everything!"

Kaylee chuckled and rolled her eyes. "You're a jerk."

"But I'm right."

It was quiet for a few moments. Spencer was ready to tell Kaylee that Brett could come back, or she could go up to her room, whichever she preferred. But it didn't take much to figure out that Kaylee had more to say.

He gave her a bit, and then she whispered, "I'm sorry about Kirsten."

It didn't surprise him that she knew about the move. Through the years, she and Kirsten had become close. It started off as mutual jabs at Spencer here and there – something that he laughed along with – and grew from there. She was losing a friend, too.

Spencer's smile melted away. He looked down and played with his hands. "I'm gonna miss her."

"Spence, you've gotta tell her."

"Tell her what? She just—"

"'Deserved better,' I know. Whatever that means. You still have feelings for her, so tell her."

He sighed. He never told Kaylee the real reason why he broke up with Kirsten. Honestly, he kind of acted like their parents and changed the subject any time Kaylee asked to know more. He had to admit, as much as he hated to do it, he used their methods a lot.

It didn't have an easy solution – through the years, he had understood his parents' reasoning there. Talking this out wouldn't make their problems go away. If it could, he'd have run back to Kirsten a long, long time ago. Or rather, he never would've left her in the first place.

He whispered, "I'm just not good for her."

One time, he had said that exact thing to Kirsten. It was the only reason he could give, even if they fit perfectly — like two halves to the same puzzle, finally solved.

"Do you love her?" Kaylee asked.

Spencer almost scoffed at the question. When it came to Kirsten, he used to be terrified of the word 'love.' But after a while, that was the only one he could use; nothing else even came close to what he still felt for her. But instead of saying that, Spencer simply nodded.

She leaned forward. "Then, don't you think that maybe this is a decision she should be able to make, too?"

"I don't know if it's that simple."

He couldn't imagine putting her through all of that. Not again. After ripping off the band-aid, why undo all that and put it back on?

"Listen to me," Kaylee told him. "She deserves to know."

Spencer didn't respond, not at first. Because she *did* deserve to know. That much ate away at him for years. But it wasn't that he was scared she'd leave this time; he was terrified that she'd say it was worth it. Then of what that could bring.

"You know she does, too, you're just too proud to admit it. Tell her at Donovan's play or something. You've always been sentimental, may as well do it somewhere big."

Donovan's play, Spencer almost forgot about it. The final performance was just days away, serving as the last production before the big move to Hollywood.

Honestly, part of Spencer agreed. His sentimental side couldn't argue with telling Kirsten everything on an important day, near their friends.

Kaylee smiled. "Kirsten's wearing that purple dress you like. She already sent me pictures."

Heat rushed to Spencer's cheeks. "How do you know about that?"

"Your conversations with yourself in the shower are very loud."

Spencer chuckled, and he looked back at his hand while doing so. He thought about how much worse it could have been. And then his mind wandered to an even darker place: to what could have happened to Kirsten if he hadn't left. The thought of potentially roping her back into it...

He couldn't believe that he was actually considering this.

"I've gotta go back upstairs." Kaylee stood up and pushed in her chair. "Just think about it, seriously. Even if you're not ready to tell me why you really left her, I think you owe it to her. She misses you." Kaylee hesitated, then said quietly, "And she still wonders what she did wrong."

Then she walked away, leaving Spencer alone in the kitchen.

Alone with a thought that had never crossed his mind, now screaming at him.

Spencer scrubbed his face with his good hand. Of everything he could've done, he never meant to hurt Kirsten. And he definitely didn't want her to blame herself.

Not ever. She didn't deserve that.

Spencer got up and went through the drawers until he found a pad of lists. It was messy — he was right-handed, the pen felt unnatural in his left — but it was good enough. He was able to write down the words that he would carry with him everywhere.

Fix this

Spencer held the pen near his ear and clicked it a few times. He read the words back to himself, as if they would tell him more. More of the secrets and riddles behind them.

Suddenly, they weren't scary anymore.

He whispered them to himself, and something rose in his chest. Maybe it was hope, maybe it was doubt.

But so much was riding on those two words.

Chapter Five

Shout It Out

Try not to apologize to her too much. You're kinda weird about that. Love you tho!!!

Spencer looked at his phone and laughed. Before he left home, Kaylee had told him a bunch of times that, while talking to Kirsten, he should try not to say 'sorry.' He hadn't expected one last attempt, though.

It was Friday, the day of Donovan's play. He was pacing outside the theater's entrance, knowing that the others would be there soon – they had to be. Donovan had given him the time he was supposed to show up, and it was already ten minutes past that.

Spencer looked into the theater and saw cast members standing around. "C'mon, Donovan," he whispered as he bounced on his toes.

Figured those three would carpool; they did it all the time. They didn't live in the same apartment complex, but they were on the opposite side of town as Spencer. Often, when they all wanted to meet up, the three would drive together and meet Spencer there.

And usually, especially if Donovan was the driver, there'd be some waiting involved.

Spencer looked at his watch again. But honestly, some of that anxiousness was displaced. If Kirsten was wearing his favorite dress, he was wearing her favorite suit. Bulking up post high school made the suit a bit snug, but it was still manageable, despite how weird it felt.

There he was, trying to impress a girl he wasn't supposed to be with anymore.

He and Kaylee had talked about it a bit more, and of course he brought it up to Donovan, who shared all the same thoughts. The feeling that Kirsten deserved to know how he felt and that he was making a massive decision for her. That it wasn't fair, hence the 'sorry' that Kaylee wanted him to avoid.

Spencer made it to one side of the building before turning towards the other.

Then he saw Donovan's red car park crooked in a parallel spot behind Spencer. Donovan got out first, tucking his shirt into his pants as he slammed the driver's side door. He muttered something to Arizona and threw her the car keys. He ran past Spencer and accidentally slammed into his shoulder. "Sorry, dude!" he yelled behind him as he sprinted inside.

Spencer straightened back up, grabbing his shoulder and making circles with his arm. When he looked back towards the car, Arizona was locking it and Kirsten was walking up to him.

Wearing the dress Kaylee mentioned.

She had some kind of big, bulky flower bracelet on her right wrist, matching the one pinned to her hair. Her eyeshadow was darker than usual, and her other eye makeup — mascara and something else, Spencer couldn't remember the name — somehow made them look even bigger.

His heart skipped a beat. He could only hope his cheeks weren't flushed like they felt. Kirsten smiled at him, and he returned it. "Hey, Kirs."

"Hey, Spence." Her eyes widened and she motioned towards his hand. "Do I wanna know what happened there?"

Spencer shook his head slightly. "You really don't."

Arizona grunted. "So," she said loudly, stepping in front of Kirsten. "Essentially, Vannie fucked up and forgot to check something with the lights before the big day. Plus he was supposed to be here, like, ten minutes ago. Sorry he accidentally body-slammed you there."

Ever since Spencer and Kirsten's breakup, his relationship with Arizona was rocky at best. She'd usually keep her cool around Kirsten, tone it down at times with Donovan. If it was just the two of them, though, she wouldn't hesitate to show she was still upset with him.

Electing to avoid an argument on her and Donovan's big day, Spencer said, "Thanks for letting me know."

Arizona shrugged. Her blonde hair was naturally straight, but she had clearly flattened it out more. It caught on her shoulders and shined with her movement.

Her black eyes were made even darker with her black eyeshadow, and her lips were the purest shade of red Spencer had ever seen. "Passing along a message." She looked back at Kirsten. "Wanna find our spots?"

"Sure, how about—"

"Actually," Spencer interrupted, "there was kinda something I needed to talk to you about."

Kirsten raised her brow and looked at him. She nodded and then gave Arizona a glance, not in a dismissive way but one that told her to give them a moment.

Arizona bit her lip and whispered to Kirsten, "I'll meet you inside." She looked at them a moment longer, like she had one last thing to say.

But instead, she hung her head down and walked towards the stage, near where their spots would be.

For a moment, Spencer reminisced about when she was like a sister to him. "She's in a good mood today, huh?" he said quietly.

Kirsten forced a chuckle. "Sorry about that. I think she's just stressed. She wrote the script, like, five times. Then there were other rewrites here and there. Think she's kinda over it, ready to see how it plays out, you know?"

Spencer nodded, lost in thought. The words were starting to go in one ear and out the other. He had rehearsed what to say beforehand, but there he was, already drawing a blank.

"Seriously, though." Kirsten asked, "Is your hand okay?"

"It is. Actually, that's kinda what I wanted to talk to you about." He rubbed his arm with his good hand. "Well, indirectly, I guess. It's kinda related. Depending on how you look at it, I—"

"Understood, Spence. It's kinda sorta related." She said it gently and Spencer knew she was kidding, but it only made his face redder. "You know you can tell me."

Of everything he could do, he *laughed*. Because no, he didn't know if he could tell her.

The lights flickered.

At first, Spencer thought there was something wrong with his eyes. But Kirsten looked up, he followed along, and within that span of time, it was back to normal.

Trying to shake it away, Spencer continued. "Do you remember what happened with my mom?"

There was a screech overhead, as if two microphones were held together, forming an earth-shattering scream that was only stifled when they covered their ears.

There was a laugh. Gravelly, dead, and painfully familiar.

The sound stopped, and Spencer quietly asked, "Are you okay?"

Kirsten slowly nodded, eyes wide as she searched for the source of the sound. When she couldn't find it, she moved her hands away.

This happened before, it drove Spencer crazy. Whenever he'd try to talk to her, tell her what happened, it seemed like nothing would let him. He clenched his fists in an effort to not incoherently blurt everything out.

"My mom?" Spencer repeated.

Kirsten's silence made his mind race.

"Whatever happened to her is happening to me."

"What do you mean? She was killed in your old house."

Spencer sighed. "I mean before that."

Every one of Kirsten's thoughts plastered on her face. Etched in her features was concern, something he knew she had been trying to suppress for so long. Because she was always worried it would happen to Spencer too — she had said so when they were still together.

Kirsten's expression softened. "Spence, what are you trying to tell me?"

"When I left you, I—"

An overhead light burst.

Kirsten threw her hands over her head, and Spencer rushed to her. He looked up just in time to see the sparks trickle down, embers falling from above.

Their breaths were labored, and he couldn't remember the last time he held her like that. She took his arms and tightened his grip. "I've got you," he said quietly.

The sparks flew. One by one the bulbs shattered, sending the theater into darkness. A pure dark that was only interrupted by the light directly above Spencer and Kirsten, forming a spotlight on them.

"Are you okay?" Kirsten asked.

"I just wish things were diff—"

There was crying over the speakers.

Familiar crying, he could remember that agonized, cold, gravelly sob from anywhere. It followed him through his nightmares, never changing since Spencer left Kirsten in the first place.

The Mangled Man. He was close.

The final light went out, sending them to darkness.

"Fuck!" Donovan yelled from backstage.

"What is going on?" Kirsten asked.

Something grazed Spencer's shoulder.

The Mangled Man's final warning, that's what it had to be. Kirsten coughed, holding her neck.

So, Spencer backed up. "I can't."

All he wanted was to rush towards her and make sure she was alright. But it was as if she'd crumble at his touch. One wrong move and she'd be lost forever.

Against Spencer's better judgment, he said, "I'm sorry."

Those two words lost their spark long ago.

The look in Kirsten's eyes was one Spencer would never forget. Never *had* forgotten; he'd seen that defeated look time and time again.

"Of all people, I never thought you would hurt me," Kirsten whispered, still out of breath. "Then you hurt the most. And I don't think I can do it anymore." The look in her eyes told Spencer that she was one slip-up away from bursting into tears. Yet, it still took so long for her to finally admit this.

She was *always* patient with him.

Spencer looked down. "I know."

No sounds. The Mangled Man wasn't crying in the background, there were no more microphones blaring in their ears.

It was a deafening silence; neither knew what to say.

Until Kirsten sniffled and hurriedly wiped a tear away. Spencer could tell that she tried to hide it, but she couldn't. "I'm gonna go find Ari."

Then she left.

And Spencer saw nothing but black. It was an all-encompassing, suffocating darkness as he stood there, hands stuffed in the pockets of the suit that he had put on just to try and impress her. Its fabric was now itchier than usual, uncomfortable.

It only got worse as a sob escaped Spencer's lips.

Chapter Six

By a Thread

Even a novice like Spencer knew that as director, before the performance Donovan should be backstage. He should have been answering last-minute questions, giving pep talks, checking the system – *something*. But instead, he was on the steps with Spencer. Donovan was above him, his back to the wall with his legs stretched out so he could take up a row.

After their conversation, Kirsten ran to Arizona. They fervently talked a while, then Kirsten grabbed Arizona by the arm and led her somewhere else.

This was according to Donovan, at least. Spencer had stayed in stunned silence, refusing to let himself try and stop her.

"How upset was Kirsten?" Spencer asked.

Donovan threw his hands in his lap. "Dude, you don't wanna know."

"What did I do to her?"

"You gave her a choice, which is the best thing you could've done for her."

Spencer shook his head. He hadn't even mentioned The Mangled Man or The Girl. Or the new visions, or how he saw the man for the first time in years. The full story was what he wanted to give Kirsten, but she didn't even know half of it.

He ran his fingers through his hair, then flattened his hands against his head. "I practically told her nothing. That couldn't possibly have gone worse."

Spencer hadn't necessarily expected it to go *well*, but he really thought he would be able to tell her more. Even if it was the only thing he could think about, he wanted a distraction. So, he racked his brain for one.

After a moment, he asked, "How's the play looking?"

Donovan scoffed. "We don't have to do that."

"No, seriously, I wanna know."

Out of the corner of his eye, Spencer saw Donovan move. He slid down a few steps until he was next to Spencer. That's when Spencer noticed the bags under his eyes and the concern that cast a shadow over every inch of his friend's face.

"Play starts in ten minutes," Donovan said quietly. "I dunno, I'm not... excited about it, I guess? Not like I should be. Ari's been stressed about it and I've kinda—"

"You were *just* excited about it. If this stuff with me and Kirsten messed it up, I really am so—"

"If you say 'sorry' or any variation of it, Spencer, I swear." Donovan's voice cut out, and he buried his face against his palms. "You've been through hell."

Spencer stayed there quietly, eyeing his friend.

"It's okay," Donovan said after a moment. "Didn't say it right. I'm not *not* excited by this, but it seems... inconsequential at the moment. And Ari's been worried because she had to change something legit yesterday, and that stressed me out, and I think it's finally catching up to me. That's all."

They stayed there for a moment, in silence. This was a sharp contrast to the play Donovan was in his senior year of high school. He was one of the leads in the drama club — and in band, where he also always made sure to put on his own show — and he loved every bit of it.

Spencer hoped Donovan could get that love back. He looked at his friend and smiled. "It's gotta be cool, though, huh? Last performance."

"Yeah." Donovan sighed and looked around. "Trust me, I'm glad I did it. Don't regret a second."

Spencer nodded, satisfied enough with that answer. He looked through the curtains, noting how the lights shone and bounced off the bright floors. And the orange hue they gave off, how it wasn't pitch black there.

How they were doing the play at all, after the lights just went out.

Even after something — whether it was a mistake or The Mangled Man and The Girl themselves — shattered them.

He furrowed his brow. "How are the lights on?"

"Uh." Donovan said as he looked at his friend, "What do you mean?"

"The lights. Didn't they, like, shatter?"

"Oh! Yeah man, it was weird. Had my guys check and the bulbs were fine. They just turned off."

"Donovan, they *shattered*. There were *sparks*."

His friend shrugged. "It just happened, I dunno. I can't explain it. They went out and then got turned back on."

Went out? One at a time, casting a spotlight on Kirsten?

"And what about the sounds?" Spencer asked, absentmindedly letting his thoughts surface.

"Didn't have to do much with the sound system."

"Arizona said that you had to fix the sound board."

"It was a quick thing with mic alignment. I didn't have to change anything in the system." He started to stand, face neutral like nothing had happened.

Meanwhile, Spencer knew what he heard. He asked, "But how could that cause the mics to blare like that?"

"They didn't."

"Yes, they *did*." Spencer stood. "You dropped the f-bomb and everything."

Donovan's face got red. "So, I *was* that loud?"

He was being so casual about it, Spencer didn't understand. He figured his friend wouldn't want him to worry, but how did Donovan not know about the bulbs shattering and the mics blaring? It wasn't just a vision this time; Kirsten reacted, too.

"It was just the lights, man," Donovan said gently. "There were no sounds."

Spencer shoved his hands in his pockets, deep in thought. He'd have to ask Kirsten what she heard. It was so loud that it hurt her.

Meanwhile, Donovan hadn't heard a thing.

"I hate to do this, but I need to finish prepping for the performance." He looked at his watch. "It starts in like, five minutes, and I've gotta give my final speech."

Trying to force his doubts away, Spencer shook his head. "Good luck, then." He pulled Donovan in a hug, throwing in a few hits to the back. "Proud of you, honestly."

"Thanks, man. I'm glad you could make it." He stepped back, looking towards the curtain. "And thanks for being so understanding with Ari. I think she just needs time right now."

"Of course."

"Look." Donovan hesitated before saying, "Even if it's your genre of choice, there's a lot that happens in the show. Lots of fake blood. Lots of screaming. Given everything that's going on, if you need to leave, I get it."

Spencer waved his hand like he was shooing the thought away. "Not happening. I'm here for you, *Donny*."

Donovan hated that nickname. So, naturally, Spencer used it whenever he could.

"Ugh. Go to your seat. Bye."

The two of them laughed, and Spencer waved at him. Any minute, the curtains would draw and Donovan would say what he needed to say. Then he could come back and watch with Spencer and the others.

He walked backstage, weaving around like it was a maze. He hadn't been there enough to navigate it well, and it was too dark to see more than a few feet in front of him. But he knew a couple of turns would lead to one room of the red curtains that went to the exit.

As Spencer walked forward, he could hear a familiar tune. It was too far away; he couldn't quite place it. But it made him walk slower as he reached the final curtain.

He slowly pushed them to the side and entered.

The Girl was in the middle of the room.

She was lying on her stomach, her elbows propping her up as her legs fluttered in the air, innocent and carefree like a child watching her favorite cartoon. Her polka-dot dress was covered in dirt – or was that gravel? – and one of her matching pink shoes were missing. The braid in her blonde hair had matted long ago, framing her black eyes affixed to him.

She was humming something, a familiar tune. It wasn't upbeat like it was supposed to be; it was slow, almost majestic. And even though it was different, he'd recognize the song that he had never gotten the heart to delete from his playlist.

It was Spencer and Kirsten's song.

Spencer tried to bolt towards the exit, but she moved in front of him like it was a dance. She reached towards her abdomen, where the dark blotch on her dress was. Where the pool of long-dried blood was so bad that it looked like there was a black crater where her stomach used to be.

Lodged in it was a shard of glass.

He fell back, landing as a heap on the floor. And her humming only got louder as she walked towards him.

He shuffled away, but she moved faster.

Until she towered over him.

Spencer screamed. He leaned against the wall, the movement in time with the song's chorus. And the world muffled around him as he uselessly threw his arms up, knowing it would never help. Images played in his head, ones of Kaylee, and Donovan, and Kirsten.

And his mom. He thought about her, too.

Powerless, all he could do was look away as the broken memories played out before him. Meeting Donovan in the stairwell of their high school, all the times he looked in Kirsten's eyes and got lost all over again. He screamed at the thought of Kaylee being left alone in the world.

There was a tap on his arm, and his eyes opened up all by themselves.

The Girl brought the glass out, then jammed it back into her torso. With a smirk, she pulled it back out and did it again. And again. And again and again.

It fit every time.

All the while, she was at his favorite part of the song that just moments ago, he had loved.

He crawled across the room, wobbly arms barely managing to hold him up. She followed him, the sound ringing in his ears.

But she let him go.

Spencer got to his feet and ran out, tumbling through the curtains. And when he caught his balance, and he looked up, he saw the crowd in front of him.

He was on the stage. All were eyes on him, having made his way through the backstage area. Donovan was next to him, eyes wide and microphone in hand. In the midst of it all, the only thing Spencer could do was try not to fall off the stage he barely registered.

And when he looked back, The Girl was gone.

He couldn't do this.

Unable to breathe, he looked Donovan in the eye and mouthed, *"I'm sorry."*

Donovan made a face. One of understanding. Then he nodded and went back to his speech, trying to redirect the crowd's attention.

Spencer made his way down the stairs and raced to the exit. He could hear his heart pound in his ears. He slammed into the door, having not stopped fast enough. Then he turned again, towards the show he was missing one last time.

He sighed and looked at Donovan. His friend saw him, his speech coming to a close. The audience started to cheer for him, but he didn't smile like he usually did. Instead, he kept his eyes on Spencer.

And he mouthed, *"It's okay."*

Chapter Seven

"Help Her"

The drive home was a distant memory. One that Spencer couldn't recall even if he tried. Same with the walk inside, and the time he no doubt spent pacing around the living room with no clue what to do.

All he knew was that he landed in front of the couch, on the ground. Not that it mattered, but the details were hazy – like whether he had stopped short or missed the couch entirely. He rested his head on the cushion, eyes trained on the ceiling, mind flooded with an overwhelming sea of questions.

And no idea how long he stayed that way.

He couldn't stop seeing The Girl. Hearing her. Never in a million years would he have expected to absolutely hate the song she chose, the one that he and Kirsten had hoped to spend the rest of their lives listening to. But now, he couldn't get its newly haunting tune out of his head.

He had been avoiding the living room, a decision he made somewhere in the back of his mind without realizing it. Its innocent, cheerful memories had long since been replaced with the bloodied visions. The Girl humming, the shard of glass, the sight of someone getting stabbed to death there in Spencer's living room. He couldn't get himself to move, no matter how badly he wanted to go literally anywhere else.

It was hard to imagine his life before The Girl and the visions they brought; they started just weeks after The Incident, when Spencer was at his worst. Though most involved Kirsten and his mom, one involved Donovan.

One where he fell.

Spencer didn't know what he saw his friend fall from, but ever since, he tried to keep him away from taller places. As far as he knew, Donovan had listened and avoided going high up. Even if Spencer tried not to talk about it too much, he always appreciated how his friend accepted this new norm.

So many signs or threats from The Girl, and Spencer didn't understand any of them. All he knew was if she said it was going to happen, one way or another it would, unless he found a way to stop it. It took him a while to trust the visions, but now they were some morbid prophecy that Spencer lived and died by.

Because again and again, The Girl had told him that something would happen to his mom. Or rather, *showed* him. And he didn't listen until it was too late.

It was one of the first visions. He was fourteen, had no clue who The Girl was, and assumed it was all a bunch of pent-up images brought on by The Incident. Kid-him hadn't thought to try and look around, see where his

mom was, but he could remember the blood. The pool of
it that she was lying in, the way it splattered on the walls.
And the stream of it that trickled down her face, the life
draining out of her in an instant.

That agonizing vision was brought to life a week before
his high school graduation. He walked into his old house
and saw his dad crying, blood all over him. Mom was
already gone, and Dad had screamed at him to take
Kaylee far, far away.

Spencer had driven Kaylee home that day. She was in his
car finishing up a text to one of her friends. He ran back
out, too stunned to tell her what had happened. Then he
drove her nowhere in particular, having no clue what he
had just seen or what he could possibly tell her.

So, he didn't.

That was when he finally learned to trust what The Girl
had to say to him: when it was too late for Mom. Now,
every time he blinked, she promised there'd be more.
That these visions would come true.

And Spencer couldn't let them. None of them.

He looked towards the center of the room, the vision
flickering in and out like a mirage. Even if he hadn't seen
The Girl's gravelly, cut-up face in so long, it felt like she
never truly left. Like she was lurking, dormant, ready to
strike when Spencer was at his worst.

And she had found that moment.

He could almost see The Girl standing over that spot,
laughing at him. Skipping around as she either showed

him another vision or a 'trick' like the one she had just done with the glass.

Whichever she preferred. Because, like always, it was her call.

The humming, the laughter, it all came back. He felt The Girl appear behind him, her black eyes trained on him.

Spencer tensed his jaw. "What do you want?"

When he tried to move away from her, he could only stay rooted in place. Stiff as a board, his heart pounded in his chest, and all he could manage was to shift his eyes over to her.

"Help her."

It echoed, just like before. The dead, decayed voice rattled between his ears.

"Help her."

He blinked, and in and out like a candle, he could see another room. One with walls he didn't recognize. With shattered glass and everything thrown around in a heap, where he could only imagine someone had fought back. He opened his eyes, and it went away.

Above him on the couch, The Girl was staring at him.

His eyelids started to close, their weight heavy like a vice was tightening them. Light peeped in between his eyelids, a blinding star that was only stifled by the returning vision. He fought as hard as he could to keep it away. To keep his eyes open. "Please."

A door above him slammed, and he could hear muffled shouts. Then the pounding of footsteps as someone ran down the stairs. "Spencer!" Kaylee screamed.

There was no hesitation to it. She threw herself at him, and he let her. Neither of them paid any attention to the glass or the blood or the way Spencer could barely stand. And what he did, he never wanted to repeat.

He sobbed in his baby sister's arms.

Even if The Girl was gone, taking the horrible sight with her, he could still picture it. Could still see the outline and the way Kirsten's empty gaze stared up at the ceiling. Kaylee's shoulder was wet with his tears. He screamed into it.

His arm was throbbing, his hand ached, and he shouted until his throat felt raw. But none of that could drown out the feeling that The Girl was still there – he could feel her gaze, hear her gravelly breaths. It was in that moment that he realized he couldn't picture a life not spent running from her.

She was watching. Always watching.

And that could have been what scared him the most.

Chapter Eight

Lost Memories

Spencer didn't know how long they stayed there. They molded into each other, their still stature interrupted only when Kaylee guided him to his feet. And when she cleared her throat, ready to say something before ultimately electing to stay silent.

All the while, they were in the living room where they first agreed to never discuss The Incident.

It was one of the first conversations they'd had there: an agreement to leave the memories in the rearview mirror. The Incident's unanswered questions had started to weigh on them, but when they realized they could look it up, they promised each other they wouldn't. Mostly because Mom couldn't stop them anymore. She wasn't strong enough for that. And they couldn't take advantage, no matter how tempting it was.

But for the first time since that promise was made, Spencer wasn't sure he could keep it.

He thought about when they first got to the new house. Spencer was fourteen and Kaylee was eight. They were in

the living room, sitting on the couch, which was one of
the few things the previous homeowners had kept there.
In between rounds of thumb wars and dumb riddles that
only kids could come up with, they had talked about how
much of a snooze fest the adults were being. How Mom
and Dad and the real estate agent were going on and on
about 'negotiations' and 'budgets,' something that Kaylee
had asked Spencer to explain.

He did, running his thumb along the couch and paying
special attention to the coffee stain that served as the
only blemish on its faded grey fabric. Minutes turned to
hours as they happily revisited the mental image Mom
and Dad had given them of where their furniture would
be placed.

For a while, they had expected to be scared. This was a
new place, and it was only a matter of time before the
mysteries showed their ugly heads.

But, they didn't.

Spencer remembered when they hung around the living
room, their parents having just signed the last of the
closing papers. The couch and its coffee stain were gone.
They were on the ground, their backs to the wall. And
they were smiling, because they were home.

"We're here," Spencer had told Kaylee.

"We are."

No matter how unbelievably cheesy it was, it felt right.
The two of them had stayed there a moment, eyes
trained on the spot the movers would put the TV.

They were where they wanted to be.

And at the time, it was all that mattered.

Kaylee had leaned over and rested her head on Spencer's shoulder. All he could think of was how while the world he knew collapsed around him, Kaylee remained his only constant. That even as Mom slipped away and Dad travelled, they'd always have each other.

Somewhere along the line, he must have said that out loud. Because he could remember finishing it in a whisper. Then he had kissed the top of her head. "I promise."

Now, Spencer thought about that promise as he rested in her arms. He was standing there, his weight on her like she could fully support him on her own. If he were being honest, he was convinced she could.

She whispered, "I'm gonna get the first aid kit again."

The warmth of reassurance dissipated as Kaylee left, and Spencer straightened back up. He looked back at the broken window and its shattered remnants on the ground. The stubborn part of his brain wouldn't stop thinking about when Mom would do that, too. It reminded him over and over, no matter how many times he begged it to go away.

Spencer walked back to the kitchen table and nodded in silent thanks when Kaylee slid the kit to him. He didn't think much of it as he cleaned his arm up and held paper towels to it. Luckily, it didn't seem to have cut deep enough to need stitches.

Kaylee sat across from him. "I think you should talk to Dad."

With how lost in thought he was, he hadn't realized he had picked up the rubbing alcohol. He almost dropped it. "What?"

"I mean, Spence, you just smashed a window. And your eyes, they…" Kaylee sighed. "Maybe Dad will know what happened to Mom."

"Thought we were trying to never mention it."

Kaylee shrugged, and the motion showed how tired she was. It looked like she was holding up a ton of bricks instead of her own shoulders. "You're more important than some stupid promise."

Spencer weakly smiled at her, knowing she was right even if he was too stubborn to voice it. "Would you wanna know?"

Kaylee looked down, her eyes unfocused. After a moment, she said softly, "No, I don't think I would."

"Okay."

He couldn't blame her. Spencer didn't really want to part with the blissful obliviousness either.

"Be careful," Kaylee told him.

"Of course," he replied. "How about I get us dinner and then I call him?"

She chuckled. "Anything to stall?"

"'Anything to stall.'"

Kaylee smiled, and no matter how many times he saw it, the sight always made him feel better. Maybe it reminded him of when she was younger, when, looking back, all their concerns were trivial. And they had Mom and Dad, Spencer was just her cool older brother who she went to for advice or help with homework or boy troubles.

He smiled back, knowing that she had that memory to look back on too. "Pizza sound good?" he asked.

"Well, duh."

They always got the same thing, which, admittedly, was the order that Spencer liked. They used to get a pizza where one half would have his toppings and the other would have hers, but then she tried his and ever since, they stuck with it.

Alfredo sauce, not that red stuff. With extra cheese, and spinach buried underneath so they could forget it was there. Then if he was feeling extra healthy, he'd splurge and ask them to throw some grilled chicken on it.

"Yes or no?" he asked, referring to the chicken. There was no need to clarify to her what he was talking about.

"Good question, but no." Kaylee motioned upstairs. "Brett doesn't eat meat."

Spencer nodded. "I'll go ahead and order it."

He got up and pushed in his chair. He went to turn away, and Kaylee grabbed his arm. "I don't necessarily want to know, but if you need me, I'm here. Just remember that, alright?"

"I know, Kaylee. And I appreciate it."

She let go of Spencer's arm, and he started up the stairs. No mention of what he was going to do before the pizza, no mention of The Incident. His phone was heavy in his pocket, the screen cracked from his bout with the window. Instead of imagining how he'd pay for that, he prepped what he could possibly say to Dad.

Ask Dad, then he could get the pizza. Ask Dad, then he could get the pizza.

But Spencer didn't know how to start that first part.

Chapter Nine

Begin Again

After hiding away in his room and going to his desk, Spencer's thumb hovered over the call button. He'd tell himself this time would be it, but then he'd hesitate and draw back from the phone. The endless loop would repeat itself until he got distracted by something he wanted to check — usually random texts or social media posts he didn't care about — then he'd go back to square one.

Talking to Dad was easy, that wasn't the problem. They checked in on each other often, usually with Spencer updating Dad on Kaylee and asking when he'd come home. Then Dad would divert the topic back to Spencer. How med school was going, his friends, that stuff. Spencer wouldn't have much to say beyond 'it's going well, I guess,' and that's when the conversations would start to vary.

Dad tried, and Spencer loved that.

It just didn't feel as effortless as it used to, and forcing it only stung more.

Spencer pressed call, not realizing it happened until he heard the dial. He probably twitched and his finger hit the mark. A small part of him hoped his dad wouldn't pick up.

"Hello?"

"Hey, Dad!"

Spencer grit his teeth. Why did he sound so dang cheerful?

His dad chuckled on the other side. "Hey, Spence. What's up?"

There was no response, not at first. Spencer ran his fingers along his desk, drawing a blank as he tried to talk to the man on the other side.

"You there?"

He shook his head, electing not to try and figure out how long he sat there in silence, his mouth hung open.

It wasn't Dad. It was The Incident. "Dad," he said after a moment, "I-I need help."

There was a sigh of relief on the other line, the last sound Spencer had expected to hear. "Oh! Son, you got me worried there, you know that? Money, I'm guessing? I was gonna give you and Kaylee something for her graduation, but I can transfer some now if you need."

"No, like..." Spencer rubbed the back of his neck. "The Incident."

As if Dad was supposed to know what 'The Incident' meant. It was a dumb little nickname he and Kaylee had given it ten years ago.

But after a moment, Dad said quietly, "I thought you and Kaylee had finally given up on that."

Spencer's eyes widened. "How did you know we call it that?"

"You and Kaylee talk a lot. It's sweet, but you two aren't too good at keeping stuff to yourself."

Honestly, Spencer was glad it was a joint effort. He didn't want to wonder what Kaylee had said to Dad, and he'd have hated to have accidentally blabbed. If Dad knew that they thought about it enough to create a name for it, maybe he would be okay with telling him — after all, Spencer wasn't a kid anymore.

Spencer said, "All I know is that some guy broke in and attacked you and Mom ten years ago — that's what she and I call 'The Incident' — and someone killed her right before my graduation. But, beyond the basics, what happened?"

"Look, Spence, your mother and I told you and Kaylee everything you needed to know. He's gone, he can't hurt us anymore."

'Gone.' Spencer almost scoffed at that word and the painful insincerity behind it. "Please tell me. Something is wrong. I think he's after Kirsten, and he has this girl with him."

"He is dead."

Dad's voice was different, almost questioning, pleading. It didn't have the assertive bite to it that had just laced every word.

"Well, something happened," Spencer insisted. "I am genuinely worried for Kirsten, and all this can't be good for Kaylee."

"I know you mean well, I really do. But she's *my* daughter, alright? And for both of you, your mother and I agreed long ago that we needed to bury this with Au—" Dad grumbled. "It's done, okay?"

But Spencer couldn't ignore that. "Bury it with *who*?"

His dad sighed. "I love you, Spencer. And Kaylee. And I loved your mother so, so much." There was silence on the other line before he said gently, "You were always your mother's son. Curious like her, too. Just know that what I'm not telling you, you don't know for a reason. It can't help you, so for your sake and your sister's, don't go digging."

Spencer didn't know what to say. How could he not try and find out more? Every day was a fight to not just type it into some search engine.

"Don't go digging," Dad repeated. "Please. For me."

But there was still so much. How was he supposed to get rid of ghosts if he didn't even know who they were?

"For your mother."

Spencer pursed his lips as he let out a slow nod, knowing it wasn't something Dad would ever see. It'd take something in Spencer to say the words, something he wasn't sure he had.

But it was a promise he had made to Mom.

How could he ever go and break the last one he made to her?

He cleared his throat and whispered, "I promise."

There had to be a different way. A way past the burning desire he had to figure everything out. With the whole thing such a mystery to him, of course he couldn't come up with any solution other than solving it.

But there had to be a way.

Dad smiled. Spencer could hear it in his voice. "I love you, kid."

"I love you, too."

"Tell Kaylee I said hey, alright? I'm gonna try to make it to her graduation."

"I will, and please do." Spencer hesitated before saying, "She misses you."

It was quiet, the only sound was their breathing. Spencer didn't know what Dad was thinking, but that wasn't much different than usual, he supposed.

"Miss you too, Spence."

The dial tone rang out, and he slammed his phone down on his desk.

His aching head blurred the sight of his fingers as they idly brushed along his desk. He had half a mind to cave and grab his laptop, figure everything out right there. But it felt like Mom was somehow both standing over his shoulder and staring him right in the face every time he so much as twitched towards it.

Someone knocked on his door, jolting Spencer out of his thoughts. The movement shot a new wave of pain to his head.

"What?" he snapped, gritting his teeth before he finished the word. He sighed and rubbed his temples with both hands, painfully familiar with the outburst his headaches could cause. "I'm sorry," he said after a moment. "Come in, it's unlocked."

The door softly opened and closed, allowing Brett to come inside. His blonde hair was tussled, nearly covering his eyes. With his brow furrowed, Brett said, "Sorry, I didn't mean to come at a bad time."

"It's not you, I didn't mean to snap like that. It was my dad."

"Oh!" Brett perked up in a mere moment. "Yup, that'll do it."

Spencer smiled weakly. Brett was never too fond of his and Kaylee's dad. Of course, as much as he loved Dad, Spencer couldn't necessarily blame Brett. To him, he was the guy who left his girlfriend in the care of an eighteen-year-old pre-med who had less than zero clues of how to raise a preteen.

"What's up?" Spencer asked.

Brett stiffly sat on his bed. "I wanted to check in. Kaylee said you were okay, but I guess I just needed to make sure. Not that I didn't trust her, but yanno."

Though he didn't admit it, Spencer understood that more than he cared to admit. He held out his arm, where small specks of red bled through the bandage. "Stings but I'll be fine."

"She said you were upset. I'm more worried about, like, mental."

Mental. What Spencer was trying to avoid.

"I have no idea what I'm doing, Brett."

"With what?"

"With literally anything. I just tried to tell Kirsten that I never meant to hurt her. But she looked like she was seconds from crying, and she acted like I could magically give us back those six years that we lost. And Kaylee... I can help her, I know I can, but I need help too. Meanwhile, there's one person left who we should count on, and he doesn't even know if he'll make it to her graduation."

Spencer faintly remembered calling Kaylee to tell her about Kirsten and leaving early. Even if he couldn't remember what he told her – and more, didn't know what Kaylee could have repeated – telling another person what happened made the whole thing seem more real.

Hearing it out loud, he realized just how insane the story was. He wouldn't have blamed Brett if he got annoyed or didn't believe him. But instead, the boy's eyes softened. Patience and sympathy laced his features.

"You know she thinks the world of you, right?"

"Well yeah, but I'm her brother. I think the world of her, too."

"No, I mean, like…" Brett sighed and leaned forward. "You can't do wrong by her, she'll never see it that way. You're, like, her superhero or something. And when people ask about her parents, she doesn't say much about them. Instead, she goes off about how she has the best brother in the world. How you're caring for her, going through med school, and managing all this other stuff."

A smile crept across Spencer's lips. He had never known that Kaylee talked about him like that. Always figured that their very successful dad or caring-beyond-belief mom would be her topic of choice. Not him.

Brett said gently, "Don't worry about her. If there's anything you can do to help yourself, just throw that thought away. Go and…" He made a motion like he was throwing something away, then brought his hands out to mimic an explosion. Finished it off with a *poof*.

Somehow, Spencer felt better. Well enough to chuckle at how cinematic Brett was about it and how he looked genuinely pleased with his joke. Growing up, he had told Kaylee over and over again that there was no one in the world good enough for her.

But maybe there was one exception.

"Thanks, man," Spencer said. "Seriously, you helped."

"Hey, I get it. I've got three little siblings. All brothers, but still. And the youngest, Tyler, bro, he is so hard to keep track of. He's seven and he acts like a whole adult when he talks back, but I'd legit do anything for him."

Even if Spencer had potential to be the most overbearing brother in the world, it felt good to be reminded that he wasn't the only one. Donovan was an only child, he couldn't relate. And Kirsten was the youngest. Arizona had one older brother, but they were close in age and didn't talk much.

So, it was Brett, and he was enough.

"I get you, I really do." Spencer motioned towards the door. "Now get outta here so I can get us pizza."

"Oh, awesome! Just remember I don't—"

"Don't eat meat, I know." He pointed at Brett like it was a warning. "But I'm asking them to put extra spinach this time."

Brett chuckled and rolled his eyes. "You do you."

"I shall."

Then Brett opened the door and hesitated near the doorway. "You really are doing just fine."

'Just fine.'

Most days, he felt he didn't come close to that, not for Kaylee or with life in general. Not after chasing the person he loved out of his life and living off his dad's paychecks. But if he was doing 'just fine,' that'd be enough. At least for the time being.

"So are you." Spencer smiled. "Thank you for making my sister happy."

"And thank *you* for making my girlfriend happy."

Brett gave Spencer one last look before getting up and going to the door. He slowly closed it behind him, leaving Spencer in the comforting silence once again.

Spencer turned back towards his desk and opened his laptop, ready to take a second to stop worrying about the ghosts and his parents and all the questions that his mom would beg him not to ask. There was a way, and he'd find it with time.

For the moment, the paper on his left was calling his name. Spencer brought it closer, eyes trained on the two words written in bold.

Fix this

He reached into his drawer and grabbed a pen, twirling it between his fingers. He idly bit his lip as he tried to stop the image of Kirsten from resurfacing.

Just one night. Then Spencer could worry about it all he wanted.

But first, he wrote the next couple of words down. The words, spoken in a gravelly, dead voice that still vibrated between his ears.

Help her

He read back the two phrases, unable to make sense of any of it.

Fix this

Help her

But soon, he would. He promised himself that, just as sincerely as he had once promised Mom.

Just one night.

Chapter Ten

Hanging Above

It felt like Mom was there.

More than usual, at least. After they finished their pizza, Spencer was exhausted. He spent the next few hours finishing up reports and case studies for clinicals the next day, mostly able to drown himself in his work instead of everything that was going on.

Usually, he was such a perfectionist with his assignments. But while he was still confident he did well, he hadn't checked them as much as he would have liked. He was too ready to shuffle to his bathroom, his eyes trying to droop shut. Their dark hazel irises laced with emerald green when he was tired or upset, or when the light hit them just right. So, when he leaned over his sink to try and take his contacts out, his eyes were earthy green.

His glasses were on his nightstand. He usually tried to read at least one chapter of whatever book he was working on before falling asleep, but as soon as he was under the covers, he knew that wouldn't happen. He had nuzzled up and expected to doze off in a matter of seconds.

That was an hour ago.

Now, as he tossed around in his bed, his usually soft mattress felt lumpy. Not that it was, but he couldn't find a comfortable spot.

And his brain wouldn't shut up.

Whispers. They were all he heard. Ones that wouldn't go away.

Some of the phrases repeated, turning into chants in the background. But when he'd get used to them enough to doze off, a new one would start the process all over again.

The voice. It was always the same.

"Spencer."

"You shouldn't be here."

"Run. You need to run."

He whispered, "Please stop."

"Get outta there."

"Listen."

"Get out of my head," he said through his teeth.

"Run. You need to run."

He slammed his hand against the mattress. "From what?"

"Run. You need to run."

"Run. You need to run."

"Run. You need to run."

"RUN. YOU NEED TO—"

"Shut up!"

His eyes shot open, sending him into the endless darkness of his room. Labored breaths filled the air as Spencer looked around, seeing nothing but black and the silhouettes of his furniture.

A body in front of his door.

Spencer yelped and ripped his phone away from the charger. He tried to keep his eyes on the figure, but his shaky fingers were so unstable that he couldn't find the freaking flashlight button until he caved and glanced down for a second.

When he looked up with the light, the figure was gone.

His heart raced in his chest. Stiff motions brought him to his feet, his joints cracking as he stood up. All he could hear was his own breathing.

Then creaking.

A little girl's laughter.

And the hallway light turned on.

Spencer grabbed his glasses, his hands so unsteady that he almost poked his eyes with their arms. His heavy feet carried him closer and closer to the sound.

"Run. You need to run."

He opened the door.

There was crying downstairs.

Not The Mangled Man's. It wasn't that cold, dead voice that made it feel like sandpaper was being scraped against Spencer's ears. It was soft, heart-wrenching.

Familiar.

Spencer followed the sounds, wincing as the floor creaked with every step. His hand squeaked against the rail, his bare feet melted into the carpet and tried to sink him into it. And part of him wanted it to. Wanted to not know.

But he kept going. He couldn't stop.

Physically, he couldn't. Like a band was pulling him down, his feet had a mind of their own.

And Spencer couldn't breathe.

"Run. You need to run."

One foot in front of the other. Slowly.

The cries got louder.

Spencer's feet met the cold, hard, downstairs floor. They turned him right, towards the living room. Where the sobs started and carried over into the main entrance of his home, the sounds ricocheting off the walls over and over again.

It was a trance. It wasn't just *like* a trance; he couldn't think of another way to describe it.

Out-of-body.

All he wanted to do was listen to the voice in his head and get away from there, but he couldn't. Something stood over him, and when he listened hard enough, he could hear breathing. Right next to his ear, so cold it made him shiver.

There was a bang. A bang and more crying. And his feet kept taking him right to it. The path led him to the living room, and when he got there, he found himself rooted in place.

"Ma?"

She was on the couch, doubled over. The window wasn't shattered, glass wasn't littering the ground. But she was there, her hands covering her face as she rocked back and forth. She screamed and cried into them, sending gut-wrenching sobs throughout their house.

And it was like when he was a kid.

He recognized the sight from when he was sixteen. The first time Mom had screamed at him, the first time her hazel eyes were replaced with black, endless pits. She and Spencer had just gone on a walk, Spencer having been so excited because Kirsten said he was 'cute.' Innocent things like that were fresh jabs now.

He had gotten home late, walked with Mom, told her everything. Then he went upstairs, leaving Mom alone in the living room. Next thing he knew, he heard screams and cries that still stabbed Spencer right in the chest.

"Ma," he repeated.

He walked over to her of his own volition. That night, he had hesitated, but there was a chance he could help her this time. Hope swelled through his body, forming a haze that swallowed him whole.

Hope that he could be fast enough.

Her cries grew louder.

Spencer reached for her. "Ma?"

He was next to the coffee table, so close that if he leaned forward, he could touch her. Her sobs echoed in his ears; his quaking hand jittered with every beat of his heart. Finally, he put his hand on her shoulder.

Her skin crumbled underneath his touch.

The cries silenced.

"Ma?"

She jolted up and screamed, toppling Spencer to the ground.

Her decayed face was white, popping against the black dots that used to be her eyes. And she towered over him, still screaming, sending this mist of what felt like death and decay into the suffocating air. She leaned over, a predator stalking its prey, her shadow cascading over him.

And somewhere between the cries, past the screams that were even louder than the ringing in his ears, he could still hear the pleas.

"Run. You need to run."

Spencer let out a scream so fast he barely processed it before shuffling to his feet. He angled his body to the left, anywhere that wasn't directly in front of her. Then when he turned...

A bloodbath. Just like when he was a kid.

She was lying on the ground, covered in blood that painted the walls. Spencer collapsed back to his knees, feeling the warm pool soak his pants. Tears dripped down his face.

And a speckle of blood trailed down hers.

He'd have given *anything* to never see this again.

It burned, just like it always had. Spencer held his shaky hands out and clasped both sides of her face.

He wasn't fast enough, he had *never* been fast enough.

His face twisted and he let out a sob of his own — an ear-piercing one that traveled around the room. And as he studied her face, his lip quivered.

She hadn't looked that calm in so long.

A tear landed on her cheek as he rested his head against hers. He apologized to her, cried for her, said things to her that he couldn't perceive. He tried to understand the words that were escaping his own lips.

But he couldn't.

When he closed his eyes, the light went out. He knew what was happening before it even finished.

Because it always went this way.

He opened his eyes again, and she wasn't there anymore. The walls weren't covered in blood, the only breeze was the idle one that seeped in from the outside world. The cold wind was biting him, trailing in from the broken window that he had yet to replace. He was on the ground, his arms sprawled out with no one in them.

Because the person who was supposed to be there had died six years ago.

And Spencer didn't know why he could still see her.

He moved his arms, breaking his hold on the person who wasn't even there. "I'm so sorry," he whispered to the empty space, his voice lacing with tears. Spencer hugged himself and stayed on the floor, no clue why the voices had found their way right back to him.

He was losing it.

Just like Mom.

That was all he could think about as he rocked near the couch where Mom once was, in a frenzy as she promised

Spencer that everything would be alright. That this would all be nothing more than a horrible memory.

It was so dark in that room.

It reminded Spencer of Mom's eyes.

Chapter Eleven

Higher Roads

It was as good a time as any to have a night owl as a best friend. Naturally, Donovan was fine with Spencer coming over, despite it being two in the morning. And Kaylee would be fine, probably safer than ever if Spencer was being honest – those things followed *him*, so she could rest easy. Donovan had said he would make sure not to go to any places that were too high up when he was around, and Spencer had forced a chuckle.

Now, half asleep, Spencer was knocking on his friend's front door.

Arizona opened it and rolled her eyes. "What makes you think you can come to our place in the middle of the night after bailing on Vannie like that?"

Spencer scrunched his brow. He was so exhausted he genuinely had no idea what she was talking about. "Excuse me?"

"The play."

He almost scoffed. Of course, he regretted not being able to stay, but even Spencer couldn't force himself to think much of it at the time.

Donovan said behind her, "That couldn't be further from the problem, babe." He carefully moved past Arizona, making sure not to push her. "Spence, you alright? You sounded pretty beat up on the phone."

It wasn't often that Donovan said something when Arizona picked fights. Usually, he was quiet, which sent a jab to the selfish side of Spencer every time.

Now, Donovan's words were enough to let Spencer finally draw in a real, full breath. And the dam that held more tears back threatened to burst, but it was just enough to keep that at bay.

He said quietly, "I really, really need your help."

Arizona rolled her eyes. "Maybe you should've thought about that before you walked out and embarrassed the hell outta—"

"I did *nothing* to *you*."

He was so sick of holding back. And for just a fleeting moment, despite everything, it made his lips twitch into a smile.

Arizona scowled at him, her dark eyes sending daggers his way. But after a moment, Donovan whispered, "Not today, okay? Please."

"Fine, but he's gonna hurt you again." She looked Spencer up and down, leaving him to ball his fists at his side. "I'll be in our room," Arizona said as she walked away, leaving Spencer and Donovan in silence until she slammed her bedroom door behind her.

Spencer walked over and collapsed on the couch. Usually, he'd have said something about Arizona and how he was sorry he had just caused another fight. But he couldn't bring himself to care.

Donovan either could tell or shared the sentiment, because he stiffly sat next to Spencer like he was standing watch, letting out enough energy to keep them both going. Quietly giving Spencer all the time in the world to say what he had to say.

Problem was, Spencer didn't know what that was. He admitted, "I have no idea what's going on, man."

This was supposed to be a thing of the past – the ghosts and the visions were gone for six years. That time was full of questions, and it was lonely without Kirsten. But it was a new, comfortable normal.

Silence filled the air as they stared at the wall in front of them. The air conditioner was loud, though its hum was overpowered by the dryer held one room over. Boxes were strewn around the apartment, their first home together about to be vacated. Every time he saw them, the boxes reminded Spencer of how close he was to losing his best friend in the world.

He looked over to his friend, whose lips were pursed. His eyes danced like he was watching something on the blank TV, though they slowed when Spencer looked. He had more to say, and Spencer knew that simply because he could always read him.

"Maybe this will help, maybe it won't." Donovan said quietly. His voice was flat as if he were reading aloud from a textbook. "I did something. Not sure if you're gonna like it, but I did it and I want to help you."

Now, that was a great start.

The hesitance Donovan displayed looked unnatural. He seemed almost scared to tell Spencer what he did, like he expected him to lose his cool at the drop of a hat.

"What'd you do?"

"I looked up The Incident."

Spencer grit his teeth, unsure of what to say. He had told Donovan over and over again about his promise and how much keeping it meant to him. He replied, "I promised I'd never go digging."

"Loophole." Donovan forced a shaky smile. "You didn't research shit."

Spencer sighed, recoiling as if Mom were there to tell him once again that she didn't want him to know. "I don't know."

But for the first time, Spencer was too exhausted to hold off. He struggled so often to not break that promise and look it up. The thing was, though, morals would get in the way and he would always resist.

A moment of weakness, maybe that's what it was, but he looked his friend in the eye and forced himself to ask, "What did you find?"

Donovan shifted in his seat, muttering something to himself. "Fair warning." He said, "It's not a lot. There are plenty of gaps. Had to put together information from a few articles, but even then, there was lots that I just couldn't understand."

Spencer nodded slightly, hoping whatever Donovan knew, it would be just enough for Dad to drop the act and just tell him.

"They were a family," Donovan continued. "The people following you around. Their obituary mentioned that they were friends with your parents and – I dunno, social media posts, you never know how reliable those are. But I guess something happened, they got into a fight with your parents, it all boiled over..."

A few seconds of silence passed. Maybe less than that. But to Spencer, it felt like an eternity.

Donovan looked down and mumbled, "It was a man, a woman, and a kid. They never found the wife's body."

Another one, Spencer couldn't believe it. He supposed it was something he was always idly afraid of. With a dad and a daughter, he figured there would also be a mother. But something in him had forced the thought away.

"What happened to them?" Spencer asked.

"Car crash," Donovan whispered. "They lived near a cliff and barely made it out of their driveway. Rounded a corner, went to brake, and just... didn't."

Spencer let out a heavy breath. He couldn't imagine.

"The man was the only survivor." Donovan bit his lip. "The daughter was thrown out of the windshield and got cut up by the glass. Bled out."

"And how did–"

"They crashed near the woods your dad lives in."

Spencer's eyes widened. After The Incident, Dad went there all the time. An obsession, almost. Then after Mom died, he went there so fast, like it was a comfort to him.

He asked hoarsely, "And the mom?"

"Went down into the water with the car. They don't know where she ended up. Cops said that she could have floated away, or she could still be at the bottom. I just know that they never found the car. It was like it never existed."

Spencer didn't know how to reply, and he hated that it made sense to him. It felt right in a way he didn't understand, like some spot in the back of his mind already knew, and the knowledge was finally resurfacing. Bringing its ugly head back, never to leave again.

"When?" he asked.

"Spence, I dunno if you wanna—"

"When?"

Donovan let out a long breath through his nose. And the worry and regret laced his voice, the words cold but still making Spencer's blood boil.

"Twenty-four years ago."

Spencer closed his eyes.

Right around when he was born.

Something happened between his parents and The Mangled Man's family. Something so bad that he found it necessary to massacre them in their own home.

The Incident.

Spencer just didn't know *why*. Suddenly, the word was heavy. But he managed to ask, "Do you know…"

His friend shook his head. "That's all I know."

Spencer closed his eyes and rested his hands over them. He propped his arms up with his legs.

"I keep watching Kirsten die. I see it over and over and over again, and I want more than anything to tell her what happened." Spencer scrubbed his face with his hands. "And if I were to try and explain it to her, what would I even say?"

Donovan put his hand on Spencer's shoulder. "The truth."

Spencer didn't know how to begin. All along, he had assured himself that at once he figured out what was going on, he could tell her. But that possibility seemed to drift further and further away.

"Hey," Donovan said. Spencer looked up at him, and his friend's face turned to stone. "She is a grown-ass adult. I think it's time you be honest with her."

"But what if—"

"We'll figure this out," Donovan said. "And you'll be okay."

Spencer was silent.

Until Donovan added, "She will, too."

Figuring it out was something Spencer had tried to do for the better part of a decade. And now that he had some answers, it only presented more questions.

He asked, "How could you know that?"

Donovan sighed and gave him a couple quick pats on the back. It was a gesture the two of them usually made as a joke. But sometimes, it was reassurance.

One that Donovan repeated then.

"'Cause I promise."

Chapter Twelve

Turned Tide

Kirsten chose this spot.

So there Spencer was, shifting uncomfortably on the couch of the café's adjacent library. Once upon a time, he'd have held a hot chocolate, and her a vanilla latte with half and half, an extra splash of vanilla for good measure, and whipped cream mixed into it because she didn't like when it settled on the top.

Spencer hadn't gotten hot chocolate like normal; there was a rush when he got in and he didn't want to add to the line. Instead, he ran his hands along the thighs of his pants, taking some kind of comfort in how it warmed his palms. It was a distraction, he supposed, and all distractions helped.

No more planning out what to say – he had run the script through his head countless times. Sometimes it involved him groveling, saying over and over again that he was sorry. Then he had thrown that idea away so fast and gotten embarrassed about even thinking of it. The next attempt had him over-explain, then he was too vague, finally too rehearsed. Nothing felt right, no matter how he tried to phrase it in his head.

Plus, he knew full well that Kirsten would never follow his script.

He just had to be natural about it, it's what everyone had told him. *Natural*, no matter how much of a condescending bite the word was starting to have. And the rest would come.

Spencer took a shaky breath and looked at the horror section again. A black cover jumped out at him, not because it was dark — most of them were — but because he hadn't yet seen it in person. It was one that people had discussed online countless times. The glossy cover made the black background stand out, illuminating the monster that he had read all about, its silhouette standing in the center. It towered over the wreckage in its wake, overlooking the ashen city.

Looming over him, the welcome distraction was the only thing that kept Spencer's heart from exploding.

But eventually, it reminded him of the way The Mangled Man stood over Kirsten's shoulder. How the blackness in his eyes grew darker than the cover before she stopped breathing.

There was humming in the background.

At first, it was so faint that Spencer was able to write it off as a figment of his imagination. But as the tune rang out, the deathly, graveled melody grew louder.

The Girl sat in a crisscross, her back to him. She was happily singing to herself, drawing on the white-painted wall in front of her. She blocked his view; all he could make out was her gleeful song. And when she moved away lightly, like a feather, she smiled at him. She gestured towards the wall.

A, M, N

She looked back and forth between her writing and Spencer, her expression giddy, full of life — growing almost inhuman. And she pointed at the *N* and herself, excitedly brandishing her artwork to the—

"That's a good one, I hear," Kirsten said as she sat down next to him. "I think you'd like it."

Spencer jumped in his spot, panting as Kirsten looked at him. And when he went to see past her, his breath caught in his throat.

The Girl was gone.

That's when Spencer realized the book was shaking in his hands. He pursed his lips and set it back on the shelf. "Maybe," he said, knowing he'd probably never pick it back up.

Spencer shifted again, and silence filled the air. He kept starting to tell her what happened then chickening out before the first syllable. It was obvious that she had noticed – she quietly showed the same puzzled expression that she'd give when she expected him to continue. Back when they were together, it was about innocent things like him struggling to explain a subject he'd learned in biology. She'd look confused, quiet. But in her eyes, he could see her encourage him to find the words.

The simplicity was one of the things that he missed the most.

When he took a break from trying to form a coherent sentence – it was a problem for Future Spencer – she caught on to that, too. She half-smiled and hit her hands on her thighs, so giddy she made the couch cushion shake. "Oh, did I tell you what Samantha did? She's one of our new regulars."

He shook his head.

She happily placed the cup down so she could lean in more. "This... this..." She made a face before straining, "*Lady*, right? She came by right after rush hour. We were finally starting to slow down, and I had to go get some more milk. Then she went and bought twelve coffees, all with special requests. And she complained because, apparently, I used fat-free vanilla instead of regular – because of course she could tell. Then after that, she ordered sandwiches."

Honestly, Spencer didn't retain the rest of her story.

He was more focused on the delivery than what she was saying. How she was so passionately ranting about something trivial, and the way her eyes lit up as she went on. Something so inconsequential meant so much to her.

And Spencer couldn't help but smile at that because even if her words were angry, he could tell she was seconds away from bursting into laughter from the whole situation.

"—and *then* the younger guy came up to me and was all like 'why'd you take so long?' And I'm like sir, did you not see the whole school bus worth of coffees and sandwiches I just shoved into bags and a bunch of drink holders?"

Spencer raised his brow. "'A school bus worth of coffees and sandwiches?'"

Kirsten huffed, then he made a face at her. She snorted and covered her mouth before erupting into a fit of laughter. "You're the worst."

"Oh, trust me," Spencer replied as he smiled at her. "I know."

The atmosphere wasn't heavy anymore. It was something only Kirsten could do.

She gave him a gentle smile. "What was it that you wanted to talk to me about, Spence? You sounded…" She bit her lip. "Upset."

Somehow, 'upset' was both an understatement and the only word he could think to use.

Kirsten sighed before asking, "Is it about the play?"

Spencer grit his teeth. It was the first time she had mentioned the play; he'd try talking about it, sometimes starting with the dreaded 's' word. Donovan joked that if he even thought about saying sorry, for good measure, he'd break up with him too – but usually, he'd stop himself.

Not that it mattered, as she was able to recognize the telltale signs that he was about to mention it. He'd shift uncomfortably, sigh, whisper 'Kirsten, I...' and she'd cut him off soon after.

But now, she was saying the word 'play' freely.

Speaking his mind is what she'd encourage him to do. The momentum was there, and he couldn't let himself stop. "It..." Spencer looked around before forcing, "Sorta. Kinda." He sighed. "In a roundabout way, I guess."

Dang, she was so easy to talk to, but the words were fighting him with every syllable.

But she was being so patient, understanding.

"I never wanted to leave you."

It came out in one gentle gust of air. One he could have missed, it was so small.

She took her hand off of his. "Please don't do that.".

Spencer opened his mouth, not sure what to say. It wasn't part of any script that he ever could have come up with. "Don't do what?"

"You wanted to," Kirsten said after a moment. She looked away, letting her gaze rest anywhere but at him. "Maybe you didn't want to do it that way. That harshly. But you did. You were acting differently before you left, Spence. Did I annoy you or something? Why didn't you just talk to me?"

"Hey, no. Please, just," Spencer said before placing his hand on her arm. "It wasn't you. It never was."

"Then why?" She asked, "Why'd you do it? I really thought we were happy."

"We *were*."

For a year and a half, and that wasn't counting when they were friends before. Because one second, she wasn't there, then all of a sudden she was, and everything started to make sense.

The Mangled Man messed that all up. And as hard as Spencer had fought to find any other solution, that well had run dry long ago.

If she only knew.

Spencer cleared his throat. "I wanna tell you what happened. I need you to know that every bit of this will sound absolutely insane but I promise you I'm telling the truth. I need you to trust me." He looked her in the eyes before asking, "Please, Kirs, can you do that?"

She searched his face for something, Spencer would never know what. Then she nodded. "I trust you."

"I was trying to protect you. When my mom died, she was killed by this guy who attacked them in our house when I was fourteen. We call it The Incident. And the guy didn't make it, his daughter was already gone. And he's..."

A ghost.

That was what kept him away from her.

"He's after me," Spencer said. "And his daughter is showing me things. I kept seeing you lying there, and you were…" The vision threatened to resurface, but he managed to force it away. "I couldn't get the image outta my head. Every time I kissed you, or went out with you, or even looked at you wrong, I'd see you there."

Dead.

Spencer would see her dead. But that was a sentence he wasn't sure he'd ever be able to complete.

His voice cracked out, "Then he started to hurt you. Strangle you."

Kirsten put her hands over her neck, a futile attempt at stifling the phantom pain that seemed to consume her.

And all Spencer could do was nod. "That night, I saw him stand over you. Kirs, you weren't choking on food, I wasn't running to get you a nurse. I was trying to get him to follow me away from you. Because with me around you, you couldn't…"

Kirsten knew what he meant, so he didn't force himself to verbalize the rest. That if he had stayed there that night, she might have taken her last breath at that restaurant. All because she was close to him.

He whispered, "And then I knew that I had to leave you."

When he left her, he acted like a jerk. Because maybe then he would have been able to get her away forever, to get her as far from The Mangled Man as possible. It was another speech that he had planned over and over again. He'd be so rude to her that she would have no choice but to walk away, deeming him a total d-bag and nothing more.

But she never had stuck to that script, either.

He couldn't read the look on her face; not only was she looking away from him, but she managed to both look stoic and like she had a thousand questions. Confusion, hurt, anger – they all collided to form this rock-hard expression that Spencer almost drew away from. He went to say her name, but it only came out as a gush of air.

"You see…" Kirsten picked her cup up and looked inside, studying it. It was like all the answers to her questions were written in there. "Ghosts?"

While Spencer wasn't a believer before he saw The Girl, Kirsten had always thought them to be real. It was one of the many reasons why she hated horror movies – the realism made them too predictable for her.

He nodded. "I promise you, I'm not lying."

"And you're sure you didn't, like…" She threw her hair back and buried the top of her head into her palm. "You didn't see it wrong? Or maybe—"

"Kirs, I swear. Him and a girl. They've been with me for ten years now."

Her eyes narrowed and she slammed the cup down, hot coffee spilling on her hands. Spencer stood and tried to look for something to help her clean it.

"Here," he murmured. "Let me—"

"I've got it," Kirsten said, her voice cracking. She reached into her apron and pulled out a cloth she'd usually clean the counter with. The table shook with how hard she pressed against it, the circles stiff. She quietly repeated, mostly to herself, "I've got it."

"Kirs, I'm sor—"

"*Don't.*"

Spencer pursed his lips and pressed his hand in his lap, sitting stiffly like he was a teenager in his first job interview. Kirsten was mumbling something to herself, incoherent as she ran the cloth over the mess long after it was clean.

She stopped cleaning and looked up at him through her lashes. "The play," she said firmly.

Spencer nodded.

"The microphone. The lights."

Another nod from Spencer, and she sat back down. She cleaned off the sides of her cup and bit her lip, blinking quickly.

"Why in the *hell* did you keep this from me?"

If earlier he was acting like a teenager in a job interview, now he was acting like one getting chewed out at a parent teacher conference.

Instead of lying and trying to justify what had happened, he gave her the most sincere truth he could. "I was scared that you'd stay."

He was scared that she'd stick around. He was scared that either they'd keep dating, or they'd be close friends again – which, he recognized, did end up happening, in time.

With silence filling the air, he said against his better judgement, "I'm sorry for not telling you sooner."

Back then, he did the best he could — he made the decision that gutted him but kept her safe. And if he was being honest with himself, he still didn't regret it. It was the only way to give them the time that they both needed.

For a long, painful moment, shared silence echoed between the two of them.

Kirsten blinked some more, looking anywhere but at him. She chuckled harshly, quietly. "I'm so pissed off," she admitted in a whisper.

But this time, Spencer didn't let the signature response pass his lips. He stayed there quietly, watching Kirsten's mind race right in front of him.

He was scared The Mangled Man would return, he was scared that The Girl's warning would come true. But while the logical part of Spencer told him to get out of there again, he also wanted to stay with her.

And that part won.

After a while, Kirsten said quietly, "Next time something's bothering you, I need you to swallow your pride and *tell me*, Spencer. We could have fixed this."

Next time.

That was what she said. She didn't tell him to get away from her and never come back.

"I understand," he told her.

"I'm very confused," she admitted. She chuckled – a forced, muffled laugh that barely laced her words, but it was there. "So, you pissed off a bunch of ghosts and now they're after both of us. Question is, how do we get rid of them?"

"I have no clue," Spencer admitted.

Kirsten took another sip of her coffee, her lips curving into something of a sly smirk. Spencer returned it in a heartbeat.

The stress and the worry melted off of him in a way that only Kirsten could manage. She looked at him like he hadn't just messed with the last six years of her life. And the light came to her eyes. One he hadn't seen since that night, and one he never thought he'd see again. For so long, Spencer had longed for the flicker and tried to figure out what had been missing for all those years.

That feeling was trust.

She trusted that somehow, they'd get through this. Spencer wouldn't search for it by himself as he hid behind some shadowy figure that threatened to choke the life out of the people he loved. He wouldn't have to do it alone, and now, he truly believed there was a way past this.

Kirsten told him, "Then let's figure it out."

Chapter Thirteen

Chaotic Joy

"This is kinda dumb."

Spencer chuckled at the sight in front of him. When his friends told him he had to check out the fair that was in town, he had accepted, despite his hesitation. The lights, the flashing, and the theatrics all cultivated into something Spencer never understood the appeal of.

But there they were anyway, all four of them. Donovan was next to him, already throwing his arms over Spencer's shoulders and laughing so hard he could be heard over the blaring music. Arizona was quiet — more so than usual — but in a different way that Spencer couldn't quite pin down.

Kirsten was on his other side.

It had been a few days since he told her everything. Things with her were going well, albeit not how he had expected. He figured either everything would be alright, or it would be the final nail in the coffin and she'd stop wanting to see him for good. But it wasn't either — glimmers of her old light would return, then somewhere along the line, it'd fade again. Spencer had no clue what to make of it.

Donovan pointed towards the middle of the fair. "That Ferris wheel is badass."

Arizona scoffed. "Babe, please don't tell me you just said that about a *Ferris wheel*."

"I dunno what you're looking at, but come on. It legit looks like it can go twen— *fifty* stories in the air!" Donovan jumped, his weight sending jabs into Spencer's shoulder. "Is that a friggin' dragon next to it? Bro!"

Spencer glanced towards Arizona and Kirsten. They both made a drinking motion, and Arizona closed her eyes and stumbled back as if she were passing out. Spencer chuckled and nodded in a silent understanding.

No wonder Kirsten drove.

"Babe." Donovan said to Arizona, "Will you please go on that Ferris wheel with me? I wanna take you up there, right, and then I can show you the world!"

Arizona smiled and rolled her eyes as she looked over at Kirsten, giving her a look that could only mean something along the lines of, '*help me*.' Her boyfriend didn't get drunk often, but when he did, they knew he'd have a show to put on.

Kirsten motioned Arizona on. "You heard the man, he's gonna show you the world!"

"Yeah, come on!" Donovan shouted as he grabbed Arizona's wrist. "You'll love it!"

Spencer opened his mouth to protest – the thought of Donovan not only high up, but also drunk, made him uneasy. But Donovan was already laughing louder than Spencer could speak, and he ran off in a flash, dragging Arizona behind him. At first, she spared glimpses towards Spencer and Kirsten, but then she turned back around and laughed with Donovan the rest of the way there.

Spencer bit his lip and turned towards Kirsten. "How much of this do you think he's gonna remember?"

"Literally none. But that's where we come in."

The two of them started to walk around the fairground, scoping out the place with no real intention to go on any of the rides. The adrenaline rushes were more for Donovan and Arizona, not Spencer and Kirsten. They were just happy to be there and get a nice bit of entertainment.

They passed a section of booths. Bobbing for apples, floating rubber ducks, darts, among other games. The sight of the darts made him grind his teeth, and Kirsten made fun of that. Not that he blamed her, he was always weird about them. An accuracy 'game' that involved throwing something at a target — he never saw the appeal.

"Wanna play darts?" Kirsten asked with a chuckle.

Spencer smiled and said gently, "Shut it."

They kept walking, making a little circle around the booths. And when they neared the Ferris wheel, they could hear laughter. It was animated, even more intense than the kids' that were running around, and deeper than them. Kirsten nudged him with her elbow. "No way."

Not that he needed any clarification, but Spencer followed Kirsten's gaze. She was looking up towards the Ferris wheel.

Where Donovan and Arizona were at the top, Donovan with his hands in the air and shouting, "*Whoo!*" and other things that they couldn't decipher. And Arizona was joining in, of course, not as animated as him.

"We're all a bunch of idiots," Spencer whispered. "Aren't we?"

"Oh, we absolutely are."

They continued on, making their way towards the Ferris wheel's exit gate. Away from the booths with all the random games and their cheap prizes. Spencer and Kirsten talked about a lot — things that he would never be able to summarize or point out — they just talked. About the dumbest topics they could think of, no matter how inconsequential.

When they reached a cotton candy stand, Spencer stopped and took out his wallet. He walked up to the operator and handed him his card. "Hi! I'll take one, please." The worker nodded and handed him a pre-wrapped bit of cotton candy and gave Spencer his card. He thanked him and walked back towards Kirsten.

"Thought you didn't like that stuff," she told him.

"I don't."

He handed it to her, and she took it happily. The smile on her face was unmistakable, with a certain giddiness he hadn't seen in years. They kept walking, and all the while, she wouldn't take her eyes off Spencer.

Cheeks flushed, he chuckled at how pure her excitement was. "What?" he asked, entranced by the way the fair's lights hit her eyes just right.

Kirsten pursed her lips and raised her cotton candy in the air. "I can't believe you remembered."

"How could I forget?"

His heart skipped a beat. The words soared out of his mouth, landing right on target.

And any regret melted away the moment she flashed him another one of her smiles.

Not much else was said as they waited for Donovan and Arizona to get off. A few comments here and there, but Spencer was lost in thought.

Kaylee was at home. She had asked Spencer if he'd be okay if Brett came over to keep her company, which Spencer accepted without hesitation. Honestly, he was just glad she asked. And part of him still didn't feel right telling her she couldn't do something. That was Dad's job.

Or, at least, it *should* have been Dad's job.

When Donovan and Arizona got off, they had their arms around each other while laughing and talking, with Spencer unsure who was getting more into it. The four of them went on, sticking as a group but allowing themselves to divert to different booths.

Eventually, they all found their way back to the games. After Spencer looked around at the prizes, he saw one that he couldn't look away from. On the top of the darts' prize collection were a bunch of stuffed animals. A giraffe, a bear, a panda.

And a monkey.

Kirsten loved monkeys.

He looked back. Donovan and Kirsten were on the opposite side of the games' section, near the bobbing for apples station. Kirsten had her head submerged and Donovan was holding her hair back, shouting encouraging words she certainly couldn't hear.

Spencer looked back at the darts and handed the attendant one of his tickets. He drew his arm back and started to aim at the balloons. It wasn't that he was bad at this, luckily. Not interested, but he was perfectly capable.

"Darts?" Arizona asked as she walked up to him. She hesitated then said, "Thought you didn't like aiming games? You said you like... You didn't get the appeal, or something."

He stopped in his tracks, just glad that the attendant didn't really seem to care and no one was waiting for a turn. "I can't believe you still remember that."

It had been years since he mentioned that to her. Years since he'd ramble about something as trivial as his hatred for a carnival game.

Arizona shrugged. "It's not like those few years just never happened, yanno?"

"Fair enough," Spencer replied after a moment.

But not even a week ago, she was at his throat like she had been for years. He wanted so badly to not care and to just take her politeness for what it was.

"I heard you and Vannie. How you talked about what happened and he told you about the attack," Arizona told him. "I don't think you two realize how loudly you talk."

Heat rushed to Spencer's face. It had just slipped his mind to be quiet, such a detail having felt inconsequential in the moment.

"Then Kirsten told me what you said." Arizona sighed. "And I realized that my best friend and boyfriend both found out something that huge and felt the need to keep it from me. Hell, I asked Vannie to see what he'd say, and he gave me the runaround."

Spencer stayed silent, fiddling with darts in his hand. He could remember back when the four of them would tell each other anything.

Arizona continued, "Do you remember the football team? That time when they made fun of my uniform?"

In high school, the four of them were in the marching band together. The football team had made fun of their uniforms quite a few times, something that had always especially bothered Arizona.

Spencer nodded.

"One time, it got really bad." Arizona sighed. "The team wouldn't shut up about my uniform, and I started to tear up. Vannie and Kirsten didn't know that part, but still." The sight of her there – about to burst into tears while running from the football team – was as vivid as ever. "Vannie just said that it was ridiculous and that I looked hot. Then Kirsten laughed and essentially said she was sorry, but it was funny because she had just said the same thing."

She looked at Spencer. The embarrassment was still plastered on her face. And all over again, he wished he could say something to take it away from her.

"But you."

Hugged her and told her she looked far from stupid. Said that she should delete the word from her vocabulary when it came to her.

He really didn't think Arizona would remember that.

"I've been a bitch to you," she told him.

"C'mon. I wouldn't say—"

"Of course *you* wouldn't, but I can. And I was. And I'm sorry."

Neither said anything for a moment. She'd open her mouth and take a breath, then she'd close it again. When

Spencer felt ready to change the subject, she blurted out, "I think what happened — and this is not an excuse, I know that — I saw her there, she was crying. And she's like a sister to me. But that doesn't mean that what I did was right." Her bangs brushed in front of her eyes, and she looked down while hurriedly moving them away. "I still think you should've told her sooner, but I am sorry for assuming like that."

Spencer didn't know what to say. For six years, he was the bad guy. He understood why she was upset with him, but his attempts at reconciling were futile.

He admitted, "I don't think it can be 'okay' just like that. But I do want us to be like we used to."

"I do, too," Arizona told him. "Can't expect you to erase all that from just one talk."

Spencer provided a silent agreement, the gesture louder than any words he could think of.

"Seriously though." Arizona asked, "Why darts?"

He aimed and threw one of them, smiling as he got a bullseye. Then he took the second of three darts from his hand and motioned to the monkey with his head. "I'm winnin' that for Kirsten."

Arizona didn't say anything. Spencer drew his hand back and hit the target again.

"Get her the panda," she said quietly.

"What?"

"The panda," Arizona repeated in a whisper. "She'd love it. She thinks they're funny, I don't know why."

Spencer looked at the panda. Its smiling face was staring back at him, calling for him. He gave one in return. "So, she's back on that?"

Confused, Arizona didn't reply. She waited for Spencer to clarify.

He told her, "She was all over pandas for a while, back when we started dating. Says they're hilarious 'cause they look like a zebra got together with a bear, and for some reason the thought just makes her laugh every time."

Spencer aimed and made the final shot.

He threw his arms in the air and cheered. Arizona joined, the excitement genuine despite everything that had happened between them. And for just a bit, it felt like old times. When Arizona used to be like a sister to him.

The surrealness of it all lasted until their cheers died back down, and he saw the prizes he could choose between. That was when Spencer chose to look back at Kirsten, who was still with Donovan. Now, her hair was dripping wet, and she was chanting Donovan's name as he stuck his head in the tank.

Arizona motioned towards the prizes. "She really would love that panda."

Spencer smiled and asked for it, and the decision instantly felt right. Like it had called for him the second he walked by, even if Spencer just hadn't heard it yet.

And while usually he'd spare one last glance to Kirsten, he instead kept his eyes on Arizona. "Thank you," he said to her.

"You're welcome."

Things were coming together; Spencer couldn't hide that fact if he tried. He was so glad he bit the bullet and finally said something.

It really seemed like things were falling back into place.

Chapter Fourteen

"Come Home"

The four kept together after that. At his request, the attendant gave Spencer a paper bag to put the stuffed panda in. Kirsten had asked a couple of times what he was holding in his hands — he told her it was a secret, and it made her even more curious — but after two or three rounds of him saying 'oh, nothing,' Kirsten had gotten bored.

There'd be a time, Spencer promised himself as he tightened his grip on the bag. It just didn't feel like the right night.

And of course, Donovan was being an idiot, almost getting them kicked out after a swim in the fountain. Gave them a laugh and a good story to tell later.

It stayed like that, with them walking around the fair together, as the sun went down to be replaced with the night sky. The darkness illuminated the fair's flashing colors, allowing a red hue to cast over the place. People were on rollercoasters, but the attractions on the ground had died down.

Out of nowhere, Spencer's head was throbbing. His friends were keeping this going longer than he had thought.

They were around the outskirts of the fair, near the picnic tables and a little built-in park. He could remember this spot, near a little hay bale where his parents brought him as a kid. They'd do pumpkin patches in the fall and take family photos with the pumpkin they each chose. Kaylee would always want to go to the park afterwards.

The four of them went near the tables and Spencer sat down. It was a faded green wire-style, with little specks of orange where the paint had rusted away long ago. At some point it had been painted over, but then that faded too, and it stopped getting repaired. Spencer placed the bag next to him and ran his thumb over it.

Until Donovan leaned over, breaking Spencer from his trance. "Y'all, I'm 'boutta hurl."

Figured. Spencer was surprised he wasn't feeling hungover yet.

"I need to go, too," Arizona said before turning to Kirsten. "Come with?"

Spencer chuckled. For some reason, they always tried to go together.

The others looked around. There wasn't a bathroom near the park, but they wouldn't have known that. Their families didn't make it a habit of coming to this fair all the time like his did. A few times that night, they had turned the wrong way before Spencer took the lead.

He smiled and pointed behind them. "Follow where we just came from and turn left. Keep going until you reach the hotdog stand — Donovan, try not to get another one while you're there — and you'll see the bathroom next to it."

Arizona moved her leftover burger from one hand to the other. "That's the closest one?"

"Yup," Spencer answered. "I'm good, I can hold your stuff when you're gone."

The three of them put their things down on the table — Arizona had her leftover food, Kirsten had bought some stuff from the gift shop, and Donovan had a stuffed lizard he won from the bobbing for apples game. They thanked him and walked off, leaving Spencer in his own thoughts.

Which, honestly, he appreciated. At that point, his head was killing him. He rubbed his temples and closed his eyes, letting out a sigh as his eyelids provided momentary relief from the flashing lights.

But then he saw more red.

A pool of it. And he could see the hardwood floor at home coated in blood, the puddle moving like a lake. Spencer opened his eyes again.

The Girl sat across from him, her hands propping her head up. She flashed him her toothy grin and waved at him.

He jumped in his seat, then he blinked, and she was gone.

And he felt this surge, this rush of anger that floated to the surface. She started to laugh at him from all sides, and then he'd look where the sound was coming from only for her to disappear again. He got up and turned towards the park, not that he could see much from where he was. The playground structure covered most of it.

"Spencer."

The voice was almost reassuring somehow, not angry like it usually was. It sent the same chill down his spine and echoed in his ears in a way that made the hair on his arms stand up.

"This way."

He took a sharp, shaky breath. And an even shakier step towards the playground.

It was only a few feet from him, though it felt like he was wading through a vat of cement. The low, cheery music from the center of the fair was distorted in his ears. As if the world was encapsulated by him, the park, and his labored breathing.

He went over a step, and mulch crumbled under his weight.

No matter how loud his breathing got or how his heart echoed in his ears, he swore he could hear something else. A creaking sound that only got louder as he walked through the playground.

Swaying.

The swing.

Spencer saw it over the play set's structure when it reached its highest point.

But no one was in it.

He took idle steps closer but barely registered the motion. Really, it felt more like his feet were growing minds of their own and propelling him forward, with Spencer not having enough of a mind to stop them. He was too busy staring at the swing in awe.

It'd reach the top, to the point where the swing was almost upside down. And every time it came back, he expected just a glimmer of a sign that there was someone on it, a kid who had jumped off.

But he never saw it.

"Come home."

Spencer scrunched his brows together and took another step.

Come home?

They were usually so cryptic; never before had they told him what to do point blank. He was used to little one-liners like '*All wrong*,' but they were never clear enough to give Spencer a real meaning.

Now, it was whispered to him again and again.

"Come home."

Spencer reached the opposite side of the structure, near the swing.

"Why?" He asked quietly, "What's at ho—"

Something dropped behind him.

"Come home."

Spencer turned, eyes darting to the mass that had landed on the ground. A man, lying face-down with a pool of blood forming around his face. With torn clothes and soaked, jet-black hair.

"Donovan!"

It was agonizingly familiar, a memory he had pushed down over and over again, no matter how many times it threatened to resurface. Part of him knew it couldn't be real.

 But the other — the more prominent side — couldn't stop his jaw from dropping open or the silent shriek as he stretched his arms out and raced to Donovan. Spencer dropped to the crimson-soaked ground, propping his friend up on his knee.

None of it made sense, he wasn't there.

It couldn't be real. It couldn't.

Donovan's head hung limp, swaying with Spencer's motions with no hesitation. His body was heavy, but it loosely followed along. Spencer couldn't look away, couldn't understand.

Because Donovan always had something to say. He always knew what he'd want to do. He wouldn't just...

Spencer choked out, "Donovan?"

But his friend didn't move.

"Donovan!

It could *not* be real.

"Come home."

Spencer's heart felt heavy. He'd heard of phrases about being broken-hearted, but there, he could actually feel the weight in his chest. The heavy pulsation that only got worse when he'd move, and Donovan's head would uselessly go along with him.

And he tried — he really did — to keep still.

Anything to stop the movements. Anything to make it look for just a second that Donovan was just sleeping.

But his cries came out in anguished gasps, and he couldn't stop the jolts anymore.

All he could do was think about when he met him. When Spencer was the new kid, a lonely sophomore who had just moved after an 'incident' ripped his family apart. He was walking the halls aimlessly, too nervous to ask anyone where to go or what he was supposed to do. Too freaked out to stop the people who always found something to make fun of. And he was too unsure to try and say anything when one day they followed him to the school's stairwell, their insults echoing. Eventually they crowded around him and yelled everything they could think of.

Until Donovan — a freshman at the time — came trotting down the steps.

And he was able to get the people away from Spencer.

Even back then, that was how outspoken he was. How sure of himself he was. Spencer remembered how from that day on, he didn't have to walk the halls alone anymore.

It couldn't be real. He knew it wasn't.

But this part of him...

Spencer closed his eyes. "I'm sorry. I'm so, so, so, so..."

Someone talked around him, people tried to shake him. But he couldn't get out of his head. He couldn't open his eyes — he could only stay there, reliving the sight of Donovan on the ground. Could only tighten his grip on his friend's body.

"Donovan," he whispered.

More talking around him. Someone was shouting, but it was so muffled he could barely make it out.

"Man, wake up!" Someone yelled.

He looked back in time to see a fresh trail of blood flow from Donovan's face, his mouth hung open and silencing the outspoken man he always was. But he was supposed to say something, *anything*.

Spencer shook his friend. "Donovan!"

Someone tried to pry his friend from his arms. But he couldn't let go – how could he ever let go? – so he fought against the motion. He kicked, and he screamed, but people kept trying to pull the heap away from his arms. He couldn't look up to see who it was, he couldn't look at anything other than his friend's face. Hands fought to pry Donovan from him, and Spencer swatted them away.

This couldn't be real.

"Please!"

The heap moved. And in Spencer's arms, Donovan opened his eyes.

Blood oozed from their sockets, adding to the crimson sea that rested below his head – this couldn't be real – and red lakes ran from his eyes, his mouth, his nose; Spencer couldn't find a spot on his friend's face that wasn't soaked. This couldn't be real. Spencer yelped, and finally, he went to let his friend go.

The heap grabbed his arm.

"Come home!"

An ear-splitting roar, one with a gush of air that felt of death and decay.

It was cold and yet felt like it would burn his skin on the spot. Somewhere along the line, Spencer closed his eyes. This couldn't be real. But that only seemed to make the heap angrier as their nails dug into his skin. He tried to fight against it, he pleaded with them to let him go.

People all around him were screaming at him to wake up
– what could waking up possibly have to do with this? –
and he fought and he kicked but he couldn't–

"Spencer!" Donovan shouted.

He opened his eyes.

His friend was there, kneeling beside him. Donovan had
both hands on Spencer's shoulders, his grip tight from
where he had tried to shake him out of it. Kirsten and
Arizona were behind him, but Spencer couldn't look
away from his friend.

There was still something in his arms, but he moved
them, and the heap dropped to his lap.

Spencer threw his arms around his friend.

Donovan stayed there motionless, and Spencer silently
begged him to show some sign of life. He was stiff, and as
much as he tried to push the thought away, his mind
would go back to the vision.

His friend returned the embrace. "What the hell is
happening to you?" he whispered.

But Spencer didn't know what to say, not in response to
the question that went one ear and out the other. "Love
you, man," he managed.

Sometimes he'd say that, usually as a joke. Because it
was just something you'd say to a friend who meant that
much. But that was the first time he'd ever said it
without adding some kind of an insult or a joke with it.

That was his brother.

Donovan took a shaky breath. "We're gonna figure this out, alright?"

Spencer nodded and slowly let go. The others stood over him, concern written on their faces whether they were trying to hide it or not.

He said they'd figure this out, but how?

The heap moved, and he looked down.

The Girl was there.

Right where Donovan was. She was looking up at him, smiling. Laughing. Her cheerful, giddy tune rattled in his ears and Spencer covered them. But like it was a game, she only grew louder.

She gestured up, towards the top of the playset where the heap had fallen in the first place.

And Spencer saw himself at the top.

Like he had pushed it off.

Pushed Donovan off.

Spencer's breath caught in his throat. He stared at the other version of himself, standing there with a smirk on his face as he admired his work. That other version of him just looked over and smiled, and in the blink of an eye, he was gone.

Spencer — *real* Spencer — was still on the ground, his mouth hung open. And he could still feel The Girl in his arms. He looked back down at her.

"Come home."

Something was wrong. He needed to leave.

He stood up, eyes wide open. "Guys, I gotta go."

"Where?" Kirsten asked, "Spencer, do you really think you—"

"I *need* to go."

Spencer scrambled away from the park, heart pounding as the others followed after him.

Donovan asked, "Where are you going?"

"Home."

"Here, let me ride with you, I can't drive anyway. I can come with you instead and—"

"No." Spencer turned around. "I can't explain it, not right now. But I need to leave."

And he would rather *not* bring any more people to the place that a ghost was leading him to.

"Spence." Kirsten cut him off, making him stop in his tracks. "We get back and you're on the ground, screaming. And now you're leaving? We're worried about you."

Home, it's where he needed to be.

"I saw something," he whispered. "And I need to go."

Kaylee and Brett were home. And as much as The Girl freaked Spencer out, one thing was sure.

She'd never lied to him before.

So, he gave Kirsten a sharp half-smile — one meant to be a goodbye — and walked past her. He had been too late; more times than he ever wanted to admit, he had waited too long.

It killed Mom.

"Hey," Arizona said sharply. "Be careful, alright?"

Spencer waved goodbye to them before breaking out in a sprint towards his car. Because something was happening. He didn't know what, but he wasn't about to wait and let it play out. Being too late wasn't an option.

He did that with Mom.

And it would never happen again.

Chapter Fifteen

Hide...

The front door was open.

That's all Spencer could process.

The front door was *wide freaking open.*

He sped down the driveway and parked crooked, not taking the time to lock his car behind him. And he nearly tripped when he got out wrong, stumbling as he regained his balance by leaning against the hood. He raced up the steps.

The door wasn't just open. It was busted in, he could see the broken lock as soon as he made it up the porch steps. He hugged the wall, ignoring every instinct that screamed at him to get in that house and carry Kaylee and Brett out of there.

Because he'd be no help to either of them dead.

Spencer took a sharp breath and glanced inside.

He couldn't see Kaylee or Brett. The Girl was in the entryway, laughing to herself as she looked up the stairs. The faint sounds of The Mangled Man's sobs rang from the living room and the house.

Kaylee and Brett had to be upstairs, locked away in her room. The only other option was that they were caught by them, or they were already...

No, he wouldn't let himself consider that.

High-stress situations at the hospital would have him talk himself through to a solution, no matter how dumb it made him look at the time. But he couldn't even let himself *breathe* with how loud everything seemed.

So, he tried to think it out, muster up some kind of plan that wasn't running in blindly with a bunch of ghosts.

I gotta go.

Then what, race upstairs? Hope that The Girl just so happens to look away and that they don't hear the sound of his footsteps?

Too freakin' bad, Spence. Got a better idea?

Right. He took a deep breath and bounced on the balls of his feet, ready to bolt – ready to tear Kaylee's door down and get them out of there, then go far, far away.

He looked down, his eyes resting on the decorative stones around his yard. The biggest one caught his eye, so he picked it up.

He aimed towards the middle of the entryway, near the living room. Away from the stairs.

Do it.

Spencer threw the stone, the sound ricocheting off the walls.

The Girl stopped laughing in his ears and walked in its direction.

Go. Now.

He rushed inside as quietly as he could and made a beeline towards the stairs, heart pounding with each footstep. Every movement seemed louder than a drum.

When he reached the top of the stairs, he turned left and tripped over his own two feet while getting there, but he found his way to the end of the hall and hugged Kaylee's door. And he let out an audible sigh of relief when he realized it was locked.

Spencer said quietly, "It's me, open up."

The sound of her frantic whispers, interlaced by what sounded like protests from Brett, filled the room. They might as well have been screams. She unlocked the door, and Spencer barreled in before closing and locking it behind him.

Kaylee threw her arms over him. "What the hell is going on?" She whisper-screamed. "We heard the door bust down, and then someone started laughing, and they've been near the stairs."

"It's okay, Kaylee, I'm gonna get us out of this."

The laughs returned, echoing from the entryway.

And the cries of The Mangled Man.

They couldn't go downstairs.

Spencer bit his lip and looked at the window. No matter what, the only option was down.

As if Brett could read his mind, Brett said way too loudly, "No way, I know that look. That's your thinking look, and a fall from that height could *kill us*, doctor guy."

But Spencer drowned out the boy's protests before he finished his sentence, instead thinking about everything he had learned in Boy Scouts. As a kid, his dad had forced him to join even though he thought it was dumb.

Now, though, there was one lesson that he replayed in his head.

Bowline knot.

Spencer walked over to Kaylee's bed and ripped her sheets and blankets off. If his muscle memory would serve him, he could make a bowline strong enough and hold it to lower Brett and Kaylee down. Then for himself...

He shuddered.

When he got to it, he'd figure something out.

After several attempts, he was able to form the knot. But then he went to pull it through, and it unraveled. His hands shook and his jaw was clenched so tight his vision started to blur.

He could make a makeshift rope out of the blankets if his hands would freaking cooperate.

And Kaylee and Brett were calling his name; he couldn't mentally muffle them no matter how hard he tried. All subtlety was getting thrown out the window in the blink of an eye, and it didn't help that the sheets Spencer was working with were made of satin or silk or whatever slippery material. Spencer bit his lip to stifle the scream that threatened to emerge, and the taste of iron flooded his mouth.

"Talk to me!" Brett yelled. "What is going o—"

"Shut up!"

Spencer closed his eyes and let out a long, shaky breath. Once more, he managed to pull the knot through. He let out an audible breath of relief when it held.

Then he threw it down when it came undone again.

Be it because of how still he was, or his visible frustration, Kaylee and Brett managed to yell louder.

Spencer clenched his jaw. "Guys, *please!*"

Their muffled words formed incoherent questions, but he finally managed to drown them out. There had to be something else he could use.

Spencer scrubbed his face with his hands. And for just a moment, he was able to clear his mind. A fleeting moment, but it was enough.

"I need a rope."

And there was one. In the attic.

Right along the hallway.

He'd have to backtrack, that was the only way.

Through the narrow hallway, no idea where either The Girl or The Mangled Man were. Part of Spencer would prefer taking his chances staying right there.

But he felt his baby sister's eyes burn holes into him, and he knew that wasn't what he'd end up doing.

"I've gotta go," he whispered, more to himself than anyone else.

Get caught in the hallway, and he was dead. Mess up the knot, and whoever went first would be dead. But do nothing, and they were all dead.

Spencer let out a silent shriek, hoping with everything he had in him that Kaylee hadn't noticed.

Then he put his hand on her arm. "I'm going to be right back, alright?"

"*No*," Kaylee protested, making Spencer wince when her voice cracked. "You are *not* going out there."

Even though she knew he would.

From the moment he found out he was having a sister, he knew he'd do anything for her. It was a self-appointed job that he had from a very young age, and the most important one of all.

No matter what it took.

He whispered, "I love you."

Then he let go of her arm, spared Brett one more nod, and unlocked the door.

Just go.

So, he did. Spencer took one more sharp breath before turning the knob, his palms squeaking against it.

And do not look back.

The hall was empty. It felt cold, huge, but at least he was alone. He closed the door behind him and made his way down the hallway, gritting his teeth when he realized just how close to the stairs the attic was.

So close.

He wasn't sure he could open it without The Girl knowing. And more, he didn't know if she was still there at all.

Exposed. Vulnerable, that's how he felt. He could barely breathe through every heavy step, the pit in his stomach refused to go away. And he was shivering, his legs turning to jelly as he struggled to support his weight with his own two feet.

A creak from the stairwell.

He crashed through the door to his left.

Spencer didn't know what he was doing until he found himself hunched in the laundry room. Something pressed up against his arm, and he let out a quiet yelp before realizing it was the cold of the dryer.

He looked through the slits along the door, begging the gaps to not give him away.

He didn't move, he didn't breathe.

The Mangled Man reached the top of the stairs, and he paused.

Don't.

The Mangled Man went towards Kaylee's room.

The door. No thought went into it, Spencer placed his hand on the knob and got ready to burst through the—

A cold hand on top of Spencer's.

And chilled, child-like laughter shrieked in his ears. He screamed and he ripped his hand away, the motion so fast and so rough that it sent him stumbling back. He ran into something on the ground and it made him trip. Before faceplanting, he managed to catch himself on the wall.

The Girl was in the corner, sitting there with an innocent smile plastered on her face. She waved at him, sending bits of gravel to fall to the ground.

Spencer's scream was deafening.

He burst through the door, sprinting the rest of the way down the hall. He made it to the attic's latch in the ceiling, and his shaky fingers found the board that would give way to a ladder.

Next thing he knew, he was scrambling up. He made it up the top and looked around, muttering to himself when he realized just how messy it was up there. The scattered boxes made his heart beat faster, eyes darting to find the buried rope.

They had to be right on his tail.

He threw boxes to the side, feeling around for the rope.

"Come on, come on, come—"

His fingertips met their mark.

And then he let out an agonized scream.

He processed the sound before he noticed the sharp pain in his leg. Blood dripped down as something clamped onto it, pulling him further as he tried to fight away.

Spencer fell and banged his head against the floor.

He rolled on the ground and the world spun around him, everything reduced to muffled lights and screams. Someone towered over him, their blurred silhouette going in and out of focus.

It wasn't The Girl. It wasn't The Mangled Man.

His blood dripped from her nails.

The sight of her was so familiar it almost hurt. Because for a moment he felt comfort in seeing her — like he was supposed to.

But then, that comfort dissipated.

Her hair was dark brown, wavy. And her eyes pitch black. She was wearing the same nightgown that she wore the last time he saw her. It was ripped to shreds, dirt-covered and wearing away at its seams, but he could recognize it anywhere. Like he could recognize her.

That was always her favorite nightgown.

"Ma?"

Chapter Sixteen

... And Seek

The light shone through the shattered window.

At first, it was just that and the pounding in his skull. Voices came from every direction; muffled, hushed whispers that Spencer couldn't place even then. They were gravelly, angry, like they were arguing about something. And as he tried to look in their direction, the dull ache in his neck intensified, his muscles screaming at him through how they had rested. He couldn't get himself to turn.

Tight, unforgiving ropes were buried into his skin, tethering his wrists and ankles to the chair in the living ro—

"Oh, no."

Spencer forced his eyes to open the rest of the way, the blurred haze disorienting him. He tried to blink it away, but a groan escaped his lips, alerting the people who hid in the shadows.

The whispers stopped — it all stopped.

And The Girl giggled before fluttering over to him, leaning in his line of sight with the biggest smile on her face. But somewhere, deep down, Spencer swore there was sadness. It was in her eyes, and then, her voice.

"Fix this."

Duct tape around Spencer's mouth stifled the pitiful screech that begged to surface. He balled his hands into fists, the chair rocking with him as he went to claw, or grab, *anything.* But the rope kept him anchored in place. And there were cries to Spencer's left, cries so muffled and unnatural to him that he didn't want to know who it was.

Because he knew, and he wanted more than anything to be wrong.

It was Kaylee.

The Girl looked in her direction, then back at Spencer. Her smile wavered as if she were deep in thought, but a playful, happy shimmer caught in her black eyes. She put her hand over the shard of glass that eternally pierced into her.

And slowly, she slid it back out.

Kaylee's screams shattered Spencer's ears.

He went to kick but couldn't. He went to rip the blade out of her hands and away from Kaylee, but he couldn't. The chair threatened to tip over — and he hoped it would — but then, there was a heavy creek as weight held it down. It anchored him in that spot, just like his arms.

A groan. A harsh, bellowed groan from decayed, withered lungs. The sound of bones creaking.

Before Spencer realized what he was doing, he looked up.

The Mangled Man stood behind him, head dangling upside down.

He hovered in Spencer's vision just enough to stare with his black, dried-up eyes, a single tear dripping to the ground. The chair stayed rooted while Spencer tried but failed to get any leverage. And he swore, there was the slightest hint of amusement from the man with every pitiful attempt. He pointed back towards The Girl.

And on cue, she raised the glass shard in the air, brandishing it for the world to see. Spencer went to scream, the taste of the tape lacing in his mouth.

The Girl brought the glass closer to Kaylee.

And the cries he heard, the ear-piercing wails, deafened him. He closed his eyes, every pathetic attempt at reaching her unanswered.

Then a soft, warm hand rested on his.

Kaylee's.

Spencer opened his eyes, tears blurring his vision. And as the world cleared and his heart pounded in his ears, he saw his sister lean towards him, her right wrist cut from its restraints.

The Girl put the glass back in her chest as simply as if she were putting a phone in her pocket. She ripped the duct tape off Kaylee's mouth, and then Spencer's. His lips burned, but he pushed the pain away.

"Are you okay?" he whispered to Kaylee.

Her cries filled the room, giving him the response he needed.

She rested her head against his shoulder and screamed into it. Her tears soaked his shirt — he could feel her warmth against his arm — and the sounds burned holes into his ears. Even more prominent than the light that shone through the window, still shattered from when he had broken it days ago.

Spencer angled his gaze up just enough to see The Girl. She stood there, stoic, fiddling with the tape she had just ripped from their mouths.

"Let her go!" he yelled.

The Girl sighed, and the bone-chilling sound made the room colder, dead. When Spencer tried to reach again, The Mangled Man tightened his grip on the chair, an amused chuckle emitting from dried-out, rotting lips.

Spencer squeezed Kaylee's hand. "What happened? Where's Brett?"

"You fell, you screamed, and then they busted the door down." She let out another sob. "I don't know where he is."

Then, as if on cue, more screams filled the house.

Brett's.

Kaylee gasped. "What the *fuck* are you doing to him?"

The Girl put a finger over her lips and started to circle around them, The Mangled Man following in her steps. Prancing, she hummed her same old melody while he complemented the tune perfectly. Like they had practiced it over and over again.

She settled to Spencer's right, giving The Mangled Man empty space near Kaylee.

Spencer tried to fight towards them, but, of course, that didn't happen; after chuckling at the useless attempt, The Mangled Man slammed a phone down on the table in front of them.

And it rang.

Tristan Levign

This time, Kaylee fought. "Dad?"

Spencer stayed in stunned silence as the ringing continued, growing louder. First it was normal, but it kept going and going, long past when it would have hung up and gone to voicemail.

"Dad!" Kaylee repeated.

The ringing turned to high-pitched squeals. Spencer's head was pounding and everything was in a muffle, it sounded like everything was in a tunnel and it fuc—

"Answer the freaking phone!"

And then, there was just the sound of Spencer and Kaylee's labored breathing. He kept his eyes on The Mangled Man, who was looking down at the phone like he didn't know who was on the other side or what Dad was going to say.

But he did. Spencer knew there was no other alternative.

Kaylee squeezed his hand even tighter. It throbbed; he could feel his racing pulse against hers. But he didn't want her to let go.

Not ever.

"Please," he whispered. "Just let us go."

More footsteps. The Girl slowly closed what little gap there was between him and her. She got so close that he could feel the small gust of wind against his hair. He could feel her cold breaths travel in his ears and send chills down his back.

He could only manage a wince. A wince to try and get away.

"Too late."

The Mangled Man looked up, and he laughed. Cackled. Snickered. Erupted in a fit of laughter that was so loud that Spencer could hear it blare in his head. Like it was traveling in between his ears, the sound bouncing through a tunnel.

The lights flickered. The TV blared. The room shook, and through it all, The Mangled Man laughed on.

Then the phone rang once more before going to voicemail.

"We didn't mean it."

It was Dad.

"We didn't mean it."

"We didn't mean it."

Faster.

"We didn't mean it. We didn't mean it. We didn't mean it. We didn't mean it. We didn't mean it. We didn't—"

Spencer choked out, "Turn it off!"

"We didn't mean it. We didn't mean it. We didn't mean it. We didn't mean it. We didn't mean it. We didn't mean it. We didn't mean it. We didn't mean it. We didn't mean it. We didn't mean it. We didn't mean it. We—"

"Shut up!"

It stopped.

Everything stopped.

And for a few seconds, all Spencer could process was Kaylee's head pressed tightly against his shoulders and her hand clasped in his. He went to say something, but the words died on his tongue before they could ever dream of surfacing.

The Girl motioned someone in.

And the screaming returned.

Brett was thrown on the ground.

He was hog-tied, blood streaming from his scalp. His blue eyes were glossed over, his weary gaze shifting back and forth between Spencer and Kaylee.

Spencer lunged towards him, barely registering the ropes that dug into his skin. He screamed, and Kaylee screamed, but it was muffled — why was she muffled? — and Spencer cried, clawed, shook in his stupid chair but for the life of him he could not get closer. He pushed on and the chair started to tip, but The Girl caught him before he could—

Cold hands slithered over his mouth, stifling his cries.

And curly, dark brown hair swayed in the corner of his vision. The remnants of dirt from a battered, frail nightgown brushed against his skin. An icy chill sang in his ears.

Spencer looked over at Kaylee again, her tear-filled eyes wide.

Mom's hands were clasped over her lips.

Even though she shouldn't be there, like how she should never have been there ever again. She was dead, she had been for six years. Spencer went to cry her name, but, well...

How would that go?

He squeezed his sister's hand, feeling their bones mesh to one. The room blurred, everything turned to slow motion as he slowly shifted his gaze back to Brett, so battered and broken.

And while Spencer wanted to call for him, to tell him to fight with everything he had in him, the words wouldn't surface.

The Mangled Man smiled, showing gaps from where teeth had fallen out. Loud stomps echoed around the room and brought him closer to Brett. The boy shook, and Spencer cried for him, but neither could move. Kaylee let out a sob that drowned them all out as The Mangled Man lifted Brett off the ground by his hair.

The sun caught the blade of a knife.

"We didn't mean it."

Brett closed his eyes.

And the knife was brought down.

Blood splattered on Spencer's face, mirroring the maroon-painted walls.

All that remained was Kaylee's agonized sobs as Brett fell, a heap on the ground. Then one last chant – Spencer knew he would remember it forever.

Despite the cries, the phrase was all Spencer could hear.

"We didn't mean it."

Tears streamed down his face, and his mom uncovered his mouth. And The Girl placed her hand on his shoulder one more time, not sending the words straight into Spencer's head like she usually did.

It didn't echo around in his mind like normal; she spoke to him.

"*You* were too late."

The cold, dead words bit Spencer. And he tried to turn back, tried to find his mom in the room again. Because she was supposed to help them — she was *always* supposed to help them. He looked on all sides, but she stood somewhere he couldn't see with the stupid restraints anchoring him to this chair.

Kaylee gasped for air.

Spencer looked up in time to see her grab her neck, eyes bugging out as she choked on nothing.

Just like Kirsten.

He cried, "Kayl—"

His throat closed. The pit formed in his chest again as he and Kaylee squeezed each other's hands so tightly he thought bones were breaking. And even more than any other time, he wouldn't dream of letting go.

The world faded to black.

But not before The Mangled Man's laughter filled the air again.

That and Dad's voice. One laced with fear and hurt and regret and so many things that Spencer had never heard from the man. In a voice never as pained or confused or fragile, a tone that was foreign when it came to his dad.

"We didn't mean it."

Chapter Seventeen

Silence

Spencer woke to the sound of distant mutters. Kaylee, he recognized her voice in an instant. He didn't pick up much of what she was saying, though somewhere deep down, he knew they weren't meant for him. All he knew was that he needed to go to her, but his eyelids may as well have been glued shut, weights thrown on his chest for good measure, anchoring him down on the ground.

He wasn't tied to the chair anymore – instead, he was lying on his back, aching limbs free. There were no footsteps to his left or creepy laughs to his right.

They were gone. *Mom* was gone.

He opened his eyes.

Blood painted the walls, the floors. Everywhere he looked there was a splatter, a puddle, a pool of it where Brett must have been. He knew how much blood was in the human body — heck, he didn't need to be a med student to know it was a lot — but *seeing* it...

Spencer rubbed his eyes and sat up. His head spun, reducing the living room to a sea of muffled, swirling crimson blotches. He blinked until his world stopped spinning, and he looked towards where Kaylee's voice had come from.

His lips parted.

There she was, cradling Brett.

She ran her hands through his hair, the matted-up bundle of ashy blonde now stained red. The motion repeated, over and over again, without Kaylee taking her eyes off Brett's. Blood webbed down his cheek, forming an intricate design against his pale skin. Another streak went down his nose.

For just a moment, Spencer's eyes directed towards Brett's torso, but the sight made him snap away. Instead, he crawled towards Kaylee and put his hand over her free one. She paused for a second, maybe even less.

Then, as if she were never interrupted, she went back to her ritual of stroking Brett's hair and whispering something to him. If she actually was forming words, they were so soft that Spencer couldn't hear them.

"Kaylee." He murmured, "Are you okay?"

No response.

He looked at her, and from what he could tell, she didn't seem to be bleeding. But with Brett in her lap, he couldn't know for sure. Spencer looked himself over too, not trusting those things to have just left him alone when the deed was done.

But nothing hurt.

Spencer looked around for his phone. "I'm calling for help."

Kaylee whispered something, a breath of a whisper that he never could have made out.

"What was that?" he whispered.

She spoke to Brett again, cradling him as she rocked back and forth. As if she could say or do the right thing and the boy would wake up, and everything would be okay. She tried, and she tried again.

"I already called an ambulance." Her voice was shallow, hoarse, as if it had been days since the last time she spoke.

Spencer nodded, and for the life of him he didn't know what to say. He thought of the visions of Kirsten and how they ripped him to shreds. But they were just that, visions – even if it felt like he could touch Kirsten, she wasn't really there. Now, Brett was swimming in a pool of his own—

Just days prior, Brett was the goofball boyfriend with a bunch of brothers and an aversion to chicken. Now, he was soaked in nothing but blood.

Kaylee scrunched her brow and ran her thumb over a line of blood that trickled down Brett's face. It smeared, the one blotch on what was a pristine network of branching-off lines. And she did it again, almost seeming satisfied with each stroke. Cleaning him, revealing more of the boy behind all that red, even if he didn't look right anymore.

Even though he would never look right again.

"Hold on," Kaylee softly whispered. "They're gonna help you."

A tear rolled down Spencer's cheek.

Help. Hold on. Those two phrases bounced around in his mind. There was no help, Brett couldn't hold on. But she whispered it to him again and again, in a chant – a spell, a quiet prayer that she repeated breathlessly. Spencer reached for, hoping to snap her out of it.

"It's okay," Kaylee whispered. "It's okay, it's okay, it's okay. They're going to help you."

Spencer bit his lip. "Kaylee..."

"You're gonna be fine. They are going to help you. It's okay."

"Come on, I wanna look you over and make sure they didn't—"

"I am *fine*, Spencer!" Her lip quivered and she held Brett tighter. So tight that he somehow managed to look frailer. Breakable.

Her voice cracked as she said to Brett, "You're fine."

Sirens blared in the distance. They were muffled, but Spencer could make them out anywhere. And he knew that Kaylee knew they'd take Brett away, she couldn't stay there with him. But he couldn't let them be the ones to tear him from her grasp.

He needed to do this.

With a sigh, Spencer held his arms out to move Brett off of her. But Kaylee resisted long enough to whisper in his ear, barely audible.

"They're gonna take you away."

Her tears started to flow freely. She wiped at them, smearing a red haze across her face.

But she stopped telling Brett he'd be alright, and her chanting stopped, leaving deafening silence to echo around the house. Words couldn't help her; Spencer knew that much. So, he curled up next to her and put his arms over her shoulder.

She leaned into him, keeping her eyes on Brett. "He just bought his little brother, Tyler, a toy superhero," Kaylee told Spencer. "Right before we heard the door break down, he finally found the collectable or whatever it was that Tyler had begged him for. He went to all the different stores he could think of, and he was so upset about not getting it, until he finally found a listing. And he was so excited to get it for him."

Spencer didn't say anything — he listened to the sirens, how swiftly they were approaching. And he felt Kaylee tense up at the sound as well.

"And now he's—" Kaylee's voice cut out. She slammed her hand against the floor. "What kind of *crap* is that?"

Her cries filled the house.

Spencer threw his other arm around her, and she let go of Brett, holding Spencer so tight he could barely breathe. Her body wracked with sobs, trembling with every breath.

Tears of Spencer's own blurred the sight of Brett, so he closed his eyes, revealing more red that lingered behind his lids. And his mind kept playing over and over again what The Girl had said to him.

'You *were too late.'*

It was a warning, a warning to come home.

"I'm sorry. I'm so sorry," Kaylee said to Brett.

Never in a million years could Spencer bring himself to understand how Mom was involved in this. How his mother was a ghost, how she had anything to do with The Mangled Man or The Girl. Or how Dad showed up in that message.

Nothing, Spencer didn't understand any of it.

"He wanted to call the cops," Kaylee said quietly. "He tried, but I told him that we should go downstairs and see what was going on. I thought it was nothing. But I..."

"Kaylee, no."

"It's my fault. I should've let him make the call."

"It's not your fault, okay? I promise you, it's not." He shifted so he was in front of Kaylee, blocking her view of

Brett. "You wanna blame someone? Blame the freaks who broke into our house in the first place."

"Spence, *Mom*..."

But before she could finish, the sound of approaching sirens rang through the house, accompanied by footsteps. Paramedics and police flooded in. It didn't take long for them to see blood splatters from the entry, Spencer could hear them march down the hall.

In a matter of seconds, they would be swarmed.

Spencer gently moved Brett off of Kaylee, and she didn't fight him. He supported Brett's head and let him lie down on the ground.

"We're gonna get through this." He put his hands on Kaylee's shoulders. "Stay with me, alright?"

She nodded. And she didn't break the stare as the people crowded around them and checked them out, she stayed motionless as they took Brett away. The people asked them questions, questions that neither of them could perceive yet.

Spencer and Kaylee were moved, but one thing remained.

Neither of them broke their stare.

The next shred of time was a blur.

Spencer didn't know how long it was, and frankly, he didn't care. It was later in the day — the sun wasn't beating down on him anymore, scorching his eyes.

A part of Spencer wanted to believe that what just happened, didn't actually happen. But then he'd see Brett collapse, and just when he thought it was finished, the whole thing would start over again.

And without exception, his mind would always find its way back to Mom. She quieted them, hurt Spencer. Never in a million years would he have thought...

He needed to talk to Dad.

It wasn't an optional way to get more information, not anymore. Maybe Mom wouldn't have wanted Spencer to dig for answers, but her daughter was about to see her boyfriend get buried. And she would have never wanted that.

Kaylee was getting checked out in the back of the ambulance next to Spencer. He could see her, but any bit of distance made him uneasy. The cops had just finished getting his description of everything, and when they asked if there was someone they could call, Kirsten's was the number he had given them.

He blinked, and next thing he knew, he saw Kirsten's little silver car. She ran out of it, mascara running down her face, towards Spencer.

The weight of her toppling into his chest nearly swept him off his feet.

"Are you okay?" She wrapped her arms around him. "What the hell happened? I could tell something was off, but then I got a call, and they said that you were hurt and I had to come and—"

"Kirsten," Spencer interrupted as he let go of the hug. "Brett's gone."

"What?" She looked over towards Kaylee, then back to him. "Oh, Spence, I'm so sorry."

"She's torn up right now. I mean, doing way better than I could ever..." He trailed off, having forgotten who he was talking to.

Spencer hesitated. Because he wanted Kirsten to hug him. He wanted to throw his arms around her again as she told him that somehow, it would be okay.

But he couldn't, not near Kaylee. Not there.

"She'd do anything to be able to do this with him, you know?" Spencer told her, "If we just be — for lack of better words, calm — I think that'd be better, for now."

The paramedics finished looking at Kaylee, and she slowly started walking towards them.

Before she got to them, Kirsten whispered, "I understand. But just know, and I'm saying this as calmly as I can, I'm so glad you're okay."

He gave her a weak smile in reply.

Then when Kaylee walked to them with her head down, Spencer held his arm out for her so she could lean on him. She silently took the offer and buried her face in his shoulder.

"Kaylee," Kirsten whispered, "I'm so sorry."

The two of them were like sisters. They wanted to have one, never did, but then they met. And suddenly, there was a missing part of their lives that was finally filled.

All Kaylee said in response was, "I don't know what to do."

One of the paramedics walked up to them. "I was just telling your sister that she's going to be fine. No injuries."

"That's great news, thank you."

"You, on the other hand, I would like to take to the hospital. Get you checked out." He pointed towards his head. "You were knocked out twice in one day."

Spencer agreed, feeling some comfort in knowing from experience that the hospital allowed overnight visitors. There was no way he'd let Kaylee out of his sight. "Can she ride with me?" he asked as he gestured towards her.

"That'd be fine."

He nodded in a silent thanks, and everyone started to ready the ambulance. Kaylee leaned in, bearing her weight on his shoulder.

And yeah, his head was killing him, he'd be lying if he said there wasn't any fear of problems or what the doctors could find. But there, in the moment, he couldn't focus on it — Kaylee was going through more than he could ever imagine. Brett had said Spencer was her superhero, the one she looked up to for everything.

But what could he do to help her this time?

All he could do was hold Kaylee and tell her it was all going to be alright. And in the process, silently convince himself that he wasn't lying to her.

He couldn't do that again.

Chapter Eighteen

Shades of Grey

Neither of them were holding it together.

It had been days since Spencer and Kaylee made eye contact, at least that Spencer could remember. There would be attempts from him, at initiating some kind of smile or glance in each other's direction. She'd try to reciprocate. The wheels would visibly turn in her head, begging to let a sign of life show.

But, like clockwork, she'd sigh and look away from him again.

That same old routine would continue with Spencer reminding her that if she wanted to talk to him, he'd always be there for her. Silence would be broken long enough for her to say thank you, and then the deafening roar of their own speechlessness would come back for vengeance.

Four days. It had been like that for four days.

Spencer had more than enough time to think. About
Brett, the ghosts, everything. But without pass, his mind
would rest on one thing.

Mom held them back and made them watch Brett get
killed. It wasn't The Girl. It wasn't The Mangled Man.

It was absolutely and unmistakably Mom.

Mom, who had been dead for six years. Mom, who, when
she was alive, did anything she could just to bring a smile
to her kids' faces.

Now, Kaylee couldn't say her name. And she winced
when anyone tried to mention her. Through everything,
seeing that made the memories of younger Kaylee and
his mom all the more painful.

They went to the hospital, but they were well enough to
not get admitted. Then when they realized that for the
second time in their lives that home was a bloodied
crime scene with police tape, Donovan had told them
they could stay over. Arizona had accepted, and Spencer
and Kaylee stayed in their tiny guest room and office
combo, using air mattresses that deflated midway
through the night.

And no words could help them through it.

Now, Spencer was laying on his air mattress, his
midsection against the ground from it deflating through
the night. His back and legs were still propped up, but
the rest of him ached from the wooden floor.

Since Brett died, this was the first time Spencer wasn't around Kaylee. And even though deep down he was sure she was fine, his mind didn't get that message.

Spencer cleared his throat, his voice deep and hoarse from lack of use. And he did the only thing he could think of doing.

"Brett," he said quietly.

Like how he had talked to Mom for years. Real Mom, not whoever it was that put them in this situation to begin with.

"I'm so sorry."

He was so sick of saying that.

Guilt wasn't the reason, it was well beyond that. Brett would never see his brothers or his mother again, never go to engineering school. His youngest brother Tyler would get that gift that Brett had bought, but it would never, ever be the same.

And Brett wouldn't get to see him grow up, wouldn't get to see the man he'd become. *That* is why Spencer was sorry.

"Everything just feels wrong now. Like, you were there, and then you were screaming, and then you weren't there anymore and…"

And he 'wasn't there anymore'.

Spencer scrubbed his face with his hands. "What am I gonna do with Kaylee? She won't even look at me."

For a moment, one that left in the blink of an eye, Spencer could hear Brett say it again. A memory of the boy helping Spencer more than he could ever know, probably with no clue that it would even be remembered for any real length of time.

But it would never go away.

'You know she thinks the world of you, right?'

Spencer sighed. "Thank you for that, Brett."

He had more to say, he just didn't know how to say it. The phrasing, the tone.

Words didn't exist, not ones that would do Brett justice. So, Spencer didn't say anything else.

He sat up too fast, and he rested his head against his palm as he waited for the world to stop spinning. Stars and patterns swirled in his vision until he managed to blink them away.

He stood up and grabbed his glasses from Donovan's desk. There would be a time to go home and get his stuff, that was something that Spencer wasn't willing to compromise on.

But he knew it would probably be a while. So, he sat down at Donovan's desk and took out a pen and one of many colorful sticky notes. His old list with the phrases was gone, but having them written down made Spencer feel better somehow. Safer, almost. Like he could look at it one day and figure it out, then this whole mess would finally be over. He wrote them again.

Fix this

Help her

Come home

Spencer softly drummed the pen against the desk, idly realizing that he was tapping out the beat of his and Kirsten's song again.

The Girl was helping him, wasn't she? As a kid, he was terrified of her. But a guide, in a way, that's what she was now. He did want to '*fix this*,' one of the most important things to Spencer was figuring out how to '*help her*,' even without specifying who 'her' was.

Kaylee had to go to her graduation rehearsal, she had left earlier in the day for that. In her absence, Spencer slowly walked across the room. He was glad that there wasn't a fake grin, or a genuine frown etched across his face. It was the closest he could get to neutral, and for that, Spencer was grateful.

He walked out and made his way to the kitchen, trying to be quiet. Arizona would be out at school, but Donovan's classes weren't until later. Knowing his friend, he probably had slept for only a couple of hours by then, despite it being eight in the morning.

It was second nature to Spencer, finding a bowl in Donovan's cupboard and cereal in his pantry. With how many times he had been to Donovan's place, he knew where just about everything was.

A second home, that's what it felt like.

Just like Donovan had no problem setting up shop and camping out in Spencer's living room when he was bored and wanted to hang out. No invitation needed, nine times out of ten.

"Pour me a bowl too, would ya?" Donovan asked behind Spencer, making him jump. "Fuckin' starving."

Spencer turned, already trying to come up with some kind of stupid, witty response. Then when he saw his friend, really there was no need to say anything. His chuckle was enough.

Donovan was leaning against his door frame, still blinking sleep away. His jet black hair was strewn about, with the word 'bedhead' giving it no justice whatsoever. One of his pant legs was rolled up, hiding the graphics from his favorite cartoon.

With a smirk, Spencer simply said, "*Nice.*"

"Ah, shut your mouth, Levign." He stretched and walked over to the kitchen. "I dunno how you wake up this early all the time. Dude, how is the sun even up?"

"It's almost nine."

"Exactly my point."

Spencer rolled his eyes, though he exaggerated the motion. In truth, he appreciated it. It almost seemed inappropriate to try and act happy around Kaylee, but with just Donovan there, all bets were off.

But then Donovan asked, "You okay?"

"I'll be alright," Spencer replied, wanting to talk about something he *hadn't* just spent days stewing in. "Honest."

"Of course you will. It's you. But do you wanna talk about it anyway?"

"I'd rather not."

"Fair."

The A/C was loud again. It provided background noise that calmed Spencer in some weird way that he couldn't place. Kinda like how people like listening to nature sounds or white noise when they want to sleep.

Donovan's face slipped into a half-smile. "By the way, that panda, you forgot it on the table. It's in my room, don't worry, Kirsten didn't see it."

The panda. Thinking about it brought an instant smile to his face, one that Donovan picked up and returned in a heartbeat.

He had his back. Always.

"Thank you for that. Of course I forgot the one thing I needed." Spencer said with a chuckle, "You know me too well."

"I know everything."

"Oh yeah? What's my birthday?"

"March ninth."

"What's my zodiac?"

"You have no idea."

"Correct, very good."

Donovan pursed his lips, a smirk forming. "You're a Pisces, by the way."

"Ugh, shut up."

They chuckled, resting their hands against the counter. It wasn't a loud, erupting fit of laughter that usually happened when the two of them went back and forth like that.

But it was something.

Baby steps, one step at a time, all that.

But, like always, his mind wouldn't settle. There was a part of his brain that wouldn't stop reminding him that Brett couldn't feel better. That he would never feel better. And even if Spencer didn't necessarily want to talk about it — the words made it seem too real too fast — he had to.

He took a deep breath. "Everything just feels different now, it's the only way I can think to explain it. He was just there, yanno? And it feels like just yesterday he was going on about stuff from his history class or going on rants about weirdo customers at the restaurant." Spencer hesitated before saying, "Now he's just, he's not saying anything. And it's not fair."

"It's not." Donovan sighed. "It never will be. I won't lie and say otherwise."

The room was fiercely quiet, the silence blaring.

Spencer asked, "I just don't understand. I know it might be a selfish question, but why us? How could we possibly deserve this?"

"You don't. Look, like I said, those ghosts were killed in a car accident before you were even born. I don't know what kind of shady shit they were up to or what happened with them, but you don't deserve any of it."

He didn't, and neither did Kaylee. Neither did *Brett*. But his mind played a chant, one that he tried but failed to escape from.

One person would know.

Spencer stood there silently. Hiding in the shadows and waiting it out did nothing other than get someone killed.

So, he told Donovan, "I've gotta go see him."

There was no need to specify to Donovan who 'he' was. His friend had spent the last six years trying to get Spencer to make the drive to Dad and finally get more from him.

Now, that option seemed more important than ever. Necessary, even.

"You do," Donovan confirmed.

And this time, he couldn't take 'no' for an answer.

Spencer asked, "Is Kaylee okay here? I can ask if she wants to go, but I think it'd be better for her to stay."

"Of course."

"Thanks, man."

"Hell, Ari's been wanting to see her. Maybe Kirsten could come over. Let them spend some time together." Donovan bit his lip. "Let you take some time, too."

Spencer couldn't argue with that, he needed to take a step back. He could actually feel his muscles relax as he let his shoulders droop, and he slouched — replacing his fake smile of deceitful optimism with a blank stare.

Donovan told him, "As bad as things might seem, come to me whenever. I know I'm not the best with this. Cheesy crap has always been a 'you' thing."

He thought his words out carefully; Spencer could see every bit of it.

An open book, written in a language only Spencer could understand.

"My door's always gonna be open for you, alright, Spence?"

Spencer shot him a smile, and once again he realized how lost he would be without his friend. His brother, really, that's what he was to him.

And, at times like this, his lifeline.

"Thanks, man."

Chapter Nineteen

Frontline

Spencer's first instinct was to pack his bag. Then, when he realized that he didn't have much of a bag to pack, he sat down at Donovan's desk.

Fix this

Help her

Come home

No more doubts. No more sitting in the shadows, hoping that the solutions to this cryptic riddle would fall right into his lap.

Soon after his talk with Donovan, Spencer called Dad again. And he asked — sternly, it didn't really qualify as a request if he was being honest — to visit Dad at his trailer. Where he and Kaylee used to go for the occasional weekend so Dad could geek out and bring the kids to work and Mom could have time to herself. Spencer hadn't been there since that week before his graduation, when he found Mom.

Donovan agreed to drive him to his house first. He'd pick up some of his stuff — what he could get of it, at least — and get his car. Then he'd drive over and hopefully get to Dad that night.

But first, Kaylee. He couldn't just leave her.

So, he waited in the room, unsure of how long he stayed there. It wouldn't usually matter, but he was so lost in his own thoughts that everything seemed to move at a snail's pace. He had already texted her, asking her to come back, to which she promised she would.

True to her word, she slowly opened and closed the front door. Spencer could hear her mutter something to herself, and then she was in front of him, with dress pants and a button-up red shirt.

It matched the twinge she had in her eyes.

"Hey," she whispered.

"Hey," Spencer replied, hating the hoarseness to her voice and how wet with tears her eyes still were. "Are you okay?"

She only shrugged in reply.

It was a lot like this after Mom seemingly passed away. They'd get through it — only, there was a fear that this would be even harder. Kaylee's world had already built itself back up, and now it had crashed back down.

Spencer got up off Donovan's desk chair and motioned towards it. Kaylee quietly walked over and sat down.

"I'm worried about you," he admitted.

"I know you are, I can see it every time you look at me." Kaylee sighed. "Spence, I miss him. And it really, really hurts. You can't make that go away."

"I wanna help you."

"And that's nice of you, but you didn't see what happened. Not like I did." Kaylee shook her head. "I don't even know if you'd wanna know. If I could unsee it, I would."

He knelt down so he could be face to face with her. The avoiding eye contact, the little moments of making brief connections before looking away, couldn't go on.

Their parents did something to make these things hate them so much, the voicemail The Mangled Man played was enough to assure Spencer of that.

"Is there anything that you could tell me?"

"Spence, I don't know if you want—"

"Please, Kaylee. I'm going to Dad's to figure out what The Mangl—" Spencer caught himself before correcting, "What that guy was showing us from the voicemail. Maybe you saw something before we were tied up."

He had kept Kaylee in the dark for so long that somewhere along the way, she stopped asking. When he finally filled in the blanks, he swore to himself he'd tell her everything she wanted to know.

After a moment, Kaylee took a sharp breath. "We heard you fall. I tried to believe that it was the people who came in, that they got hurt by you somehow and it was all over. But Brett, he just, he knew, yanno? He always did."

She shook her head, longing eyes flickering the moment she said Brett's name. It was like she managed to fall for him all over again.

"Like I said, Brett wanted to call the cops. But I wanted to see you so badly, make sure they didn't get to you and I—" A tear trickled down her face, and she wiped it away. "So, I went out anyway, didn't even wait. And you know Brett, he saw me leave, so he came with."

It was like everything played out in front of Kaylee's eyes. A movie, a dream, something.

"Then I woke up in the living room."

Spencer nodded, not needing her to fill in the blanks. They got knocked out, tied up, and all three of them were taken to the living room. But he still had no clue why, of all of them, Brett was the one they took.

"Why him?" Kaylee asked quietly.

He could only offer a slow shake of the head. "I don't know," he admitted.

A small part of Kaylee looked satisfied with that answer. She continued, "That guy played the tape, then he and the girl looked at each other. That's when Mom came up behind us."

He shuddered at the thought. It was the first time in so long that Kaylee said the word 'mom,' and there was a bite to her voice.

Spencer decided to take a shot. His sister was always more observant than him.

"What did Mom look like?" he asked.

"What?"

"Humor me."

"Pale, she still had her nightgown on. It was torn up, her hair was all over the place. Why?"

"And her eyes?"

"Her *eyes*?"

"Yeah, like how did they look? Were they black?"

Kaylee considered that before saying, "Yes. Like, black-black. Even worse than they used to be, which, frankly, I didn't even think was possible."

Pain crept up in Spencer's chest, a fresh knife wound to the heart. He had hoped that Kaylee wouldn't remember that side of Mom. Hoped that with her being younger, her subconscious had rejected it. And Mom's legacy was the real her, not whatever she became.

Reckless optimism.

Spencer almost shuddered at the thought.

"I'm sorry," he said to her. "I should've warned you. I hoped that you would just forget how she was towards the end."

"I didn't."

This time, it was Spencer's turn to break eye contact. When Mom was getting worse, he'd be the one to talk to her. To take the hits in the hopes that maybe, just maybe, Kaylee wouldn't see what was happening to their mother.

She asked, "What the hell happened to her?"

"That's not an easy question."

"Spence."

"I honestly don't know." The words spilled out of his mouth like a burst dam. "It wasn't her."

"What do you mean, 'it wasn't her?'"

A soft sigh escaped him. He really was about to tell her everything, wasn't he? He had spent years trying to keep this from her. It would seem like the right time to tell her, he'd end up giving her a bit longer anyway, then that cycle would repeat itself.

Until eventually, reopening the old wound never seemed right.

Now, though, he supposed it was opened *for* him.

"Something happened with those people in the living room, they died years ago. I think Mom and Dad had something to do with it." Spencer fiddled with his collar as he continued, "Then they controlled her — possessed her — all the way up until she died. And now, I don't know how, but she's back."

He had never said that out loud, only glimpses of it to Donovan. Kaylee bit her lip, stifling whatever remark no doubt threatened to surface.

"I know it sounds ridiculous," Spencer spouted out. "But c'mon, Kaylee, you saw them. They weren't human, at least not anymore. Mom's—"

"A ghost?"

"Yes."

And he needed to know why. His love for horror taught him that ghosts always wanted something. What she wanted would remain a mystery until he asked Dad. Because he could blame his dad for a lot of things, but his parents loved each other. Knew each other in a way that no one else did.

Spencer finally looked his sister in the eyes again.

"Please trust me."

All he knew was that Mom would beg him to do this if she could.

Chapter Twenty

Left in Darkness

With much more effort than Spencer would care to admit, he was able to park next to the forest that held his dad's trailer.

It had a decent enough path, one that Dad had tried to plow back when Spencer was in high school. That — one of Dad's more ambitious 'fix-it' projects — started off well, then contracts and life got in the way, resulting in a path they could only walk through.

Spencer glared at the forest, having never been as outdoors-y as his dad. He got out and locked his car, giving it a couple extra clicks and pulling on the handle just for good measure. Through all that, he caught himself watching as the setting sun caught on the trees and formed a silhouette along the orange sky.

The trailer was about two hours away from home. Dad would move it around if his work assignment was too far away, but usually, he'd settle it in the same spot along the lake. It called to Dad, made him feel 'where he was supposed to be.' When Spencer would ask what *that* was supposed to mean, Dad would keep his lips sealed.

Spencer started through the trail, listening as the leaves crunched underneath his feet.

Though he'd need to do it alone this time, usually someone would come along. It was so familiar to Kaylee that she could probably find her way through the path with her eyes closed. Donovan had tried once, but he freaked out when he saw a ladybug and realized the forest wasn't for him.

It only took a minute or two for Spencer to reach the point that wasn't paved anymore. He was met with a group of trees, the occasional one marked with a long-faded red '*X*' to help guide the way. He saw a root to his left, recognizing it in an instant. One of his first walks through the forest, he had stumbled over it and nearly broken his ankle.

Truly, he got a lot of his traits from Mom.

He followed its path, his muscle memory leading the way. The marked trees every few feet let him settle down and try not to think about every rustle or broken branch around him.

Now that he was back here, the vision was stronger than ever — it was engraved in his memory, just as vivid as it was when he was fourteen. When Dad got this patch of land and decided to settle after The Incident. Spencer did what he did best as a hopelessly optimistic kid and set out to explore the forest with Mom's encouragement, smiling face and beady eyes and all.

All until he walked into a little girl's path.

That was the first time The Girl showed up, bringing the vision of Mom with her. Now that he was there, in the forest, he couldn't even blink without seeing it again.

He grit his teeth and took heavy steps forward until he made it to the clearing that housed Dad's trailer. The clearing was about a half an acre, with the old, dingy trailer in the middle. The lawn mowed and the yard empty, save for one tree to the left.

Spencer' tree, where they got a treehouse built for him.

He looked up at it, in awe at the fact that, despite the wood rot and holes in its floor, it was still there. A standing death trap, even for someone who wasn't clumsy like him, but there. Spencer gave the tree a pat on one of its branches like it was an old friend before directing his attention back to the trailer.

Back to Dad. Back to answers. A few more steps got him there. And the door opened before Spencer even had the chance to knock, replacing the wood with his dad's smiling face.

His green, plaid shirt made the color in his eyes pop. His hair was brown like Kaylee's, same as his stubble from not wanting a beard but hating the process of shaving. Just like he always looked, only a bit more rugged and muscly than Spencer remembered.

"Spence!" Dad held his arms out for Spencer, but the motion wasn't returned.

It had been far too long for that.

Sometimes, Dad would act upset. Others, he would be so dang cheery that Spencer wouldn't know how to handle it. It was like that when he was a kid too — there were two ways Dad would act, and it was a flip of a coin of which Spencer would come home to.

"Hey Dad," Spencer replied after a moment, having moved away from the man without meaning to. "Thanks for letting me come over."

His dad kept his arms out a moment, then gently lowered them to his sides. Head down, he waved it away. "Ah, you're always welcome here. Come on in."

Spencer nodded in a silent thanks when Dad stepped aside.

The inside looked massive to him, especially in comparison to how tiny the place looked from the outside. There was a couch against the wall, with reclining chairs next to it facing the TV. One of the chairs was Dad's, the other, Mom's when she'd come to visit him for the weekend. And the couch was for the kids or guests or whoever was not Mom or Dad.

Whatever happened, no one sat in Mom or Dad's spot.

Out of habit, Spencer walked over to the couch and stiffly sat down. Dad went to the attached kitchen, leaving Spencer to look at the TV and whatever random fix-it show Dad was watching at the time. He had either muted it when Spencer showed up or a while beforehand.

Something started to brew, and the strong smell of coffee filled the trailer. Spencer's nose scrunched, just like it always did when people brewed that stuff.

After a while, Dad walked in with two mugs in hand. He passed one to Spencer.

"Thank you." Spencer hesitantly took it. He winced before saying, "I really appreciate it, but I'm not into coffee. To me, it tastes—"

"'Like burnt water,' I know. You're allowed to be wrong." Dad chuckled and settled on his chair. "That's hot chocolate."

Spencer smiled and took a sip. Maybe he was too quick in thinking that Dad had forgotten.

"I'm sorry to hear about Brett, he was a good kid. Really made Kaylee happy." Dad sighed and put his cup on the table between his spot and Mom's. "How's she doing?"

"As well as she possibly could be. She's hurting, but she'll be alright."

His dad nodded. "And what about you?"

"Fine. We got along pretty well, but he—"

"No, no 'buts,' we don't see each other enough to waste time lying."

Spencer almost chuckled at the mention of him needing to not lie or bend the truth, but Dad either didn't notice or decided not to acknowledge it.

"Knowing you," Dad continued, "you probably found a way to blame yourself for it. Someone broke in and stabbed Brett, but that's on you somehow, right?"

One thing about Dad was that he always knew what was on Spencer's mind. Speed, it was the thing that he had messed up with both Mom and Brett. The Girl showed him what he needed to see, but more time was spent doubting her and trying to get away from her than trying to help.

And then it was too late.

He dropped his guard just enough, and Dad knew he had struck the nerve he was aiming for.

He told Spencer, "I do the same thing with your mother, you know. Hell, I knew something was wrong. And yeah, she could tell me all day that she was fine and she didn't need help. But eventually, I should've stepped up, you know?" He shook his head. "Instead, I left you and Kaylee to figure it out. You guys were just kids."

As if every path he could've taken to save Mom played in Dad's head — and knowing him, he had come up with plenty — his eyes danced around and started to water. He tried to blink the tears away. Like always, if he could help it there would be no cracks in Dad's façade.

"I need your help," Spencer whispered. "It's not just a curiosity thing anymore, I need to know what happened with The Incident. And Mom, how did she die?"

"Your mother and I agreed—"

"Yeah, the two of you agreed when I was a *kid* that *kid*-me was too young to handle it. And you know what, I probably was. But now, I need to know."

"Spencer."

Spencer wasn't about to back down, but his dad shared the sentiment. A long moment of silence passed, their mutual stubbornness filling the air.

Part of Spencer wanted to say it was like old times, but he managed to keep the snarky thought from surfacing.

"Dad, please."

Stifled, low-pitched grunts were what Spencer got in response.

But at the same time, his dad's eyes softened. And he looked over at the table next to him, towards the chair that he still guarded like a hawk six years after losing her. He picked up a picture, one that Spencer recognized instantly – it was a framed photo of him and Mom from their wedding. Dad looked at it with wide eyes, taking it in like he was looking at it for the first time.

And, there in front of Spencer's eyes, something seemed to flicker in his dad.

"His name was Austin, the guy who killed your mother."

Spencer took a sharp breath, and he felt his gaze soften. His dad finally let the tears flow free, refusing to look away from the picture that he had a death grip on.

"Same guy from The Incident, but I think you and Kaylee already figured that out."

Austin. That one man broke into their home and messed Mom up so bad before she started to slam her own kids into the glass tables.

Spencer asked, "Who is he? I saw him on the ground. I thought you said they confirmed it. He died."

"He *did*," Dad's voice cracked. "I don't understand, but he came back. And it was like he was able to tell your mother what to do; she was operating but he was calling the shots."

"Why? Did something happen between you?"

Dad recoiled like he was hit with a bunch of bricks. Then he stayed there, flattened against his seat. "When we were in high school, your mother and I were friends with him and his wife, Megan. They got in a wreck on the way to see our graduation. The two of them were in the car, along with their daughter, Nikki." Dad pursed his lips. "Austin was the only one who made it."

Spencer silently soaked in every tear-filled word from his dad. Donovan had told him the basics of this, but the names just made it more real.

"The girl was only five," Dad said quietly.

Nikki. He could feel her presence, like she was there next to him.

Spencer took a shaky breath. "Dad, I—"

"Please, Spence." He put the picture down and buried his face in his hands. "You need answers, but I need time to give them to you."

And in the blink of an eye, The Girl — *Nikki* — was in Mom's spot. She looked tiny there, stretching fully to rest her arms on both rests. She glanced at the picture, black eyes laced with something that Spencer could only describe as sorrow. Pity, even.

She stood and walked towards the door and motioned for Spencer to follow.

He took a deep breath and leaned forward so he could rest his hand on Dad's arm. "Take the time you need. But please, there's more. And I need to know."

"I know you do, kid. Just give me a minute, alright?"

Spencer tightened his grip and turned towards Nikki. He followed her outside, her light steps making no sound at all. Meanwhile, his sounded like a hammer being dropped. Every move was heavy to him when she was so light. Airy.

Fragile.

She gestured towards the treehouse. The branches near it swayed in the light breeze, causing a few leaves to fall and land at Spencer's feet.

He hadn't gone up there since Mom passed away. It was a gift to him from her.

"Nikki," Spencer whispered, "I don't know if—"

When he looked down towards her, she was gone.

Not sure why, he turned his attention back to the treehouse. Maybe it was him finally trusting her or him being too naïve — probably both. But he slowly made his way towards it. With every step, he heard whispers, speaking over each other in a hushed, fast ramble.

He heard the word '*help.*' There was no mistaking that one.

He made it to the ladder and gripped it, the wood soft from years of elemental damage. But against his better judgment, he climbed upwards.

The whispers only got louder.

And when he reached the top—

"M-Ma?"

The whispers stopped.

She was staring out the window, her gaze affixed to the massive expansion of forest and the lake that extended below.

The floor creaked as Spencer inched off the ladder and swung his legs to stand. Seeing her made the cement blocks on his feet heavier, and time slowed as he made his way to her.

"Run," she whispered, her scratchy voice drilling nails into Spencer's skull. And she turned towards him, her sullen eyes glittered with tears. "*Go.*"

Spencer trembled with every breath, and he didn't think to move away from her. He was terrified the ethereal sight of his mom — standing there in front of him — would slip away.

"Run, you need to run."

But he couldn't possibly leave her again.

Spencer reached for her. Reached towards the empty air, knowing that either his hand would go right through her or she'd fade or do whatever it is a ghost—

His hand met her arm.

Her *warm* arm.

"How are you—"

She smiled a toothy grin, so large, so unnatural that Spencer could feel his own muscles ache. The hazel in her eyes was replaced with the same black, but somehow, even deeper.

Darker.

The air was suffocating.

She tried to come closer but every motion was met with an unnatural, violent twitch. Something would draw her towards him and she'd jolt away. Her lips quivered, agony etched all over her face.

Spencer tried to grab her, to talk her out of it. And he put his hand on her shoulder again — how was it *warm*? — but she let out a shriek.

She raised a knife.

"Run," she choked out.

It all happened so fast.

Mom brought the knife down and Spencer moved out of the way, but she raised her hand back up. She fixed her grip on the blade, he shielded his face...

Blood.

All Spencer could register was the sound of his scream.

He doubled over and clutched his arm, gritting his teeth as red gushed between his fingers. He pushed harder to stop the flow, but it only shot more pain throughout his body.

Mom raised the knife above her head. And as much as it hurt, Spencer was able to shuffle away, towards the ladder.

But not before her face twisted. "Get *out!*"

She clutched her head and dropped the knife. Spencer could barely breathe as he found the ladder with his feet, keeping his eyes on Mom.

It took everything in him not to scream.

With shaky hands, he closed the latch on the treehouse and locked it. Then he started down, making it halfway before his arm gave out on him. He couldn't fix his grip in time.

He fell the rest of the way down.

The wind was knocked out of him. Spencer rolled on his side, his mouth open in a silent cry. He wrapped his arms around himself, every movement sending fresh jabs to his wound. When the air finally came back to his lungs, he did the only thing he could think to do.

He let out a blood-curdling scream.

One that traveled through the forest and echoed back into Spencer's ears. He forced himself off the ground and ran back to the trailer, limping with every step.

The tears made the trip a blur that didn't even register. One moment he was there, then the next thing he knew, he practically ripped the trailer's front door off its hinges. He barreled inside, caught sight of his dad, and finally, he slowed.

"Spence?"

He crashed into Dad. And he threw his arms around him, letting out anguished, muffled cries against his shoulder.

"What in the hell happened to you?" Dad yelled, tightening his grip on him.

Every bone in Spencer's body ached. He shivered with each motion.

And there, he swallowed every bit of his pride. The distance he had once forced between them came crashing down. Through the anger, the pain, and everything else he felt towards the man — Spencer let everything out, soaking Dad's shirt with his tears.

Mom just—

"Please help me."

Chapter Twenty-One

Breaking Point

Spencer couldn't remember the last time he was truly vulnerable around his dad.

Granted, he of course didn't hide his pain during Mom's funeral. But the crying, the incessant realization that he couldn't imagine a world without her? The mentions of how he wanted to talk to her about every mild inconvenience, only to feel that pain all over again when he knew that would never happen? Those conversations were reserved for Kaylee — and after her, Donovan and Kirsten.

But Dad? Never.

Now, his shoulder was soaked in Spencer's tears.

Tears which caught the blood on Spencer's hands, causing it to smear against Dad's sleeve. A design melded there, with red clashing against the green of his shirt. It changed shape every time Spencer clawed at his dad's shoulder and smeared the blood elsewhere. Everything was throbbing, and between his cries and the fall, he couldn't catch his breath.

Dad slowly led Spencer over to the couch. He tried to get him to lie down, which Spencer silently protested, insisting on sitting up so he could breathe. Dad took the hint and let him, arms stretched in surrender as he backed off. He paced around the living room, shooting questioning glances at Spencer like he was supposed to spout out the answers.

Mom's touch was still warm.

And even if it wasn't quite her anymore, she wasn't pale like the others, and he swore she still had life in—

Spencer stopped himself in his tracks.

There was no way.

It was well beyond his usual reckless optimism — that thought was in a different realm entirely. He couldn't consider it because when a different explanation, a reasonable one, would inevitably arise, he'd get hurt all over again.

"Can I use your first aid kit?" he fought out.

His dad perked up a bit, no doubt relieved that he could be useful. "Oh, course!"

Dad made a beeline to the kitchen and hunched underneath the sink. He rummaged through and muttered something to himself.

All the while, Spencer managed to gather his breath. His heart beat at a less alarming rate, no longer making every pump known as it pounded against his ribs. He leaned back, his head against the top of the couch. His good hand rested against his forehead.

His dad returned, a clear container in hand. He snapped its white lid off, looking through it for just a moment before handing it over to Spencer.

"Figured this is more your jurisdiction than mine."

Spencer nodded in silent thanks before taking it. There wasn't much, but he found bandages that helped to hold pressure in the meantime. They were quiet as Spencer cleaned his own wounds for what felt like the hundredth time — he really was far too clumsy for his own good.

Dad spent his time pacing again, looking anywhere else. Blood was never 'his thing,' as he explained. Spencer took a few minutes and kept his jaw clenched so tightly he swore he ground a bit of his teeth away.

All the while, he couldn't get a question out of his head. One that he managed to quietly ask when he was finally done fixing the wound that — somehow — *Mom* had given him.

"How did Mom die?"

Dad stopped pacing. The color drained from his face as Spencer asked a question that should've had a straightforward answer.

No backing down.

Not even when his dad tried to mumble incoherently before changing the subject.

"I need to know," Spencer insisted.

"I told you what happened," Dad murmured, refusing to make eye contact. "The guy who tried to kill us during the Incident, Austin, did it."

"'Did it?'"

"Yeah, he must've been mad at us 'cause it was on the way to his graduation or—"

"*Stop*." Spencer clenched his jaw and leaned forward, making himself appear in Dad's eyeshot. "You're trying to tell me that a guy went on a killing spree because he got in an accident on the way to see his friends' graduation ceremony." He made sure to exaggerate every word, how the lies would never sit with him like Dad hoped. "And further, the dude died then killed Mom? Years later?"

"Spence, you know your mom and I always considered the possibility that there are—"

"What aren't you telling me? What does 'it' mean?"

Spencer loosened his shoulders as he tried to calm himself down. The lies were killing him but he hated being like this.

His parents' opinions on ghosts were more similar to Kirsten's than his own. Before he came face to face with one, Spencer hadn't so much as considered the possibility. Even after he met The Girl, he was fourteen and trying to scrounge up any alternative. His parents, on the other hand, were believers.

But even if his parents so wholeheartedly believed in them, why'd the ghosts come back?

Dad spoke with a meek, shaky voice that Spencer had never heard before. "The blood you saw in our house? It was mine, not your mother's."

Air caught in Spencer's throat. He tried to swallow, but nothing came of it.

Not as Dad's words brought him back there, back to when he was just eighteen and came home to a house of blood. With a messed up, grief-stricken Dad, no mother in sight. He had asked where Mom was, Dad had told him she was dead.

But it wasn't even her who was hurt?

The room was heavy, suffocating. But Dad went on anyway. "One second, we were fine. We were in the kitchen, and she was showing me a funny video she found. Then her eyes turned black, she had this smile."

Dad covered his eyes like it was all a horrible sight he could hide away from. Like he could hide behind the comfort of his own hands, retreat to a world where his wife was still alive and ghosts weren't lurking at every corner.

"And she wasn't your mother anymore."

There was no reply. How could that be met with anything other than dead air?

"She grabbed a knife and stabbed me. I got away, but she followed. I didn't want to fight back, of course I didn't.

But I was scared for my life. I swung here and there, not sure if anything connected." For the first time, Dad looked up and made eye contact with Spencer. "She tried to kill me. Then her eyes cleared up for just a moment. She dropped the knife, broke the window, and ran out. I never saw her again."

'Never saw her again.'

The words echoed in Spencer's mind, cultivating to the fact that his mom tried to kill his dad and then stopped. He asked, "And why did you say that 'the guy' did it? Mom did, to you."

"You're gonna think I'm crazy."

Spencer let out a dry chuckle. With everything going on, the concept of something being 'too crazy' was incomprehensible. "Try me."

"Austin made her do it."

"What do you—"

"Unfinished business. He wanted us dead, but he died during The Incident." His tone was sure, instinctual. Like he was a teacher giving a lecture he had long ago memorized by heart. "With him gone, making your mother do it for him was the next best thing."

Dead air.

Nothing more, nothing less.

Spencer found himself simmering in the fact that although it was hard to process, this wasn't the most ridiculous thing he had ever heard. That fact hit him like a ton of bricks.

There was no telling what was going on in Dad's head, but he seemed to be trying to read Spencer like a book.

How did this not sound completely unbelievable?

Spencer sighed. "How sure are you?"

"Completely."

"Why didn't you tell me this?" Spencer asked. "Dad, come on. I get that you didn't know if I could handle it back then, but you lied."

"I didn't lie."

"You told me that my mother was *dead* when she wasn't."

"C'mon, be realistic." Sympathy and pity etched themselves in dad's features. It was infuriatingly familiar, his go-to since Spencer was young. "She's gone. How much time it's been, she is long go—"

"No, she's not! She's alive!" Spencer raised his arm, brandishing it like the blood was a weapon in itself. "She's alive and she just freakin' stabbed me!"

All this time.

All this time, and she wasn't gone.

Spencer wasn't talking to her every single night while he tried to go to bed, he wasn't one-by-one scratching off each of the 'final talks' he dreamed of having with her. He wasn't talking to his dead mother.

He was talking to *dead freaking air.*

He hadn't realized before, but he was shaking. It only became evident when Dad held his hands up in defense. When he looked deep in his eyes, they showed something that Spencer could only describe as fear. Familiarity, maybe. But there was fear.

Fear of Spencer.

"She *stabbed you*?" Dad's voice cracked, the panic scratched in permanent ink as he grabbed his arm.

Spencer limply let it follow Dad's motions, gritting his teeth as it moved. It didn't take long for Dad to catch on and use his free hand to stabilize Spencer's wrist.

That was when Spencer realized that his dad was tearing up. His macho, lumberjack-like dad was crying again, and this time, while holding his only son's arm.

It was the sign Spencer needed to finally loosen his shoulders.

Dad must have noticed, softly asking, "Are you okay?"

Spencer let out a deep breath. He found himself shutting people out when he was upset, but Dad was even less open about his feelings — if that were even possible.

So, seeing him there, shaky and uneasy, Spencer didn't know what to do. He held his arms out and dropped them, being careful with the hurt one. "No, I'm not.

Mom's alive and I don't know where she is. Brett's dead, and Kaylee is…"

Broken. But judging by the look on his dad's face, he didn't need to elaborate.

"I don't know who's next," Spencer continued. "Could be Donovan, could be Kirsten. Austin's hurt Kirsten before, apparently *I* might hurt Donovan." He still found himself wincing at the thought — felt like he was risking Donovan's life every time he went near him. "Point is, I don't know. And I'm not about to wait around and find out."

His dad went back to pacing.

And as he watched, Spencer bit back the idle fear that maybe The Mangled Man would come back for him. That he was chipping away at everyone one by one, waiting to strike at the man in front of Spencer.

As if the thought surfaced without his knowledge, Dad stopped pacing. And his skin was pale, his words forced.

"Your eyes do it, too."

Spencer opened his mouth, but only gushes of air came out. Eventually, he managed, "Dad—"

"It scares the crap outta me." Dad winced as if the thought were playing out in front of him. "Why do you think I left? I didn't want to leave you and Kaylee alone, of course I didn't. But I thought that if I got away from you, maybe Austin would cut you some slack. Maybe…"

He grumbled into his hands before he could say anything
else.

But there wasn't time for waiting anymore. Spencer
asked quietly, "What happened?"

At that, Dad sighed. He went back to his chair and found
his picture of him and Mom again. Found it with ease.
Probably because, just like when Spencer was younger,
Dad would look at it daily, sometimes more. He stared at
it, a longing look in his eyes.

"She fell first. We were in math class together; I didn't do
too well, so I needed a tutor. Our teacher paired us
together and..." He took in every bit like he was seeing
her for the first time. "She was so beautiful."

Spencer found himself smiling at the sight and how a
small hint of red washed over Dad's cheeks. It was the
same thing that happened with Donovan when Arizona
would kiss him or whisper something in his ear. Both of
them would blush and melt into themselves like the
woman had solved all their problems.

Which, once upon a time, Kirsten did every single day for
Spencer.

"Of course, I was completely oblivious. Afraid you got
that from me." Dad chuckled. "But what you got from
your mother was that unrelenting optimism. Seriously,
even in the worst situations, she'd always see the good —
she'd *make* there be something good. It was one of the
first things I loved about her."

There was a spark to Dad's eyes, the last shred of her
light shone directly on him. Even in her absence, Mom

could make his dad smile in a way no one else had ever managed.

She was Dad's world.

And that world was ripped away from him.

"I don't know what happened to the optimistic girl I fell in love with, but she's in there somewhere."

Spencer leaned forward, sparing the photo a glimpse before shifting his gaze back to his dad. "What happened?" he repeated, softly this time.

Dad didn't look up.

"We didn't mean it."

With the same cadence as he did in the voicemail, as tired and shrill as before.

Dad told him, "Austin and I were friends since we were kids. I was a few years younger, but our moms were like sisters. You know how it is; between all the playdates and the hangouts, we became best friends, too."

Dead air. For just a moment, and then Dad continued under his own volition.

"When Austin started high school, he met this girl, Megan." Dad shook his head. "She didn't like him for a while. Didn't even know he existed. But lemme tell you, my man knew how to flirt."

A genuine smile broke through, followed by a tearful chuckle.

"They had their daughter, Nikki, their senior year. She was five when I graduated." A long, painful moment of silence passed, cut off by his shaky breath. "Your mom and I were friends with them, best friends. Hell, to Nikki we were Uncle Tristan and Aunt Emma."

His words cut out, and he put the picture down. Muttering to himself, he used his free hand to secure a deathgrip on the ends of his hair.

"Then we had to go and mess it all up."

A primal, deep cry stifled against his palm. The sound traveled towards Spencer and cut him deep.

Dad said through his teeth, "It was so stupid. Your mother and I's senior year of high school, we'd pick fights with them here and there. Dumb, juvenile stuff when they started maturing, you know how it is."

Spencer swore that Dad was just seconds away from ripping hair out of his scalp.

"Then one day, soon before your mom and I were set to graduate, they showed up at the store we worked at. Showed up drunk even though they didn't really like drinking — that was how badly they wanted to come across as 'fun' to us again." There was a bite to the word 'fun,' one that made Spencer wince. "They got us to walk out on our shift — not that we really needed much convincing. We were fired the next day, 'too many strikes' kinda thing."

Silence screamed between the two of them. Spencer saw the rage in his dad's face, knowing it wasn't directed at the stupid mistake or the job. It was much more than that.

Dad told him, the same bite in his voice, "It wasn't their fault, but we *made it* their fault at the time. After all our little fights throughout the year, your mom and I were so pissed with them."

Now, it was remorse that was written all over Dad's face.

"What did you do?" Spencer finally managed.

"We just wanted to inconvenience them, annoy 'em. We didn't mean t—" He banged his hand on the table before standing up. "We were kids, just trying to play a prank on them! We didn't know." Dad's voice cracked out, "We didn't know. I swear, we didn't know."

The picture shook in his hands.

"Your mom and I decided to get back at them. We went to their house."

Their house.

"Dad—"

"We cut something in their car."

The color drained from Spencer's face. A prank – an extreme one. Mom and Dad had always hated pranks.

"We just wanted to slow them down."

A prank started—

"But we got their brakes instead. And then right out their driveway, they had to take a sharp turn to get to us. They lost control, they crashed, and there was this lake and—"

And then Dad broke down.

For the first time in twenty-four years, Dad collapsed in front of Spencer. Tears poured freely, the sobs agonizing.

He went to his dad in a heartbeat, he always would. Spencer threw his arms over him and let Dad cry into them.

Words were said, Spencer wasn't sure what they were. Lots of apologies, pained attempts at saying over and over again that he killed his friend and he never meant it. That his friend buried his wife and daughter for something so stupid.

'Sorry' was thrown around so many times that it didn't even seem like a word anymore.

They stayed there for a while as Spencer tried — and failed — to make sense of it. There was still so much to ask, but for a moment, the room was too thick to begin. Questions, doubts, concerns, they all filled the room.

Along with dead air.

Chapter Twenty-Two

Call It

Before long, Spencer and his Dad silently went back to their spots. They adopted the same sullen pose — meaning, they leaned forward and stared blankly at the ground.

Both were lost in their own thoughts, though frankly, Spencer was pretty sure they were thinking the exact same thing, just too proud to admit it.

They didn't know what to do. Plain and simple.

And Spencer was terrified that one moment they'd be there in silence, and the next, Mom and the ghosts would bust the door down. Maybe drag Spencer and his dad by the hair to bear witness as another one of Spencer's visions came to fruition.

There was fear in that. Fear of Spencer seeing his mom, fear of Dad seeing his own wife.

Fear.

It still didn't sound right with Mom. He had never imagined being afraid of her.

Spencer broke the silence by clearing his throat. "Are you okay?"

Dad slowly shook his head in response. "Austin was my best friend."

His words were slow, almost robotic. Like he was blandly reading it off a script. All over again, Spencer couldn't imagine what that would be like.

He thought back to the vision of Donovan, how real it felt. Then he thought about that being his reality. Of waking up every day and knowing he couldn't see his friend again.

The thought nearly took his breath away.

"Our moms were like sisters; we grew up together. Then one drunken mistake later..." Dad shuddered. "I can't tell you how badly I wish I could take it all back."

The story unraveled, and so many parts of Mom and Dad's methods made sense. They raised Spencer to believe in pacifism and not much else; they'd get upset with him if he had arguments with his friends – Donovan in particular. With pranks and generally messing around, Spencer had always wondered why they were so strict.

Dad looked like he was in a different world.

It killed Spencer to see his dad like that.

He didn't even show much emotion over Mom. Of course, Dad had locked himself away and let it all out behind closed doors, but the vulnerability was something that he never showed Spencer.

"There's something I still don't understand," Spencer told Dad. "You cut their brake line, how'd he find out? He must have if he's after us now."

Dad nodded and pulled a phone out of the drawer next to him. "He called me. Sometimes I answered, sometimes I didn't." He sighed. "I still have the voicemails he left me. After your mom died — or, after she disappeared, I guess — I tried to erase them, but they wouldn't go away."

Wouldn't go away.

Spencer furrowed his brow.

"I even went to get it looked at. They'd get rid of them for a moment, then five minutes later they'd be back."

A chill sent down Spencer's spine. "What?"

"Yeah. I even changed phones, but they followed me."

"They follo—" Spencer ran his fingers through his hair and stood up. "Dad, that's not a thing."

"For me, it is. I can't get rid of them." He stayed quiet for a moment. Then he said tearfully, "And I don't want to completely clear the memory — it's the last thing I have of the texts from your mom. The voicemails."

Spencer's frustration dissipated, sending a tired chill down his body. He stopped pacing and whispered, "Dad."

"And, I don't know. A lot of what he said scared the absolute hell outta me. But some things, about how he and his wife used to hang out with me and your mother, it just..." After a moment, Dad forced out, "I listen, and it feels like old times. There's so little I have left of them, but with *this*...."

Dad tightened his grip on his phone like someone would pounce on him and steal it.

Spencer knelt down next to him, trying to be at his eye level. "What did he say?"

"I don't know if you wanna—"

"Please, Dad."

The room was silent, even if only for a moment. Spencer could see in his dad's eyes while he wanted to help, talking about this was almost too much. Letting all of this resurface was tearing him apart.

But, regardless, Dad told him, "Austin talked about your mother a lot. And sometimes, he'd remember little things that she said or ways she helped him out. It was all I had to remember them all for the longest time."

Spencer didn't say anything. He waited silently, watching his dad fight out more words.

"But then, he found out more. I don't know how — he ranted about it, but..." Dad shuddered. "There was one last voicemail that I never was able to listen to. It just doesn't play. You know me, I'm stubborn as hell, so I eventually caved and took it to get looked at. See if we could get it to work."

"But nothing?"

"'But nothing,'" Dad echoed. "He sent it to me on the day of The Incident, right before he went after me and your mother. "

Spencer took a sharp breath. Ten years, and no one managed to get that voicemail to play. Like The Mangled Man — like Austin — was hiding it from them, the last thing he sent before he died.

It wasn't like Spencer was some tech guru; he was the tech guy of the family, but that wasn't really saying much. Mom and Dad were oblivious with electronics, and Kaylee knew how to work her phone and laptop, but that was about it. If it came to glitches or fixing phones, it was Spencer who they'd go to.

But even he knew it wouldn't be that simple.

"I listen to the first one a lot," Dad whispered. "He left it the day after your mom and I first visited him."

Spencer would have asked to hear it, but Dad's thumb was already hovering over the screen. And he could tell from the look in the man's eyes that he wanted to hear it, likely for what was the thousandth time. Even if it felt like a first all over again.

That's how it always felt for Spencer when he listened to Mom's voicemails.

His dad pressed down on the screen, hard. And a voice fillcd the room.

"Tristan, hey."

It sounded like The Mangled Man. Spencer could recognize the deepness anywhere, even if he had only spoken a few times. The gravelly tune was missing though — in its place, Austin sounded hoarse, exhausted.

"Look, I can't thank you and Emma enough for coming to visit the other day. My parents are working on getting a flight over here, but you know how they are with traveling.

I was trying to arrange stuff, help my parents find out how to get here from the airport and where they would stay."

Dad was looking down at the carpet, his silent stare deafening.

"But that was Megan. The planning, yanno? She did that stuff." Austin was quiet for a moment. Then he sniffled before saying, *"I feel so lost, man."*

Every tear laced Austin's voice; they were just as loud as the words themselves.

"And I do appreciate that you showed up and we were good. Thought at first that you were still pissed with us about everything, but I guess it just put things into perspective, huh?"

There was no attempt at hiding it, Dad recoiled at the fresh blow to the gut.

"Megan would be happy that we're still hangin' out, she was pretty beat up by how mad you guys were." There was a forced chuckle on the other side. *"Maybe we could meet up and grab something from the cafeteria. It's*

crappy, but it's not as crappy as the food in high school, which of course isn't saying much."

They had plans to meet up, they had plans to do something together again.

And Austin had no idea what happened.

"For a second, it felt like the four of us were together again."

Dad's lips quivered.

"Anyway, I'm gonna go. Talk to you later, alright?"

The voice cut off, and silence flooded the room.

Neither Spencer nor his dad moved, not for a while. Spencer could say he was sorry that he had to go through that, but that much would be obvious. All he knew was that Dad lost his best friend.

The vision threatened to resurface, but he forced the notion away; it was genuinely painful to think about.

In a calm, soft voice, Spencer asked, "Can I hear the other ones, too?"

"Do you really think they would help you with whatever it is that you're doing?"

"More than anything."

The Mangled Man was trying to say something too, Spencer knew it. Maybe there was a way to talk to him.

Dad sighed and rolled the phone around in his hands. He said slowly, "Then take it."

Spencer backed away as if it were a weapon. He didn't mean to take it *from* him.

"Dad, I—"

"Please, Spence." There was so much hesitance in his voice, but Spencer could actively see as he tried to suppress it. "She was your mother. I shouldn't have hidden this for so long."

Dad shook the phone lightly and nodded, so Spencer reluctantly obliged.

It felt heavy somehow. Not just with the messages from the guy who took Mom away to begin with, but it was one of the last things Dad had of her. Spencer kept all her texts and had backups of any voicemails and pictures she had left of him. He'd have to help Dad figure out how to do that too.

"I'm sorry," his dad whispered. "For so many things. When I lost her, I just didn't know what to do. So, I ran."

Ran to the woods. Ran far, far away from the people who needed him the most.

"That wasn't fair to either of you."

Spencer slowly nodded in response. He loved his dad, that much never changed. But the resentment was something that he idly held in the back of his mind, and it was something he had no idea how to express.

"I suck at this," Dad whispered. He drew back and hesitated, but then he said, "I love you. Which, I know I don't say much. Kaylee, I blew her childhood all to hell, and I sure didn't do you any favors."

The dumb look on Spencer's face wouldn't go away. He had imagined this conversation before, dreamed of it. Pictured the day where Dad would admit that he was wrong for leaving Kaylee with Spencer.

And he imagined what he would say when Dad apologized. The angry words for not helping Spencer find his way through school, his absence through relationships and everything that Dad had sworn he'd be a part of.

But none of the spiteful words came out.

None did at all.

"I miss her," Dad said quietly. "I tried so hard, I kept saying one more day, and I'd come home. Then — and this isn't an excuse, I don't have any — without your mother, I…"

Didn't even know how to breathe.

Spencer knew it, because that's how he had felt for so long. Without Kirsten, without Mom.

He wouldn't say it was okay; he didn't want to lie. Instead, there was only one thing he could think of. And he couldn't remember the last time he said it.

"I love you, too."

Chapter Twenty-Three

Etched in Empathy

The drive was a distant memory. One that Spencer couldn't be bothered to try and remember.

It was reduced only to scattered, hazy pictures that refused to go away. There were brief glimpses of a tearful goodbye to his dad. After that, Spencer had stumbled through the woods and tripped over his own two feet more times than he'd care to admit. He got to his car, but he had trouble getting back on the road. And he was pretty sure The Girl freakin' materialized somehow, almost making him crash as he swerved to miss her. Then she gave him this look like everything was going to go horribly wro—

The one thing he didn't have to think about was the route he was taking; he knew it by heart. He had for longer than he could remember.

Now, he was walking up to Donovan's front door.

The sky was dark, the nighttime critters played the same song that they did when he and Mom went on walks all that time ago. The cadence still managed to provide the slightest bit of comfort, something he concentrated on as he hugged his trembling frame.

Some of it was the cold — he zipped up his jacket and hugged himself — but honestly, most of it was more than that. He knocked on the door, barely sparing it a moment before he grit his teeth and pounded on it. Loudly, as if to punish the barrier that stood between him and his friend.

After a few moments, the wooden door went away, and Donovan stood in its place. "Spence?" His voice was already concerned, but his eyes widened when he saw more. "The hell? You alright?"

Spencer's heart was racing and he could barely stand. His friend held his arms out, ready to catch him.

Donovan was in the living room, blinking sleep from his eyes. It must have been late, but time was a concept lost long ago. The checkered blue leg of his pants were up, exposing his right calf. He clutched his jacket, the black shade matching his disheveled hair. And above all else, his eyes wore more worry than he had shown in a long time.

Spencer said in a tearful whisper, "My mom's alive."

That was supposed to be impossibly good news.

Mostly as a kid, he had held on to hope that, maybe someday, he'd see her again. Even as an adult, sometimes he'd imagine what it would be like for those last talks on solitary outings to be more, to be real.

To think that *this* is how that hope would play out...

"What are you talking about?" Donovan asked.

"She's alive, I saw her near my Dad's trailer. My parents played this stupid prank and it caused the crash. And the girl who died, Nikki, she's been the one showing me stuff this whole time."

The words blurted out, and while Donovan's face was still an open book, its contents may as well have been written in a different language.

 "I went to see Dad, he told me this stuff, and Nikki led me up to the treehouse Mom made. I went up and she was just there, then she pulled out a knife and she stabbed me in the—"

"The fuck do you mean? Your mother *stabbed you?*"

"Yes. And she is alive. That's why I'm here, I need your help. I wasn't fast enough last time, didn't help her in time. Now, I can."

He hadn't even realized that was what he wanted until he said it out loud. His voice cracked and his body quaked at everyone he had lost because he wasn't fast enough.

"I don't have to be too late this time."

Donovan didn't say anything, not for a moment. Then when he opened his mouth to reply, a door shut from inside their apartment and Arizona walked over.

"What happened to you?" She brushed past Donovan and looked at Spencer's arm. "Fuck, that's a lot of blood."

The world fell back into its jumbled blur. Donovan's words muffled as he told Arizona whatever it was that he had managed to pick up from Spencer's earlier ramble. The one that ended in the same solitary concept that kept echoing in Spencer's mind.

Mom was alive.

All those years ago, he had stared into her tear-soaked, black eyes, their hazel hidden away. Pain-stricken and battered, she had still promised Spencer that he would be alright, like she always did. In response, he had clutched her tighter and told her — promised her — that he'd look out for her.

This was his chance to bring that promise to fruition.

If she needed help, of course he would give her that.

When Donovan went quiet, Arizona looked Spencer up and down. Her face was laced with something he had not expected — there wasn't judgement, or anger, or anything like that. She was worried, it was etched in her features.

And empathy was in Donovan's.

Arizona said carefully, "You need to go to the cops."

"Those are the last people I would go to." Spencer shook his head. "She would charge them with a knife! She'd get shot."

"It's better than her stabbing someone else to death."

"Oh, come on, that's not fair. She couldn't help it."

"I *know that*."

She forced those words out, then she put her hands over her face and groaned into them.

"Look, I'm sorry." Arizona said, "This sucks. It sucks so hard, and I wish that it wasn't happening to you. But come on, you know she can't get past this one. You're talking about trying to get her away with murder. She killed someone, and you think everything can just go back to normal? C'mon, you're smarter than that."

But calling the cops on her? Throwing her to the wolves? How was Spencer supposed to do that?

"Maybe if I just talked to her."

"You are going to get yourself killed!" Donovan yelled. He walked a small circle around his living room with his face buried in his hands. "Look man, be realistic. She can't come back from this."

"I can't give up on her."

Because the last thing she did was warn him to run far, far away from her.

"I can't do this," Arizona grumbled.

Donovan sighed. "Ari—"

"What, now you're saying he's right?"

"No, I'm saying I'm not gonna let him run off without—"

"You don't get it, Vannie! We're talking about a murder here. Covering it up. Then she's gonna hurt someone else, and he is going to go down with her. Are you really willing to take the fall for that?"

"*Yes.*"

Spencer's eyes widened. He hadn't expected Donovan to side with him – to try and protect him, sure. In an argument, though, Spencer thought he'd take Arizona's side one hundred percent.

But all Donovan wanted to do was help. He turned to Arizona. "Babe, can we have a minute?"

She looked at Donovan, then at Spencer. And she went back and forth with that a moment before sighing and landing on Spencer again.

Now, she just looked tired. Defeated.

"You're smarter than this."

And she went back inside without another word.

Spencer and Donovan stood outside, both of them shivering as Donovan motioned with his head towards the rails near the steps.

His apartment was on the fourth floor. The view from there extended towards a park that, while deserted, usually served as a good distraction to look out at. Donovan leaned against the rails and looked out, and Spencer followed.

Sirens blared through the night. Hidden by the small road that separates them from downtown, it was just them. Instead of meshing with the outside world and all its problems, they stood stewing in their own disasters.

Drowning.

"You know you have to go to someone about this," Donovan whispered.

"She's my *mother*."

There was a difference between what he should do, and what would let him sleep at night.

Spencer took a chance and asked, "C'mon, man, you really telling me you wouldn't do this for JJ?"

That's what Donovan called his mom, JJ. He was her only child, and she always wanted to be cool to him. And no matter how much of a tough-guy Donovan tried to be, he'd never been quiet about how cool she was in his eyes.

Donovan sighed and looked down at the rail, idly running his finger along the cold steel. While Spencer would have assumed he was angry, or at least frustrated, he didn't look that way in the slightest.

"She's not your mom anymore, you said so yourself," Donovan's voice was calm, firm. "Can't have it both ways, man. She's gone."

"But she's still—"

"If she were standing here right now, do you really think she'd tell you to face this head-on? Knowing how likely it is that you could get hurt, or worse, what do you think she would want?"

Spencer grit his teeth. Because she would want him to run, she said it herself.

But he couldn't leave her again.

As if he could read Spencer's thoughts, Donovan continued. "She's gone, there's no way around that. But think about Kaylee, if nothing else. She already lost her mom, she doesn't have to lose her brother, too."

The two stood in silence, and Spencer's gaze remained affixed to the park. It reminded him of the one Mom would take him to as a kid, free to be as innocent and naive as he was back then.

Now, as an adult, how could Spencer with a straight face say he'd grow up to feed her to the wolves? Not just throw her towards them, actively trap her in their den and watch them tear her apart?

Donovan said, "Hell, right now, Kaylee still thinks your guys' mom is dead. There doesn't have to be another loss to her at all."

"I need to talk to her. Maybe we can do what we did with the last vision. I told you everything, and we tried to see what it meant." Spencer bit his lip. "I need your help to find her."

A few moments passed. Then, his friend slowly shook his head. "I'm not doing it."

"I'd never ask you to come with me. You wouldn't get hurt."

"Yeah, but it'd sting pretty fucking bad to find out that you got killed, wouldn't it?"

Donovan's voice was low, a bite of anger in the calm demeanor he was trying to maintain. "You're like a brother to me," he whispered. Though it was so high-pitched he may as well have screamed. "A stupid, recklessly optimistic brother who is too damn nice for his own good. I'm not helping you dig your own grave."

But all Spencer could think about was all the plans, all the ridiculously stupid schemes that he and Donovan had managed to conjure up together. How they worked — they *always* worked.

How Donovan's 'door was always open' for him.

Spencer said, "You promised me."

"Yeah, well, I'd rather you be pissed with me than in a body bag."

"Donovan, I—"

"And I'm not gonna do that thing where I promise to look after Kaylee and make sure she'll be alright if anything happens to you. I'm not gonna swear to check in on Kirsten or water your plants or whatever the hell else it is that you'd ask me to do with you gone."

"I just mean—"

"*Stop.*"

Donovan banged his hand against the rail. A dog from a neighboring apartment howled at the shrillness in his voice.

He finally looked Spencer in the eyes.

He blinked fast. And never in his life had he looked so desperate. Donovan shook his head and looked back out at the parking lot, gaze trained on a random spot.

"It's not because I wouldn't do it, but because that's for you to do. This could kill you." Donovan's voice cracked as he said, "And I *can't.*"

They stayed there quietly, their silence broken only by the sounds of the nighttime melody and Donovan's labored breathing. Everything was screaming at Spencer to listen. To Kaylee, it'd be the closest thing she could possibly get to a return to normal. She'd believe she wasn't losing anyone else because she buried her mother six years ago.

Back when the world crumbled around them, and ever since, Spencer tried to glue it back together for her.

But Mom was still in there.

He felt that way when she shoved him into the glass table. And again, that thought surfaced, even past the throbbing where he was stabbed.

She was still in there.

And there was no way he would be too late to get to her. Not again.

Donovan whispered, "Please do the right thing."

One phone call to the cops could stop Mom from hurting them again. Then Spencer could go from there with the ghosts. He could make the decision to ensure that no matter what, Kaylee would always have someone to be there with her.

He could make that decision, or the wrong one.

Too bad his heart had settled on the latter long ago.

Chapter Twenty-Four

Running Home

Spencer's feet took him there. That and his car, but it wasn't what stuck out to him at the time.

Maybe because while the short drive only served as background noise, the walk to her apartment was full of murmurs. Some were his, most were The Girl's. But all were accompanied by doubts and all sorts of other things that Spencer forced out of his mind. Even for just a bit, a short moment of weakness, this was where he needed to be.

Once upon a time, he'd have said it was his heart that took him there.

Be it by his heart, his feet, whatever he wanted to say, there he was. His forehead rested on Kirsten's door, his knuckles just below on the cold, wooden surface.

He knocked on the door, in a familiar little tune that he didn't realize he was making until it was done. It was the dumb beat he'd drum out on Kirsten's desk at school when their teachers stepped out.

He made the same rhythm, albeit slower than usual.

After a few moments, Kirsten came out. "Hey, you alright?"

It hadn't hit him how awful he must have looked. The fall, the stabbing, the way he haphazardly drove all around town this late at night after days of barely sleeping.

But she didn't look disgusted, and she didn't recoil.

Spencer threw himself in her arms.

He rested his chin in the crook of her neck, fitting just like he remembered. All the worry and pain and doubt seemed to melt away, its absence finally letting him breathe.

Even if for a fleeting moment, Kirsten's touch always managed that.

"Do you wanna talk about it?" She asked.

He shook his head.

Not yet, but in time, he knew he'd want to spew everything out. Even if he had rehearsed it more times than he could ever count, he needed a moment.

That was enough for her. Kirsten took him by the hand and guided him to her living room. He'd never been there before; she still lived with her parents when they were together, and they made it a point not to be at each other's places since they broke up. Too intimate, they reasoned, even if they knew it was just as friends.

Kirsten lived in a student apartment. She had mentioned roommates before and complained about them, but they were either in their rooms or not in the unit. They made their way to a couch — beige and in between two matching arm chairs. A coffee table was in front of them, along with random decorations and a television.

Kirsten fished a remote from between the cushions and turned the TV on. She flipped through the channels, making disappointed groans every time she found a new show.

"What are you looking for?" Spencer whispered.

"Don't worry," she replied. "You know."

She went from channel to channel before changing her mind and pulling up a streaming service. She silently pressed play.

The show she chose was perfect, but he couldn't believe she remembered. It was this dumb, old cartoon that Spencer was obsessed with as a kid. He had watched every episode and its low-quality made for TV movie multiple times. His parents would put it on if he was upset, just like if he was happy or bored or if they needed him entertained.

It was still a comfort show in adulthood. Kirsten knew that much.

But for the first time, he didn't laugh at a single one of the jokes.

There was too much on his mind, somehow, despite how empty it felt. He stared through the box in front of him, and he may as well have been looking into blank space itself.

"Brett's dead."

Spencer said it to himself more than to Kirsten. What stuck even more wasn't that Brett died, but instead, *how* he died. *Who* did it.

"I know," Kirsten replied softly.

Tears welled in Spencer's eyes, making the show blurry. Everything was muffled except for Kirsten's voice; she served as the only break from the static. He wished she'd keep talking.

And he realized that wanted to listen to her voice every day for the rest of his life. The way every syllable sounded like a pleasant chirp — soft when she was neutral or bell-like when she was excited.

It always enthralled him, much like the way she'd nerd out about her favorite music or go in detail about the authors of her books of choice. How she loved romance and fantasies and knew how her favorite movies were made. She learned about the actors and directors and how this makeup artist also worked on this other project, or how that person got an award.

All things that he would never retain, because he was too entranced by the way she managed to actually *glow* every single time she rambled about it.

It reminded him of how he could listen to her rants for days. How she came up with the dumbest analogies that made no sense but still were perfect for the situation.

How he felt safe near her, accepted in a way that he never had before. How once he got talking to her, no one could get him to shut up. They'd rattle off for hours in talks that he missed more than anything.

But those talks would always end with him saying one thing.

"I love you," Spencer told her.

Finally told her.

In one breath, a blink and you'll miss it gust of wind, the words were said. They had been on the tip of his tongue, buried inside of him for so long that he had almost forgotten that the words themselves existed. Now, they were tangible, and Spencer could breathe.

Even though he had expected to recoil and run for the hills the moment he managed to say it, he was surprised at how badly he wanted to stay.

How he could only think to say more.

"And not in a friend way. I love you like I loved that shy, dorky girl in band class." Every word felt like a boulder being lifted off his chest. "And my girlfriend who gave me the best year and a half of my life."

"Spence—"

"I made a decision for you that day. I didn't ask, I ran." His face flushed, and for a moment, he had to break eye contact. But then he looked back at her, and all the nerves washed away. "I miss you."

Not five minutes ago, he thought this was a moment of weakness. But it didn't make him feel weak, not anymore.

It only made him think about the eighteen-year-old who broke this off in the first place. How he cried and looked out the window, encapsulated by the world that once helped him write a love letter to the girl he thought was cute.

Spencer finished it off by saying, "And every time I look at you, I realize it all over again."

In anything but a moment of weakness.

Kirsten let out an airy breath and muted the show.

She'd try to find words, they'd come to her, and she'd open her mouth, then she'd lose them again and she'd stay quiet. Spencer knew that much simply because he knew *her*. How every thought turned to words that may as well have been written across her face in a language that only he could read.

Except there. For once, she was unreadable.

"Please say something," Spencer whispered.

Like a prayer, one phrase and he could know what was on her mind.

"Of course, I still..." Kirsten said with a soft voice. She blinked and tucked her hair behind her ears, breaking her stare. "I never stopped."

Spencer took a sharp breath. He had imagined this conversation, the way he'd tell her. Of course, it was less grand and perfect than he had pictured.

But, despite everything that Spencer had thought, Kirsten *did* follow the script after all.

Then she asked, "Do you promise me you won't run out this time?"

All Spencer could do was smile.

So big and genuine that it told her more than his words ever could. She returned it, and with that toothy grin that he hadn't shown in so long, he inched closer.

He whispered, "I promise."

Kissing her was just like he remembered. As if no time at all had slipped since the last time he felt her lips against his.

Home.

That's the only word that Spencer could ever use to describe it. He felt like he was home.

They broke away and stared into each other's eyes for what could have been forever. And he learned all over again that they *could* make this work. Her moving to California and him tagging along, the logistics and having to figure everything out — it'd all be worth it, Spencer had no doubt in his mind.

The confirmation he didn't even need, staring him in the face.

Kirsten turned the show back on, and Spencer looped his arm over her shoulders. She leaned in, resting snug against his chest, seamlessly, like they hadn't just spent years apart.

Both of them laughed at every joke, even the ones that didn't land. And for just a moment, everything felt right.

Because they were home.

Chapter Twenty-Five

The Brightest Light

The random conversations continued well into the night. In the time it took for their talks to slow, it was four in the morning, maybe later. He expected to be tired, but he was far from it. Every new talk gave him this spark that had long since been put out.

Between random topics — the regulars at Kirsten's work that she didn't like and this weird guy in Spencer's class that always gave him dirty looks — and more serious ones, the pauses Spencer had long-dreaded were nonexistent. When it got to the topic of California and her dream taking her halfway across the country, they came to the same decision that they made when they were younger.

She'd go, and he'd follow. Whenever he could, whatever that entailed, they'd find a way.

Which was more than enough for either of them.

"–they're all like Miss Jade, Miss Jade, we love you!" Kirsten raised her voice, breaking Spencer from his trance. She was telling him about her last day of student teaching, down to each individual student's reaction. "And I'm like, I would literally teach you guys every single year if I could, you're all so awesome."

Spencer smiled at her. "So happy for you, Kirs."

They went on for a while longer, with Kirsten telling him about all the tests she'd need to take, but Spencer didn't retain it. His attempts at explaining med school were met with a similar stare — happy, but confused.

And those conversations continued until it got to the point where Spencer could barely keep his eyes open.

Then, somewhere in the middle of being awake and passing out, his gaze drifted to the window.

Where The Girl stood, her sullen eyes staring in at them.

She shook her head slowly, tracking them, not once looking away. Like one wrong move and they would be lost to her forever.

Spencer blinked, and she was gone.

A shiver went down Spencer's back, big enough for Kirsten to stop talking and look at him with a furrowed brow and a clenched jaw. Spencer went to wave it off, but then he stopped. Lying was *not* the way he wanted to start this off.

"I should get going soon," Spencer whispered. "I'm tired."

"I can see you're tired, you look like you're about to pass out."

"Don't worry, I—"

"Spence, I genuinely am not sure if you're okay to be behind the wheel." Kirsten slowly blinked, then she murmured, "I'd feel better if you stayed here tonight."

He went to disagree, but he quickly realized that he didn't even have the energy for *that*. So, he nodded, closing his eyes while doing so. "Sounds good, but we're gonna have to wrap this up soon. I'm about to pass out."

Kirsten chuckled and took his hand, with Spencer letting himself get dragged along for the ride. A few steps brought them to her room, and Kirsten's giggles were contagious as she closed the door.

Her room was full of posters and decorations — she had heard the phrase 'make yourself at home' and taken it seriously. A few boy bands and movie posters, and the debut album cover of her favorite singer. A curtain light hung across the room opposite to her bed, covered slightly by a small bookcase and dresser. On the corner near her attached bathroom was her desk, littered with textbooks and notes. Then, for the corkboard above, artwork that her students had made for her.

Spencer's gaze traveled to her bed. Its blue, patterned sheets were in disarray, flickering lights dancing off the silk covers. And above her bed where a headboard was at her old house, she now kept pictures. Ones of their little group of misfits, all together. A bunch of her and Arizona.

And one of her and Spencer.

Their first date, when they went to an amusement park together. It was a close-up shot of the two with their mouths open in the goofiest, widest grins they could imagine. Spencer's sunglasses shielded his eyes and Kirsten had on a fake monocle she had found at the gift shop.

Spencer chuckled. "Can't believe you kept this."

"Honestly, I thought I took it down after, well, you know." Kirsten put her hands in her back pockets and shrugged. "So glad I forgot." She hesitated a moment, considering her words. Then she said murmured, "Bet you tossed that letter, huh?"

The letter. Spencer was so glad she actually remembered it. It was something he'd alluded to but never shared — he wanted to give her years down the line, and of course, that plan got blown out of the water when they broke up.

He held up his wallet. "Think again."

"Seriously?" Kirsten asked happily as she reached for it. "Lemme see!"

"Heck no, you know the rules. No grey hair, no letter."

Kirsten rolled her eyes, and Spencer found himself in awe of the way they caught in the light, like he was seeing it for the first time.

"I'm gonna go get ready for bed," Kirsten said while motioning towards her bathroom. She kept her smile on her face as she got pajamas from her dresser and closed her bathroom door.

Alone, Spencer looked back at Kirsten's collection of pictures — one with her in the middle of both her parents. They looked strikingly similar to her, all staring at the cameraman with their massive, dark eyes that were outmatched only by their darker hair.

Spencer remembered taking that picture. It was taken when they all went out to dinner for her seventeenth birthday.

When Kirsten left the bathroom, she wore her hair in a braid and had an oversized shirt that fit her like a dress. She climbed into bed and told Spencer about an unused toothbrush she had in her drawer. He thanked her and walked into her bathroom, looking around at how basic it was compared to her bedroom. Soaps and products were all around the sink, everything else was white.

He took out his contacts and threw them away, knowing they were officially lost causes with no lens solution. Somewhere in his car, he kept a pair of his old prescription glasses for just this occasion – namely, somehow losing or ruining his contacts.

Getting them was a Tomorrow Spencer problem, though.

He brushed his teeth and splashed some water on his face, savoring the cold as it brushed against his skin. A calming, deep breath erupted through his chest, his eyes closed as the water droplets trickled down his face. Kirsten's voice echoed from her room and he found his eyes popping open at the sound.

The Girl stood behind him.

On the toothpaste-splattered mirror, Spencer could see himself hunched in front of her, her head cocked to the side as she stared daggers into him. A cold, frail hand gently slithered on his forearm.

Tremors littering his body as she stood on her toes, getting as close to his face as she could.

"You're running out of time."

He turned towards her, and as suddenly as she appeared, she was gone.

Spencer sighed and rested against the counter, uselessly searching for a girl who wasn't even there anymore. He had half a mind to drive home and figure this all out later, but he just couldn't get himself to. This chance hadn't presented itself in so long.

It was a moment of weakness.

So, Spencer shook the doubt away and went back to Kirsten's room. Her main light was off, amplifying the yellow, intricate design that bounced off the walls from her curtain lights. They flashed, set just dim enough for it to not be overwhelming.

Spencer crawled in bed next to her and placed his arm over her shoulder. She fit snug against his chest.

Kirsten chuckled. "You stink."

"Hey! Gimme a break. I've done, like, a lot today."

"Mhmm, sure."

Spencer smiled and took a whiff of her hair, melting at the familiar scent. Vanilla: it was always her shampoo, conditioner, body wash, perfume, candles, air freshener...

"Okay, I'll bite," Spencer said, purposely exaggerating his words. "On a scale from one to ten, how bad do I stink?"

"You do *not* want to know the answer to that, trust me."

He held her tighter, snickering at the playful bite in her voice. "Suppose I don't."

"Well, since you *insist*." She straightened up and drew her arms out like she was framing a photo. "Picture a dead fish got thrown into a rotting dumpster and the sun was beating down on—"

"Oh, hush."

She dramatically rolled her eyes and threw herself back against Spencer's arms.

He furrowed his brow. "Did you say a 'rotting dumpster?'"

Kirsten pursed her lips, stifling a chuckle. Then it escaped and emitted a loud, sailor-like roar.

"The *heck* does that mean?" Spencer asked between his own bursts of laughter.

"Thought I was gonna get away with it."

"Kirs, I would never let you get away with *that*, come on now."

What followed was enthralling, perfectly comfortable shared silence. And every time Kirsten blinked — every time her hair moved or he caught a new whiff of her perfume, he was entranced all over again.

But, after a while, the magic started to stifle. His tired mind would bring him back to reality, away from the perfect world he had convinced himself he had paved his way to.

Seeing The Girl brought back everything — the ghosts, his mom, Brett. The way every move seemed to be wrong and his best friend, who always found a way to help him, essentially said there was no way that he'd back Spencer up with this one.

And Spencer thought about how, as much as it frustrated him, he couldn't stay mad at Donovan.

Because he was right; his plan was at least fifty-seven brands of stupid, and Spencer was the only one who could look past them all.

"Kirs, about everything that's going on…" Spencer sighed before reaching into his pocket and grabbing his dad's phone. He had explained everything to Kirsten in the hours-long ramble they had back and forth earlier. "Do you think you could listen to some of these with me? I dunno, you always get it. Maybe you'll pick up on something I can't."

She nodded, he felt it against his arm. "Whatever you need."

Spencer kissed the top of her head in reply. He scrolled back to the voicemails and hovered his thumb over the

second one. He had explained in such detail what Austin
said in the first one, that he figured he may as well skip
it. He pressed 'play,' and Austin's voice filled the room.

"Hey, been a few days."

The man on the other side sounded meek, exhausted.
Like he could be blown away by a simple gust of wind,
sand destined to turn to nothing.

*"Doctors finally let me out, parents drove me home. I
ended up asking them to leave, I'm supposed to be
watched over right now, but I just couldn't do it. Needed
to be alone."* Austin sighed. *"But between you and me, I
don't know if I want that anymore.*

*"I see them everywhere. Hear them. At first, I thought it
was just something that happens, yanno? I miss them, I
wanna see them, so they're showing up in my mind."*

Spencer's grip on Kirsten tightened.

"But I'm not so sure."

Ghosts.

Austin saw them, too.

*"Nikki's in her room. She's cut up, there's a damn hunk
of glass in her chest. Megan is soaked, like she drowned.
Do..."* Austin took a shaky breath, and his voice cracked
as he asked, *"Do you think that's how she went?*

*"Listen, I hope you stop by soon. I know it's been a bit
weird, but I really did mean it when I said that you've
helped me through this. Without you, I'd be a—"*

There was a chuckle on the other side of the line.

"Fuck, I almost said I'd be a wreck."

Spencer closed his eyes as if that could shield him from the knife that drilled into him.

"I've gotta go, Megan's trying to tell me something. Take care, man."

Silence filled the room: deafening silence that remained until Kirsten placed her hand on his chest. The pressure made his heart's pace known, and it was painfully fast.

Kirsten whispered, "You didn't do anything wrong. Never forget that."

And just like that, it slowed to the point where he knew he was finding out how to relax. How to breathe right, not in the concerning gasps he barely even registered he was taking.

Spencer placed his hand on top of hers as his eyelids started to droop, giving way to the world around them.

"I know."

The world faded to black, his fight to keep his consciousness finally lost. But he lulled over the fact that he could do this over and over and over again for the rest of his life. Just like the kid he used to be had hoped for, a dream that he thought had slipped from his grasp forever.

A fight fought, a battle won.

"I love you," he murmured.

What followed, Spencer was ready to spend the rest of his life hearing.

"I love you, too."

Chapter Twenty-Six

Darker Skies

The birds chirped.

It was almost funny. That sound was so true to how Spencer felt as he held the sleeping woman in his arms. His muscles screamed at him, the lack of circulation sending pins down the length of his arm.

But he didn't care.

He kissed the top of her head. "Good morning, hun."

Kirsten didn't reply, still sleeping soundly against his shoulder. He buried his face against her shoulder and planted a soft kiss on her neck. No, he didn't want to wake her. But he longed for a morning like this for so long that he honestly couldn't help himself.

He had just had one of the best nights of his life. It was complete with a dream he couldn't quite remember, but Kirsten loved sharing that stuff. He always thought it was dumb to share dreams — no logic behind them, so they seemed too random — but he longed for the chance to tell her all about it.

He nudged her, though she didn't stir.

A quiet laugh escaped Spencer. "Good morning," he said again.

Nothing.

Spencer furrowed his brow.

Something was off. Where was the sailor-like snore he'd made fun of time and time again? Without exception, every single morning, he would wake up to that sound.

He shook her, and her head bobbed with his movement. Spencer brought his face away from hers.

The Girl stood by the foot of Kirsten's bed, a tear rolling down her face.

"I tried."

The world itself seemed to stop spinning.

All Spencer could hear was the pounding of his heart that echoed between his ears. He moved, and Kirsten's head went with him again

That's when he finally looked at her.

And the sight was just like he remembered. The one that had plagued him for years. Kirsten's lips were parted, skin ghostly pale. Her dark, sullen, empty eyes stared at the ceiling, all semblance of light ripped out of—

"K-Kirs?"

Hands trembling, Spencer ran his fingers through her hair. Her loose braid had come undone, curls free around her neck. He caught sight of a tear, one that rolled down her cheek, hidden away. It was fresh, new.

She had *just* called out for him, *just* tried to get him to help her.

The room was a mess. Just like he always saw, with the lamp thrown across the room and the blankets on the ground.

"You're okay," he promised her tearfully. He ran his hand across her face. "You're okay, you're okay, you're okay."

A chant, that's what it was. He said it again and again.

But she didn't move.

He choked out, louder, "Kirsten?"

Nothing.

A hand was placed on his — pale, streaked with blood and dirt and gravel. Nikki. She tried to rip Kirsten from his grasp, with her cold touch burning his skin.

 "Don't!" Tears sprang to his eyes, blurring the nightmare that he could still see every time he blinked. And every time he moved, Kirsten started to slip from his fingertips.

He was supposed to have one more try. He was supposed to figure this out.

"Kirsten!"

The Girl sighed as she took away her hand, the sound sending a cold, empty chill through Spencer's ears and down his back. He shivered and looked at her with pleading eyes.

All he got was a blank stare.

Then blank space; she disappeared in a heartbeat.

Spencer screamed, letting everything out as he lifted Kirsten up. It took everything he had in him to not watch her head dangle and sway with his motions as he brought her down on the floor.

Gently, carefully.

Because she'd wake up. She had to.

"She's okay, she's okay, she's okay."

That's what he kept repeating to himself — that same prayer-like chant — as he took out his phone and called for an ambulance. The world muffled as he rambled off on the phone that his girlfriend was attacked, and he vaguely remembered looking up the address of her apartment building before rattling it off so fast that he had to repeat himself. Then he hung up, dropping his phone somewhere on the ground.

Spencer's lip quivered as he put his hands on her chest. The procedure had been drilled into his head so many times that it felt like nothing.

But not there with her — unnatural, wrong. Spencer went up and down, wincing as her ribs gave way.

"Come on, come on!"

This couldn't be it. They were supposed to grow old and start telling each other the same stupid, mindless stories that still got them blue in the face from laughing.

That was how they were supposed to be.

"Please, baby!"

Please don't leave.

Don't make him be in a world that didn't have her in it. And if they couldn't have that ending with them old together, then let him have the chance to break her heart all over again. Let him make the choice to make the right one this time, and he wouldn't back down.

She was alive. She was *just* alive. Don't change that.

Her ribs snapped.

And she didn't do anything about it.

Spencer couldn't see her anymore; she was a fuzzy haze hidden behind his tears. He cried for her, pounded against her chest as the bones broke underneath him. And he went harder, and harder, and harder and harder.

Don't do this.

It echoed in his mind, and the sight of her gave way to a memory.

A time when he was hanging out with Donovan, who mentioned his girlfriend's friend and how he just *had* to meet her. Spencer remembered joining the band with him, and how the first thing Donovan did was take him over to the shy girl with her spiral-curled hair pinned up, loose strands gently resting on her shoulders.

Then he remembered how any awkwardness had melted away the moment he saw her.

How she looked at him and smiled, and her polite greeting quickly turned into a ramble about her flute and a microphone she'd need to be hooked up to.

His response? Of all things, he stammered out the way microphones work. His rants of 'nerding out' usually were met with eye rolls or groans, or blank stares if they were feeling nice.

But Kirsten had latched onto every word.

Smiled at his jokes, appreciated his stupid analogies. He felt normal with her in a way he never had in his entire life.

That was when he realized that he loved her: when she was sweating and covered in dirt after doing run-throughs for the band.

The shy girl understood him in a way he never thought possible. And the awkward boy would lose himself in her eyes every single time.

Now, out like a candle.

That's how they remained. Sirens blared in the distance, he could hear them get closer. They'd try to restart her heart, get her going again.

One more chance.

He pleaded with her to give it to him.

"Please don't do this."

Chapter Twenty-Seven

"I'm Sorry"

"What happened?"

At first, Spencer didn't register Arizona's voice. He was leaning against the wall next to Kirsten's hospital room, reliving everything in excruciating detail. When the ambulance took her, they said they found a weak pulse.

But Spencer knew that with how long she was out, there could be brain damage, her body might not be able to...

'The next few hours are critical' was a clinical term, one he heard so many times that it used to feel empty. But with the tables turned, it was a dagger. A painful dagger that was anything but empty.

Arizona repeated, "What happened?"

He slowly looked up at her. Her eyes were red, her face soaked with tears. She was wearing her pajamas, as was Donovan, who was rushing behind her.

"I don't know," Spencer managed in one quiet breath. "We were asleep, and she must've—"

"Look me in the eye and tell me that you *still* won't go to the cops."

"Arizona, I—"

"*Years*! For years, she cried for you. For *years*, she would go on dates with douchebag guys, but none could live up to how perfect Spencer *Fucking* Levign is." She raked her fingers through her hair. "Damnit, Spencer, I *told* you that you were smarter than this. I told you that we could avoid this!"

Donovan put his hand on her shoulder, and she trembled so much that Donovan's arm moved with her. He said gently, "Ari, it's alright."

"*Don't*." She closed her eyes and said to Spencer, "Does she have a chance to wake up and be okay?"

"I don't—"

"In your medical opinion, could she get through this?"

Spencer grit his teeth and pushed himself off the wall. He didn't feel like it was him inside his own body, but he needed to give Arizona the answers. She deserved that much.

He did his best to speak calmly, but every syllable was shaky, laced with tears he could no longer hold back. "She has a chance. I did CPR, then they were able to keep her heart going." Spencer hesitated before saying, "I honestly don't know beyond that. I haven't seen her."

The doctors had asked if he wanted to come by and hold her hand, talk to her. He knew that she may or may not be able to hear him, but for some reason, he'd start to walk in and then stop.

One more minute, he kept telling himself. He'd take one more minute and then go in.

Knowing full well that in that one minute, she could flatline.

Arizona drew in a sharp breath. She visibly forced her frustration away, doing whatever she could to snuff the fire out before it suffocated all of them.

Kirsten wouldn't want them to fight.

A few quiet seconds passed, and then Arizona took Donovan's hand in hers. She whispered, "I wanna see her."

"Of course, babe."

Her voice cracked out, "Help me?"

Donovan slowly nodded in reply. He looked at Spencer, as if to comfort him for even a moment before turning back to Arizona.

When they quietly slipped into Kirsten's room, Spencer didn't take a look inside. A few steps brought him to a bench nearby, and he plopped down on it. He doubled over and buried his face in his palms.

And then he screamed into them.

People walking around and all, Spencer let everything out — every cry and shout that smothered his heart to the point of nearly breaking it. Someone asked if he was alright, but he didn't respond.

He stayed just like that.

Until someone sat down next to him and put their hand on his shoulder.

Spencer didn't need to look, her touch was enough.

"Nikki."

And he realized there that somewhere along the way, she had become a comfort. Somehow — though he felt so far from safe and so lonely that it physically hurt — she made it feel better. But there was a truth that Spencer hadn't been able to put into words.

He asked, "Your dad did this, didn't he?"

Austin, The Mangled Man. Strangling people was practically his calling card.

"*I'm sorry.*"

Spencer's shoulder drooped more. He didn't know that was even possible. "Why?"

Ghosts wanted something, that's what he knew. Be it revenge or a place or for something to happen, they had to be after it. Austin wanted something so badly that he was willing to do *this*.

"*I'm sorry.*"

That was her only reply.

She kept her hand on his shoulder, forming little circles as she gently tried to provide any kind of support, any kind of sign that it would be okay. A reality that at one point, he was so optimistic that he truly believed it would happen.

But Spencer wasn't sure if he had it in him anymore.

He asked Nikki, "It wouldn't have been as simple as calling the cops, would it? Wouldn't end with Mom?"

She shook her head.

Spencer sprang up and ran his fingers through his hair, pacing back and forth. He vaguely made out people looking at him with various expressions of concern or annoyance, but it was so fleeting that Spencer barely noticed. Definitely didn't care.

"Then what in the hel—" Spencer grit his teeth. "What can *I* possibly do?"

His head was killing him. Pounding. He could feel the blood pulsating through his temples, felt every compression. A chill sent itself down his spine and cut him so deep that his body jolted against it.

Ringing in his ears.

Stabbing in his temples.

Doubling over, he buried his head in his hands and squeezed. "Please," he begged through his teeth.

But after a moment, a new voice rang through. His dad's.

His wife, Megan. They never found her body.

They lost control, they crashed, and there was this lake.

That was what he could hear. Not the concerned people around him or the world in general. Just the racing of his heart, drowned out by his dad's voice.

Then Austin's.

Megan is soaked, like she drowned. Do-Do you think that's how she went?

It stopped. Everything — the ringing, the sharp pain digging into Spencer's skull. The voices, all muted at the flip of a switch. People stood around him, but all he could do was look at Nikki.

"Sir." Someone asked, "Are you alright?"

He felt something tickle his nose, and he hurriedly wiped it away. When the annoyance subsided for a moment, he lied, "I'm fine, thank you." He looked at Nikki, who was sitting on the bench like a statue. He said through his teeth, "I fell."

"But, you're bleeding."

The feather-like brush against his nose returned. He wiped away at it and looked at his fingers.

Red.

He looked up at Nikki, as if to say 'what's happening to me?' But he didn't verbalize it, not there. "Nosebleed. I'm fine, thanks."

When the person left, they might have said something else. But Spencer wasn't paying attention anymore.

There was this lake.

She drowned.

They never found her body.

Spencer fell to his knees.

"You're looking for your mom too, aren't you?"

"*I'm sorry.*"

He must have looked insane, but frankly, he didn't care. He put his hand on her shoulder this time.

"Show me."

Nikki shot him a glance and raised her brow, as if to ask if he was sure. And Spencer nodded at her.

Sure enough, it came back. The ringing, the pain, but stifled. She held his hand and he squeezed, holding on as the nails drilled into his skull again.

He saw a forest. One that by the looks of it hadn't been traversed for years, or longer. Overtop it, a cliff that led its way to a massive running creek. His view panned to the right, overlooking the mass expansion of trees until he saw a gap and—

"Dad."

Spencer saw the clearing for his dad's trailer, just a few miles from the lake.

The spot in the woods that he clung to.

And the vision faded to nothing. Spencer was still there, upright as he held onto Nikki. She looked back at him with tears in her eyes, a look of longing. For once, she didn't look like a ghost or some terrifying figure with blood littering her body and glass lodged in her chest.

She looked like a scared little girl.

"Your mom's in the lake by Dad's trailer."

Spencer didn't ask, he *said* it. Because he knew, she was telling him even then. Planting it in his head, little seeds destined to sprout at just the right moment.

That was where he needed to be. Where it all started twenty-four years ago.

After a moment, her gaze hardened.

"*I'm sorry.*"

"Nikki?"

He blinked, and...

It was nothing like before. Whatever he saw, he wasn't in the hospital anymore.

"*I'm sorry.*"

It faded in and out like a mantra. A ritual that he couldn't begin to understand. The sound was just as foreign as the place he was in, like the feeling against his face.

He was lying face down on the ground. Everything was cold. Except for his upper half — it was covered in something, a pool.

Something warm, something sticky.

"I'm sorry."

His head jolted up, turning the world to muffled static. Everything blurred as he pushed against his ears, trying to make the ringing go away. It was all a jumbled-up mess of nothing as he trembled and squeezed his eyes as tightly as he could, fighting away from the—

Spencer's hands slipped.

Instinct, that's what it had to be. One moment, he was doing everything not to look. But then he opened his eyes and caught a glimpse.

His hand was stained red.

He gasped and tried to push away, but his tired arms grew heavier until they gave out entirely, sending him to face-plant into the pool in front of him. He slammed his hand against the ground and resorted to rolling on his side. He frantically patted himself down, in search of cuts or gashes or anything.

Nothing.

It wasn't his blood.

He forced himself to sit up.

The world spun. His hair was matted against his head, and his button-up shirt was in disarray, clinging to his abdomen. The sight of it came and went; all he could see clearly were the bright walls around them, burning holes into his eyes. Red splotches scattered on them. He blinked. Quickly, aggressively, he blinked.

And when he looked around at the walls, their painful patterns combined to form something he knew.

Something familiar.

He knew this place.

Just like how he knew the layout, the musty feeling of the outdoor bathroom whose air conditioner had broken long ago. The cracks on the walls, random graffiti. And he recognized the image, a little paw print.

Ridgeback logo.

Spencer was in his high school bathroom. The outdoor one by the football field.

"I'm sorry."

As if on cue, the place's scattered remains formed into one. He could make out the way the blood painted the walls. Glass fragments littered the ground, trailing toward the stalls. Not sure what compelled him to do it, Spencer looked to the right. And his heart skipped a beat.

A girl was lying there, face turned away from him.

In the midst of the maroon sea, her brown hair sat in crimson-soaked clumps. Her hand rested against her abdomen, but past it Spencer could make out gashes that littered her torso. Gashes that matched her hand, where she must've fought back. Crooked was the only word he could use to describe her.

Crooked, and bent, and matted, and—

Her left leg was broken, bent back towards her ear.

"I'm sorry."

Something glimmered in her other hand — her good one, resting against the ground.

The necklace.

The one with the paw print charm that he bought her with the biggest sense of pride. It matched her valedictorian sash.

Spencer remembered fishing it out of his closet and bringing it to the dry cleaners, ironing it out more times than he could count. Because she deserved the best. She always did.

He remembered loving her more than words could ever describe.

"Kaylee?"

"I'm sorry. I'm sorry. I'm sorry. I'm sorry. I'm sorry. I'm sorry."

No reply.

"Kaylee!"

"I'm sorry. I'm—"

"Shut up!"

"I'm sorry..."

He held his hand out for his sister as he screamed into oblivion. Begged and pleaded for her to wake up and come back to him; he would do anything to protect her.

Always.

Tears soaked his cheeks as his heart-wrenching sobs bounced off the walls. They streamed down and his voice cracked in the name of every lie he was told, every promise and all the *hope* that his painfully optimistic brain once held.

That for one *freaking* time in his life, he wouldn't be too late.

And he screamed at how it all ripped away in a heartbeat. It went on until his voice cracked and drew into hoarse gusts of air, then faded to nothing.

All he could manage was a tear-filled whisper.

"Kaylee."

He wanted to say something to her, but words couldn't
do her justice. Not any that he could ever find.

But then, the voice found them for him.

"I'm sorry."

Chapter Twenty-Eight

Emptied Home

It was time to go.

Spencer was getting ready to head back to the forest, only this time, with no intentions of telling his dad. Whether he knew he lived close to the accident or not — and Spencer had a tough time rationalizing the latter, as much as he wanted to — he couldn't see mentioning it.

Dad would try to talk him out of it.

And honestly, Spencer wasn't sure if he had it in him to defend his choice.

That's what he was getting ready for. Most of his stuff was gone, the rest in his car; it wasn't like he needed to suit up or run around, finding more information. He'd go find Megan, and maybe even Mom. And The Mangled Man would be there, which Spencer knew essentially meant he was going to uncharted territory to confront ghosts.

He might not make it out of this one, that much was obvious. So, in one last moment of weakness, there was a final stop.

Kirsten's room.

Spencer stood outside of it, his hands balled into fists. He rested his head on the wooden door, painfully aware of how similar of a position he was in when he went to talk to her. How she was on the other side, and at the time, the world seemed to be falling apart. If that was the case then, Spencer didn't know what to call this.

He knocked quietly, a generic, bland beat that was lifeless in comparison to the little tune he had drummed out for Kirsten.

On the other side, Arizona said quietly, "Come in."

Man, she sounded exhausted. It ripped his heart to shreds. It reminded him of how confident Arizona was, how assertive. She was the youngest of the four, but she always had such a powerful presence. Wilted, now. That was the only way to describe it.

Spencer walked in slowly, lips parted as he opened and closed the door, unable to look away.

There Kirsten was: hooked up to monitors and IVs that Spencer knew the purpose of and could handle. But somehow, he forgot what all of them did.

She was lying there, still motionless, with Arizona on one side and Donovan on the other. It was quiet, save for the beeping of Kirsten's heart monitor. It kept a steady pace,

Spencer kept reminding himself of that. He had prepared himself for the worst, but at least it wasn't the case.

For now, that was all he could hope for.

"I'll give you guys a sec," Donovan whispered as he stood up. He slowly walked over to Spencer, then spared Kirsten one more glance. "Let me know if you need anything."

"Hey," Spencer forced out. "Thank you for everything. Seriously, I—"

Donovan threw his arms around Spencer.

And he felt the floodgates open, the dam broken beyond repair. His tears soaked the collar of Donovan's jacket. He didn't say anything, he only thought about how, despite everything, he was able to get his friends back.

Even if this could be one last time.

"Love you, man," Spencer whispered.

"This isn't your fault."

Spencer's lips twitched, momentarily forming a half-smile. He wasn't sure if he'd ever be able to tell his little group how much they meant to him. Donovan tightened his hold before letting go and sparing Spencer a warm flash of a smile.

Then, he left.

Left Arizona and Spencer.

Spencer quietly walked over and took Donovan's spot, grabbing Kirsten's hand. Delicately, as to not nick any of her IVs. He bit his lip, unable to rest his gaze on a part of her that wasn't hidden by equipment.

In the silence, Spencer couldn't help but remember Nikki's warning. Time was running out — he hadn't listened for Mom, not with Kirsten either.

He couldn't make that mistake again.

So, in an attempt to start the most painful goodbye imaginable, Spencer whispered, barely aware of his own words, "Are you okay?" Even though he knew that of course, Arizona wasn't. It was almost condescending.

But if Kirsten could ask Arizona that question, she would.

"No," Arizona whispered in reply. She sniffled, using one hand to wipe away her tears, the other still tethered to Kirsten's hand. "I keep trying to 'look at the bright side,' that's what she'd want. But she's always been better at that motivational crap than I am."

"Tell me about it." Spencer forced a chuckle. "She'd probably say something along the lines of we're 'crying enough to fill up a medium-sized aquarium and need to bring up the mood.'"

"Yup, medium-sized specifically."

"You gct me."

He swore he felt the slightest shift from Kirsten, a squeeze of his hand, something. The logical side of Spencer knew it was just him making things up.

But the optimistic one liked to believe she heard it and laughed.

Kirsten always did like that optimistic side. She'd want him to hold onto it, no matter how much it threatened to slip from his grasp.

Another moment passed. But not an uncomfortable silence; instead, one shared between Spencer and someone he used to see as a sister. One whose pain he wished he could at least stifle.

"She's been my best friend for ten years," Arizona whispered. "I'm just so…" Lost, broken, confused. Spencer could no doubt finish her sentence with any of those and still hit the nail on the head. "What are you gonna do?"

"It's dangerous and stupid and absolutely could get me killed," Spencer admitted. "Would you want to know the details?"

She slowly shook her head, eyes still glued to her friend. "No. I guess not."

Though, given the look on her face, she wouldn't have tried to stop him. Maybe because Kirsten wouldn't have picked that battle either; it was a losing one.

"Listen," Spencer said as he shifted uncomfortably. "With everything going on, I might not—" his voice cracked, and he found himself not sure how to say the rest. He closed his eyes and forced out, "I might not ever see her again. Please, do you think I could talk to her?"

"Yeah, I get it. She'd want you to say goodbye."

"Thank you, Arizona."

"Ari, just…" She stood up and squeezed Kirsten's hand before gently placing it back on the bed. Her eyes glittered with tears, voice cracking out, "Call me Ari."

Spencer smiled and nodded, unable to remember the last time he called her that.

"Okay, Ari."

She walked over to the door, and hesitated as she put her hand on the knob. "Whatever it is that's dangerous and stupid, try not to go overboard." She motioned towards Kirsten with her head, and her voice cracked as she told him, "She needs you."

Coming back wasn't something he could promise, as much as he wanted to. But trying not to do anything stupid? For once, he could say it. "I promise."

"I really do hope you come back. And not just because of her."

Spencer smiled. "Bye, Ari. Thank you."

"Goodbye. And good luck."

Without another word, she slipped away, leaving Spencer and Kirsten alone.

Like always, Spencer didn't know how to start. He cleared his throat.

"Hey, hun."

Spencer flipped her hand around in his, gently, making sure not to snag anything. He looked at her machines again, mind slowly clearing as he remembered what they did and how they worked. How they were helping her, it was something he had to remember.

He also remembered how much she hated hospitals.

"Gosh, this would freak you out."

As she always said, anything 'medicine-y' was 'gross.' And when either of them got hurt, she'd start to ask what was going on, claiming that she didn't want to have any surprises. Then when he'd start to explain, she'd recoil and say she didn't 'think that one through.'

Unsure of what she'd want to know, Spencer decided it was best to change the subject. Best not to describe every intricate detail like his mind defaulted to.

"You're the best thing that ever happened to me."

The plainest, simplest truth he could ever tell.

"I'd never be able to tell you how much you mean to me. Just—" He kissed her hand. "Thank you. For-for everything."

'Thank you.' Spencer almost laughed at it. Because the awkward kid would've said that, too.

At least she always liked his brand of awkward.

Spencer sighed and took out his wallet. "Alright, you win." Without needing to search for it, his fingers found the note he had written all those years ago. "I know, Kirsten one, Spencer zero. We all saw it coming."

Gently, he unfolded the letter. By then, it was torn at the edges, but it meant the world to him just the same. His best attempt ever at putting his thoughts into words, something that he could only hope would do her justice once finally spoken aloud. Spencer looked down at it, though he didn't need to.

He had memorized it long ago.

"Kirsten, it's been a year. And after all this time, I still never know how to start talking to you. Then you say something, and you always seem to know what I need to hear. After you start, you can't get me to shut up.

You're always there.

After Donovan told me about you, and that we had to meet, I didn't know what to say to him. Now, I almost want to thank him for it. Even though he'd never let me live it down.

I love you, Kirsten. And I hope that maybe you feel the same way about me.

You've done more than you could ever know. Since the day I met you, I knew that I would always have someone in my corner.

And for that, as dumb as it sounds, thank you."

He remembered how weird he felt saying it, and the irony behind him repeating it didn't elude him.

"Spencer"

Like every time, he gave it a couple more reads. But his gaze started to settle more on the paper than the words themselves, part of him hoping that she would wake up and say something about it. Whether she said it was dumb or the best thing in the world, it wouldn't matter. Just as long as he could hear the chirp in her voice again.

"There you go," he whispered between tears. Tears he hadn't realized were there but wasn't surprised to feel as they flowed down his cheeks. "Just, do me a favor and let me read it to you again, alright?" He forced a smile. "Hope you took notes, there will be a quiz later and…"

Silence.

Nothing but silence.

And he needed to leave. With a long, shaky breath, Spencer managed to stand. "I'm so sorry, baby." He planted a soft kiss on her cheek. "Please come back to me."

His heart skipped a beat as he turned. Turned towards a path of unknowns and fear and who knew what else. Away from everything he knew.

In the hopes that somehow, that path could lead him right back to where he wanted to be more than anything.

And even if it was battered and broken, there was still a part of Spencer's mind that said it would be alright, that there was a way, and he'd find it.

That's *exactly* what Kirsten would tell him.

Spencer looked at the way her chest rose and fell. Rhythmic, steady. And the alarms weren't going off, her vitals didn't have any blaring issues. She had a chance, a real one, and Spencer would never let himself forget that.

"We're gonna see each other again, do you hear me?"

He swore her lip twitched, forming a smile. One that Spencer returned.

"I promise you."

And he'd take that with him through questions and fear and everything else that Spencer had spent years running from. All so it could lead him back to his promise. The one that he'd hold onto through everything.

The awkward boy *would* see the shy girl again.

Chapter Twenty-Nine

Runaway

"Tristan, listen to me. Nikki said you did something to the car. She insists, but I keep sticking my neck out for you and telling her that's insane. She keeps going and — What was that?" There were murmurs in the background — hushed, bone-chilling whispers. As soon as they left, without so much as a pause, Austin whispered, *"I gotta go, Megan needs me."*

Spencer let out a shaky sigh as the voicemail cut out. He was driving to the forest, having settled on parking where he would if he were visiting Dad. At least that way, he'd spend some part of this trip knowing where he was.

Music didn't seem right, but the silence was killing him, so the voicemails were what was left.

"This was the right call, wouldn't you say?" Spencer asked while glancing towards the passenger seat. "The more I know before doing – well, whatever you need me to do – the better, yeah?"

Nikki was seated next to him. He didn't know when she appeared or why she did it, but there she was, buckled and all. Her void stare was trained towards the road, her mind somewhere else entirely. It wasn't that she looked angry or disinterested, far from it — 'sad' was the only word Spencer could come up with.

All he knew was that he was glad he didn't have to do this alone.

"Surprised you came with," Spencer said with a slight chuckle. The silence was making him uncomfortable and his mouth worked faster than his brain. "I mean, after the crash I didn't know if you'd be, like, inherently scared of cars or..."

Nikki slowly looked over at Spencer and shook her head, her stiffened bones creaking with each motion. Bits of gravel fell on the seat.

"Sorry," Spencer mumbled.

He quietly drummed out a random beat against his steering wheel, catching glimpses of Nikki here and there.

A half a mile or so later, he wasn't sure if it was him deciding it or if Nikki somehow put the thought there, but he elected to play the next voicemail. The only other one he and his dad could get to — just like Dad had said, the last one couldn't be played. Not yet.

Austin's voice filled Spencer's car.

"Hey, so, what in the fuck is Nikki talking about here?"

The man's voice sounded aged, winded as he spoke with one breath of air. Nikki flinched at the sound.

"Call me back."

Before the message silenced completely, there was a bang. And that was all Spencer had to go off of, a crash and then nothing.

"Stop."

Spencer's foot hit the brakes before he knew what was happening.

He looked around, panting, soaking in the overwhelming darkness of the empty road in front of him — the road that had led him just short of Dad's trailer. It was better than looking to his left, where the vast expansion of uncharted territory took the form of acres upon acres of woods.

"Are you sure that this is where I need to—"

But Nikki wasn't there anymore.

Spencer bit his lip. "Right."

A few more moments passed, and Spencer found it in himself to pull over to the side of the road like Nikki told him. Part of him would have preferred to blindly scale the cleared expansion near Dad's trailer and just hope he'd come across the lake — all for the sake of seeing something familiar, even if it was fleeting. But he could tell Nikki would remain with him, even if it wasn't always in the physical sense.

He still couldn't believe how much comfort that gave him.

All the comfort in the world, though, still might not have been enough. He stayed there, with a death grip on the steering wheel.

He found his arm aching from where Mom stabbed him, felt the lingering pains from every time he fell while trying to get away from her and The Mangled Man.

That brought his mind to an even darker place: how Brett died, the thought of Kirsten unable to breathe on her own. He thought about the stab wounds and The Mangled Man.

What if he couldn't get away in time? Just like how no else could?

There were so many goodbyes that were missed, so many things he should have done. Donovan came to mind — yes, he said goodbye to him, but neither of them had even scratched the surface. Spencer hadn't stressed to Donovan just how much he meant, or how serious he was when he said he saw him as a brother. He always assumed there'd be a next time.

But he wasn't sure about that anymore.

Kaylee.

Spencer closed his eyes and let out a shaky breath. If something happened to him, Kaylee would be able to handle herself, Spencer knew that much.

But she should never *have* to do it.

And he thought about what could be the last time she'd hear his voice, and the fact that he couldn't remember what he said — that whatever it was, it wasn't enough.

She needed more.

Spencer took out his phone again, his shaky hand making the screen dance in his vision. It was all muscle memory as he pulled Kaylee's contact up, one of the people he talked to most in the world. It rang a few times before sending him to voicemail. Spencer rubbed his eyes and listened to Kaylee's message, one he knew by heart.

For some reason, she had always been bad at answering her phone.

That one was all Mom.

When the message ended, Spencer heard a beep. And suddenly, he was met with trying to say goodbye to her.

Words couldn't express this — not the lifetime worth of comfort that they were supposed to give each other. In their eighteen years, already she had been the one constant that got him through everything.

All to be condensed into one final voicemail.

"Hey, Kaylee. It's me. I just wanted to say I'm sor—" Spencer clenched his jaw. "I'm proud of you."

Those two words he almost said had lost their meaning long ago.

And of course he had told Kaylee that he was proud of her. But he needed her to have a reminder of that every day, ready to go whenever she needed it.

"Life's dealt you a lot of horrible cards. Heck, looking outside of Mom and Dad — which frankly, I admire how well you've done with that — there's so much I've watched you go through and just, freakin', excel."

So many examples popped in his head. But if he listed them, he'd be there all night. Little, every day victories flashed in front of his eyes. He'd heard of someone's life flashing before their eyes, but it wasn't his. It was hers danced in his vision.

To summarize the lifetime of pride that she gave him, Spencer said, "I knew you'd be valedictorian, I knew you'd get into that school, all of it. Mom and Dad knew it too, they told me all the time."

He smiled.

"Brett would be proud, too."

No hesitation there.

Not just because Brett spoke of Kaylee with so much pride that he would practically glow at the mere mention of her. It was also because Brett had point blank said it to Spencer more times than either of them could count.

"Kinda spoiling the surprise here, but..." Spencer sighed, then he forced out, "*Just in case*, we've been putting away money for you, for college. Didn't want to tell you about it 'cause we wanted to make sure you'd put aside your own. But it's there, and you can have it, there's a paper in my drawer that'll tell you how. Just use it right, okay? Promise me?"

He ran it through his head, the account they had put money into every month for years. The paper was supposed to be made into some kind of a scavenger hunt or something else dumb, but things change.

It hit him how quiet he was being, how time had passed and empty silence was filling the message. Tears sprang to his eyes as he tried to bring his message to a close.

Just so that if this *was* it, the last time could mean something.

"I just want you to know that you've been the best little sister I could ever ask for. You have meant more than I could ever..." Spencer cleared his throat and looked at the roof of his car, vision blurring as he tried to blink the tears away. "I love you, Kaylee. Always."

His lips quivered, and he knew that was because there was nothing more to say. It hadn't scratched the surface, but Spencer had done the best he ever could with words.

Kaylee would know that, which is what mattered to him.

"Goodbye."

Nothing more to say, Spencer hung up the phone. And deafening silence was all he had to keep him company.

He looked at the mass of the forest and all the secrets it held, in awe of how much things had changed. The graduation that he had once looked forward to was only a day away. Now, he knew what would happen if he didn't 'fix this.'

One last attempt.

This time, he wouldn't be too late.

Spencer got out of his car and rested his hand against the hood. He kept his eyes trained on the forest, shaking his head to try and rid it of every single thought about how this could go wrong.

A cold hand rested on his arm.

"You can do this."

Because of that — because of the voice that he used to fear more than anything else in the world — Spencer managed a shaky smile.

Then he forced himself off the car and walked towards the forest, with his feet stamping down like they were caged in cement blocks.

A few steps in, Spencer could already hear the running water that hopefully led to the lake. He looked around, though not much was visible past the night's sky. He had found his spare pair of glasses in his glove box, but they didn't do much; only providing slight clarity to the miles upon miles of silhouettes of trees.

The more he looked, though, the more he remembered some of them. Back when they were kids and afraid of practically nothing, he and Kaylee would run around in these woods, sometimes going way further than the trail.

It was much to Dad's discontent, but in the moment, Spencer was so grateful for it.

A tree root in front of him was familiar: the way it shriveled up and swirled into an intricate mess of patterns. And the one next to it extended towards a tree marked with a red rope, a warning to them that they were well past the boundaries of the clearing and needed to get back to the trail.

Familiarity. Spencer had it after all.

Which was all he needed as he walked in the opposite direction, keeping in mind every familiar bit of the forest and the fact that he had explored this place more times than he could ever imagine. He went past another root, through a group of trees that had caved in towards each other. He knew to listen to the lake and the idle sounds of the moving body of water.

He kept going, unsure how much time passed.

Then he stopped.

Whispers, that was all he could hear; gravelly, angry whispers that cut Spencer to his core. His body froze, eyes uselessly searching the place for a hint of what he heard. But all he saw was black.

"Where is she?"

The Mangled Man.

Spencer's throat closed.

Like he was sucking through a straw and the other side was held shut. He threw his hands to his neck and clawed at it, trying to pry off a hand that wasn't even there. And he could hear The Mangled Man's cries, interlaced with laughter.

He doubled over and slammed his hand against the ground.

Everything inside him screamed for air. Spencer's ears started to ring, and he threw wide his arms to push off a man who he couldn't even—

The hold on his throat ripped away. He could feel the force against it.

"Run."

He took off before Nikki even finished her word.

Spencer gasped for breath as he sprinted along, the trees a blurred mess. It was just as hazed and distorted as the sounds behind him, the sounds of leaves crunching.

As the cries continued behind him, all Spencer could do was be faster.

Be faster, and no matter what, never look back.

Not even as The Mangled Man's sobs chimed in his ears like bells in a morbid orchestra. No matter what, as Spencer tripped over tree roots and pushed himself deeper into the forest, he couldn't let himself look.

Even as the cries grew more distant, as The Mangled Man stopped gaining ground.

Do *not* look back.

Spencer kept going, his heart about to burst out of his chest. And then before him, something caught his eye.

And finally — *finally* — he slowed.

Nikki was there, her back to him as she carved something into a tree. He wasn't sure if she heard him or somehow sensed he was there, but she stepped away.

M :-)

And next to it, an arrow pointing to the right. It was towards a clearing just big enough for Spencer to slip past.

He ducked around a couple of trees and barreled past the arrow. The sound of running water intensified, the cries of The Mangled Man lost in the distance. Spencer doubled over, knees on his hands as he took in gasping breaths.

With The Mangled Man lost for the time being, it was just Spencer and Nikki near the lake, its mass extending beyond eyeshot in either direction. Spencer had no clue where to go. And when he glanced towards Nikki, she sighed and looked away.

"It's okay," Spencer murmured, both to himself and her. "Let's follow the stream."

Which is exactly what they did, with Spencer leading the way. It didn't take long for him to take out his phone and turn the flashlight on.

Leaves crunched underneath his weight, The Girl's soft steps in tow. They glanced at the trees and the endless secrets they held. And they kept going, with Spencer jumping at every other sound while Nikki remained unbothered.

Until eventually, Spencer didn't know why at the time, Nikki froze.

There was a cry behind them.

And as the air caught in his throat, he managed a hard, pained look at Nikki. She pointed behind him.

He turned stiffly, robotically.

The Mangled Man's dangling neck swayed in the wind. Tears escaped the man's blood-shot eyes.

And his head grazed Spencer's shoulder.

"WHERE IS SHE?"

Chapter Thirty

Road of Ashes

One second, The Mangled Man's cold touch could be felt against Spencer's arm.

The next, Spencer was running – *flying* – through the woods, following the will of the icy hand that led him further and further along.

The Mangled Man trailed behind them, his steps silent like Nikki's. But in Spencer's mind, each stomp into the ground sent shockwaves. Violent, thunderous beats that vibrated in his chest and made him struggle to breathe as he tread further into the woods.

Nikki turned a corner and hid behind a tree, jolting Spencer's hand with her. The two stood there, both with their hands covering Spencer's mouth. Her hand was overtop his, her icy stare drilling holes into him.

"Don't move."

The footsteps weren't there. The forest itself was eerily quiet, as if it was hiding right along with them.

Through gaps in the trees, Spencer could make out the stream leading to the lake.

But the running water's idle sound was lost to him as well, muffled by the heartbeat racing in his ears. He could hear his own labored breathing, felt its shaky heat trap itself against his palms. With each breath his glasses fogged, allowing only a solitary moment for him to savor before the world blurred again. A scream threatened to escape, and he was met with Nikki's cold touch as she clasped him tighter — so much that he was running out of gaps to gather panicked breaths from.

With how small she was, Nikki seemingly meshed herself into the tree, finding effortless camouflage.

The only other sound was from The Mangled Man, the one thing he couldn't stifle. His sobs, they boomed through the hushed forest. They bounced off the trees, their low, desperate groans stabbing Spencer in the temples.

And they were getting closer.

They went from muffled cries at the end of a tunnel to static against Spencer's left ear. He could practically *feel* the movement, and he couldn't stop himself from recoiling.

One more low groan, so close that he could feel the cold breath against his skin.

"Where is she?"

The next thing he knew, Nikki was gone.

Spencer's legs turned to mush. He had to catch himself against the tree to stop himself from falling, the soft graze sounding like fireworks. And he held his breath as he pitifully shifted his gaze through the forest, pleading for it to not be so.

He begged that he wasn't alone, not there, to run from The Mangled Man in a forest he didn't know. His one anchor in this couldn't have up and left him when The Mangled Man was just feet away.

"Austin."

The cries stopped.

Everything stopped.

Spencer narrowed his eyes, searching for any sign of what could've called; the voice that was familiar but laced with something he didn't know. He looked more, squinting through the endless abyss in front of him.

Then, he saw her.

Nikki. She stood atop a hill in the distance, in the direction they came from. The voice she used was deeper, as if to not give away who she was.

She smiled.

And then The Mangled Man went towards her.

Away from Spencer, taking his cries with him until they returned to muffled sounds at the opposite end of the tunnel.

Nikki appeared next to Spencer before he had the chance to take his hand from his mouth.

For a moment, Spencer couldn't speak. But everything rushed back, and he threw his arms over her, shaking as he fought out, "Thank you." When he realized how close The Mangled Man still was — far enough for him to breathe but too close for Spencer to talk normally, he whispered, "He can't hear you, not if you don't want him to. Find her, lead me to her, and I will do whatever you need me to do."

Nikki looked at him sadly before shifting her gaze to where The Mangled Man disappeared. Spencer grabbed her by her shoulders.

"One wrong move," he said quietly, so soft he could barely hear himself, "and he'll hear me. We don't know where she is."

Hide and don't make a peep until they knew where Megan was. That's the only plan Spencer could rationalize.

"Find your mom," Spencer whispered to Nikki. "You can do this."

The cries were moving again, closer but not to the point where Spencer could feel The Mangled Man's suffocating touch against him. It was just enough for Spencer to try to melt into the tree and wait for Nikki to show him the way.

All she had to do was find it. Nikki nodded at him. *"Be careful."*

And Spencer was alone once more.

He let out the shakiest of breaths and curled into the tree, listening to the cries and how they maneuvered through the forest. Some moments, they were far. Then, so near that Spencer found himself biting his tongue until iron flooded his mouth. Time seemed to still, and the cries settled close by.

All Spencer could manage was a slight tilt of his head as he looked back, where the sound was coming from.

The Mangled Man was feet away.

His back to Spencer, he was viciously storming through the clearing and looking past every tree. The Mangled Man howled, a bone-chilling wail erupting from his throat. He shoved a tree aside, peaking near it.

With a crack, it fell to the ground.

"*Where is she?*" He shouted again as he searched where that massive tree just stood.

Spencer's heart felt like it was about to burst. A tree – The Mangled Man managed to knock over a tree with his own bare hands.

And he kept coming.

He didn't falter, he didn't hesitate. The Mangled Man kept along his path.

Right towards Spencer.

Until, silence.

Time slowed. He didn't move. He didn't breathe. Maybe, just maybe, The Mangled Man had given up the chase.

A twig snapped underneath Spencer.

He stood there, mouth agape as he didn't dare to try and look back. He held his breath above the weight of the twig that he had only twitched on.

But something turned his head for him.

Black, chasm-like eyes met his.

Spencer took off, The Mangled Man on his tail. His legs burned as he sprinted further and further into the forest, away from the lake and Nikki.

He'd fall back for a moment, then he'd think about Donovan or Kaylee or Kirsten and he'd pick up his pace. The overarching branches and leaves smacked him in the face, sending blood over his eyes. He squinted and made out a clearing.

Dad.

Spencer was taking The Mangled Man right to him.

For just a moment, he slowed.

Then, when he looked back, The Mangled Man wasn't there anymore.

Spencer toppled forward and fell to the ground, his body jolting with the thud. The world blurred, and he took shallow breaths as he blinked away the haze.

The Mangled Man formed in the corner of his vision.

And Spencer shuffled back, heart racing in his ears as he watched the man's blackened gaze affix to him. Words were thrown from his mouth, but Spencer couldn't perceive what he was hammering out.

All he knew was the looming and hardened ghost stood at his feet.

The ghost knelt down and fixed his hold over Spencer's body, stifling every attempt at so much as a twitch.

He stared into the endless chasm of *nothing* where The Mangled Man's eyes should be. Through them, this pit of sadness and hurt and emptiness spewed out in a look of what Spencer could only explain as misery personified.

He couldn't breathe.

Toying with his prey, The Mangled Man gave Spencer just enough strength to throw his hands over his throat, clawing away at it like he could pry the invisible hands off of him. He gasped and writhed on the ground, leaves scratching against his skin and grazing against his eyes. He uselessly clawed against the hold that wasn't even there.

Everything in him screamed for air.

His pulse raced in his ears. He held one hand towards The Mangled Man, pain shooting through his chest.

In response, The Mangled Man smiled. A fit of laughter replaced the cries, flooding the space between Spencer's ears and echoing around in his skull.

He curled up into a ball, his once-frantic agonized attempts turning slow. He tried to call for help, but all he could manage was a faint, "Please."

That was only met with more laughter.

Spencer's movements turned to faint twitches; his attempts at gasping turned shallow. And his ears rang as the pulse that used to race turned to weak, sporadic thuds.

Everything sounded like muffled nothing at one side of the tunnel, and Spencer was trapped on the opposite end. Completely and breathlessly unable to claw himself away from it.

Memories flooded his mind as he laid there, only managing pitiful twitches. The darkness that surrounded him gave way to images of Kaylee, images of Donovan. He thought about how lost to the world Kaylee would be. All she'd have of him was the stupid voicemail and a check that wouldn't scratch the surface of what she needed. And Donovan, he thought about their goodbye, how didn't have one last chance.

Kirsten would wake up, he knew in his heart that somehow, she'd come back. But instead of seeing him by her side —where he wanted to be more than anything — Spencer agonized over a broken promise.

His final one.

The world faded more and more into nothing.

A gasp, and a tearful cry.

"Mom?"

Nikki, he could recognize her even there. The Mangled Man let out a cry of his own and looked up before standing in one fluid, weightless motion.

And Spencer took in the sharpest breath.

He rolled onto his stomach, gasping as he brought his knees towards his chest. Blades of grass rubbed against his eyes and dirt clung to his skin.

Acid dripped into his lungs and pulsed to every cell in his body.

He screamed into the dirt. Again, and again.

Cold hands rested against his shirt, sending light thuds against his back. Spencer drew in another breath and looked up at Nikki, his tears blurring her. But he was able to make out her expression, how frightened and sickly she looked.

She held her hand out to him. *"I need you."*

Slowly, with time he wasn't sure they had, the world started to come back. Clear, grand trees overlooked them, forming from what used to be hazy green dots that splattered in his vision. The sounds of nature clarified, just as true as the orange of the sunrise that cascaded over them.

And clearer than anything else was the girl's hand in front of him.

Nikki, that's all she was to him now. All she'd ever have
to be.

He took the child's hand, and the two of them shared his
weight as he got up off the ground. She smiled at him
like a kid would. With a breath of innocence as their
wildest desires came to fruition.

It was a gleeful, hopeful smile.

"You found her," Spencer said breathlessly.

And the shared feeling between them confirmed it,
though he didn't truly need that confirmation to begin
with. Spencer inched and rested his hot hand on her cold
shoulder, sending a comforting chill through his body.
With The Mangled Man going the opposite direction,
Spencer felt safer, even if for a moment.

"Then, let's go to her."

The two of them ventured back through the forest,
Nikki's hand clasping Spencer's. She effortlessly skipped
around each stump, humming to the beat of a kids'
cartoon he remembered hearing from reruns when he
was younger. He'd slow here and there to go over a tree
root, and she'd glance back at him and wait patiently for
him to clear it. Then she'd go back to her little dance as if
she wasn't ever interrupted.

Spencer didn't know where The Mangled Man
disappeared to. The cries and groans were off in the
distance, the man having gone the wrong way. He was

lost in those woods, further and further from the one woman he wanted to see more than anything.

And, despite it all, Spencer's heart couldn't help but ache for him.

Any hesitation from him was met with Nikki tightening her grip and picking up the pace. It continued until the stream grew louder, bringing them to the mass of the lake, its vastness extending in every direction. But Nikki didn't falter — she turned to the left and skipped on, guiding Spencer towards a different patch of water.

Then, and only then, she started to slow.

Her gleefulness melted away, replaced with a serious scowl as she pointed towards a group of rocks.

And when Spencer looked in that direction, when he squinted towards the collection of jagged boulders, he saw a hand.

He took a shaky breath and looked at Nikki. "She's trapped there?"

Once again, the silence answered his question.

"Come on," he said as he carefully nudged her forward. "It's alright."

This time, Spencer guided Nikki. Her gaze remained trained on where her mother was, her light steps turning to heavy stomps. Not as forceful as The Mangled Man's, not laced with anger or booming with earth-shattering grief — more childish, like she was stalling.

But Spencer carefully guided her, which she allowed. He led her all the way there, the two of them slowing just short of the clearing.

Megan was in the lake, body sprawled out, her brown eyes still open. Her red, curly hair looked like straws that clung to her body and wrapped around her neck. Mangled, battered clothes formed with her skin, soaking for so long it practically formed to her. And her skin was sickly pale. Clear and with no blemishes in sight, but void.

Empty.

Nikki shriveled up and clung to Spencer's side.

He couldn't take his eyes off her — he didn't understand. He hadn't expected her to be so... *whole*, for lack of better words. It was as if Megan or the forest itself had managed to preserve her.

Spencer could only hold the woman's daughter in a silent wonder of what he was supposed to do. He thought about what he would want there, what would help.

And a sharp breath erupted from his throat.

He'd want to say goodbye, to know where she would be. And if it were his mom, he knew she'd want that, too. She'd want to spend the rest of forever not in that lake, waiting for the water to finally fade her to nothing.

Spencer turned to Nikki, who was looking at a spot in the woods. Her gaze more went through the place than anything else. "Stay with me, alright?" he whispered to her.

And she did. Unmoving, she remained close to Spencer as he dragged Megan away from the water. Her sullen eyes looked up, lifelessly glaring holes into him.

He wanted to look away. Somehow, her gaze was almost pleading.

There wasn't too much he could do, only see if she had any living family. He repeated that promise to her as he laid her out on the grass, collecting flowers here and there for her to hold. He untangled her hair, laying it out as best as he could. It was long, just past her shoulders. The curls were still there despite everything, and Spencer watched how, as more time passed, it started to dry. The curls started to idly sway in the wind.

He didn't know why he did it, not beyond it feeling right.

Maybe it was because he knew she must've hated to spend the rest of eternity like that, or maybe it was some other reason he couldn't understand yet.

"I know I didn't do this, but my parents did, and..." Spencer grit his teeth. "They never meant to hurt you."

It wasn't enough, it never would be. But Austin had heard it over and over. It was her turn.

"Whoever else misses you, I'll find them, I promise. I'll let them know that..."

Her story, he could make sure that people knew it. Spencer stole a glance towards Nikki, who was still looking away. Then he faced Megan again. "She misses you."

He gently closed her eyes.

Spencer stood and made his way back to Nikki. His gaze met hers and he crouched down, meeting her face to face. As black as her eyes were, he could still see the kid there. How her porcelain skin meshed with her blonde hair, the gravel permanently affixed to her skin serving as the only blemish.

"You should say goodbye to her," he told her after a moment. "I'll call your dad over, too." Spencer chuckled before saying, "Just as soon as I'm in the clear, I don't think he likes me very much."

That was met with a faint laugh and an exaggerated shrug from Nikki.

After hesitating a moment, Spencer asked, "What about *my* mother?"

In the blink of an eye, a vision came to him.

It was met with a dull ache in his head and ringing in his ears, but it was manageable. He made out the familiar sight of a living room with black hardwood floor and a white-painted wall that still had blood on it.

It was home.

His living room. And he could see his mom there, in a brief shot before the vision faded to nothing. Then he blinked and he was back in the forest.

Spencer had to go home.

"Thank you," he murmured as he took her hand. "Thank you for everything. I know I fought you a lot, and my lack of speed probably drove you crazy." A knowing chuckle from Nikki made him smile. "But you got me there, and I appreciate it, and…"

There was still much to do, and time seemed to sprint faster than Spencer could ever manage to keep up. But things were feeling right again. Austin and Nikki would get to say goodbye and see her one more time. The Mangled Man could be regular Austin.

Spencer didn't have to be too late anymore.

"I couldn't have figured out how to 'fix this' without you."

He squeezed Nikki's shoulder and watched as the cheerful smile found its way on her lips once more. And he walked back, watching as she slowly went over to her mother and took her hand. A smile crept on his lips, and he found a mass of trees and bushes he could hide behind and be invisible to the world.

For just a moment.

When he was ready, he tilted his head back, and at the top of his lungs he screamed to the world, "Austin!"

The crying came back, and Spencer screamed again.

He shouted until the sounds came close enough. He kept his eyes on Nikki, who talked to her mom and shot Spencer glances.

The world slowed until they saw The Mangled Man emerge, face boiling over with rage. Then he saw Nikki, saw his wife.

And all the hate, the rage, and the pain erased itself in the blink of an eye.

"Megan?"

He ran towards them. Nikki stood and threw her arms around him, and he returned it. From a distance, Spencer couldn't make out what they said. But they talked to each other and knelt down towards the woman they had both spent the better part of two decades searching for.

Then, they both stiffened.

The expansion of trees swayed faster in the wind, and the orange of the sun beamed down on them. Something in the air changed, Spencer didn't know what it was. He could only hold his breath as he watched the two ghosts look around.

And he heard dripping.

Loud droplets outshined the peaceful sway of the breeze. It crept closer, echoing, as if it were dripping in a cave. Fear found its way back to Spencer and traveled up his spine.

But Nikki and Austin both looked towards the water and smiled.

Spencer couldn't see the body anymore. Just a woman, she walked over to the two of them, her arms outstretched. Water dropped off her dress. Her hair still clung to her skin.

Megan.

The three ghosts embraced, a lost family glowing in the light that now flooded the entirety of the clearing.

Finally, they had found each other.

Spencer stayed motionless as he watched Nikki talk to her parents, her gleeful smile so pure and so whole it looked like it would never leave her face again. For a few moments, he swore he could see a hint of a beautiful, light brown envelop the blackness that used to consume her eyes.

With that look, and a sparkle that Spencer had never seen in her before, Nikki spared him one last look.

And she tearfully mouthed, *"Thank you."*

Chapter Thirty-One

One Last Time

Spencer could hear his mom's blood-curdling screams from outside.

He stumbled up the steps to his house, the same ones he had traversed countless times with Mom by his side. But, he couldn't let himself slow to relish on that. Spencer looked at the busted-in door and saw a trail of blood, and he realized he didn't know if it was his own, Kaylee's, or Brett's.

Another scream. A deafening one.

He made it atop the final step, feeling like he had traversed a mountain. Spencer's palm squeaked against the doorknob, and his face curled into a pained scowl as he prepped himself to go in — to see her.

The scowl only deepened when he realized that, of all people to be afraid of, it was his *mother*. In his wildest dreams, Spencer would have never pictured that.

But — figuring one last foiled plan wouldn't make much of a difference — he pushed the door open, not needing to use the handle he held.

Ten, maybe fifteen steps took him there, but it may as well have been miles as the screams continued to emit so harshly that it shattered his heart like glass. Spencer's feet were heavy as he trudged towards the living room.

The way there was a straight shot, but it seemed like a maze. One that he had gotten lost in time until Mom appeared, ready to have his back at a moment's notice.

At the final step, his foot planted wrong, almost sending him tumbling towards the floor.

Mom was on all fours, screaming into the ground. He wouldn't have believed the sound was stifled if he didn't see it for himself. She clutched her head, her arms trembling so fast her shaking body could hardly catch up.

Spencer took a sharp breath. His voice cracked as he whispered, "Ma?"

His heart shattered as her movement came to an abrupt halt — along with her crying, her breathing, all of it. She stared, and two black pits where her eyes used to be drilled daggers into him.

With another step, Spencer repeated, "Ma."

She blinked faster than he thought possible, snapping her head away. "Go away," she strained.

Spencer took another step in return. "I'm-I'm here to help you. It wasn't you; it never was. I know about Austin and how you—"

"Go away!"

"But I wanna help you! I have always wanted to help you."

Fumbling, heavy steps took him to her side, and he saw her more clearly than he had in six years. Her brown hair was ragged, a frantic mess after having been pushed back and raked through. There were scratches on her face, crimson streaks trailing in fragments. Slowly, Spencer knelt down and put his hand on her shoulder, his touch meeting bare skin where her nightgown frayed to nothing from years of wear.

"Mom, please."

In response, she buried her face back against the ground and screamed, hands clasped over her head. Spencer didn't think much of it at first, but then he saw how hard she was pushing into her skull.

"Hey," Spencer said harshly. And she started to flinch, only to glance at him and close her eyes tighter. His eyes widened as blood started to seep between her fingers. "Hey!"

"Go away!" She screamed, her voice lacing with something he had never heard before. Something inhuman. He stumbled to the ground and Mom stood. A tear trickled down as she painfully, meekly whispered, "Please, while you still can."

In a passing moment — blink and you'll miss it — all the color drained from her face. And she stood straight, stiff.

Unnatural.

A smirk plastered itself on her face.

She brandished a knife, its blade's shine hindered only by dried blood.

His blood.

And a laugh rang through the room, harsh and pitchy. Spencer's mom towered over him, blood streaking out from her nose and falling to the floor with every cackle. All Spencer could do was shuffle back, heart pounding as he raised his hand to his face.

"Mom!"

Her pain-filled face twisted, letting out a harsh roar as she managed to slow, but she didn't stop.

 Tears sprang to Spencer's eyes and, as he shuffled further back — further away from her — he kept his hand out and said whatever came to mind.

Anything to get through to the *real* her.

Because she had to still be there. It was the only option.

"I just wanna talk to you!" Spencer screamed. "I miss you. I-I wanna tell you about my friends, like before." He racked his brain for something that his mom used to ask him about on their walks. "M-Mark! From my chemistry class, remember? *He* was the one who stole from the—"

It went in one ear and out the other. Spencer started to get up off the ground, shaky arms barely managing to hold his weight as he pushed up.

She pushed him back down.

Spencer's heart raced in his chest. And when he tried to stand again, and Mom sent him toppling like nothing, he stammered, "Don-Donovan's still being Donovan. Remember how you used to ask about him?"

Nothing.

He shuffled back more.

"I tripped while walking across the stage in undergrad! What do you think about that?"

But she advanced faster than Spencer could move. His vision reduced to nothing more than the blurred mess of his mom and the blood that laced her knife. He shuffled back.

And he hit the wall.

Spencer slammed his eyes closed. "Mom, please!"

Mom raised the knife in the air.

"Kaylee!" Spencer shouted.

Time slowed. That's all it could be. The two of them were still, his mom poised like she was a statue presenting her knife to the masses. And the look of hatred and grief and agony etched on her face, frozen there for all time. Then, before Spencer's eyes, it started to melt away.

Maybe she managed to smi...

Reckless optimism.

But Spencer let himself take a breath. "She misses you," Spencer said softly. And when the blurred mass in front of him started to lower her knife, he shakily told her, "We *all* miss you. I've been trying, I-I really have. But I was drowning, still am, and she needs you." Mom gripped her head again, and he forced out, "For her, Ma, please."

Time didn't slow — it pressed faster than ever before.

"Come back," Spencer tearfully whispered.

But Mom pulled the knife out and swiped at him, the blade cutting across his chest. Spencer yelped and put his hands over it, blood gushing between his fingers.

He stood up stiffly, every motion a fight. But she was graceful and light as a feather. They stood toe-to-toe, tears streaming out of Mom's eyes as she plastered on the most unnatural smile Spencer had ever seen.

And for once, he couldn't bring himself to say anything.

This was it.

Mom drew the blade to Spencer again, the rush of air grazing his abdomen as he jumped back. He stepped to the side.

A swift swipe from the blade caught Spencer's arm.

She moved in a frenzy, motions wild as she swung the knife. Spencer's face, hands, *everything* stung. Blood trickled towards his eyes, and all he could think was to scream.

He slammed his arm down when he saw her move forward again.

And she stopped.

He looked down at her arm, caught between his hand and waist. And when he looked at her, the way she stared back at him with nothing but hate…

"This isn't you."

Spencer tried to yank the knife away from her. The motion was met with a jolt from Mom, but he pulled harder, and pressure went against his foot.

He didn't know what happened.

Mom fell.

And she landed on the blade.

The thud to the ground was deafening. Spencer collapsed to his knees, the warmth of her blood coating his pants. And he leaned towards her, hands shaking as he laid eyes on the vision he was tormented by.

He thought it had come true years ago. He thought…

Spencer's lip quivered, and he forced out, "M-Ma?"

He took her in his arms, her head loosely following his every move. Spencer pressed against her chest where the knife had lodged, and she painfully drew away.

Blood painted the walls. Tears dripped down his face.

And a maroon-painted speckle trailed down her lips, spider-webbing towards the floor.

He'd have given anything to never see this again, the portrait that flooded his eyes. It was impossible to breathe as he tried to wake himself from this nightmare, stop himself from reliving what he had watched over and over and over.

He wasn't fast enough.

His voice cracked, "It-it's okay! It—"

But the words he was searching for were never found.

Spencer's mom laid there in his arms, breaths shallow as she rested her hand on his cheek. And when he leaned into it, his tears trickled on her face. They blotted the design, washing the streaks of blood. He watched in silence as the blackness in her eyes went away, the grip on her chest visibly melting.

The hazel in her eyes was always beautiful.

Spencer shakily smiled and whispered, "Hi, Mom."

She looked up at him silently, and past the pain, he could recognize her expression. The look she gave him was one much like when they'd go on their walks and Spencer would spout out the most trivial of things he could ever imagine. And she'd look at him in a way no one else ever had.

Pride. It was written all over her face, the ink leaving a permanent mark.

She said hoarsely, "I'm so sorry."

Spencer's lips curled, and all he could do was silently shake his head at her, with the river continuing to flood his face. It wasn't her fault.

He pushed down on the wound — maybe he could get her to a hospital in time.

Maybe he wasn't too late.

"Don't," Mom said softly. She meekly tried to move away, the pain against her chest taking over. And through her teeth she said, "It's okay."

But it wasn't, Spencer didn't understand. He was supposed to figure this one out. He was supposed to come home and talk her out of it, then slowly, everyone would start to understand. Kaylee wouldn't take too long, he knew it. Maybe Mom could even watch the graduation in a few hours. Then she should be there to send Kaylee off to college, and she and Spencer could call her every single day and finally see the mom that she always knew she could be.

"There's so much I wanted to tell you," Spencer's shaky voice managed to crack out.

A small smile formed on her lips. It was weak but gentle, a tame version of the beaming grin that used to plaster itself on her face. But it was there. And it was enough.

"Then tell me."

Spencer let out a silent sob and rested his head against hers. One more time, that's what he was getting.

The chance he had begged for every single day.

An excruciating thought rattled through to his core, momentarily stifling everything that he had wanted to say for six years.

He'd always want one more time.

But he had to make do with this.

Spencer picked his head up and looked at her, blinking his tears away. For a moment, he could imagine the two of them outside, carefree as he told her everything.

If he could take back just one time that he said no to those stupid little talks…

The nighttime song rang in his ear, its melody somber and faint. He tightened his grip, her stare affixed to him. "I made it into med school. Top-choice, which surprisingly enough, I didn't change my mind on fifty-seven times." Spencer weakly smiled when his mom chuckled, then she winced behind it. "I know, it was a shock to everyone."

When he tried hard enough, he could imagine the numerous sly remarks Mom would've made at *that* one.

"Kaylee's doing great," Spencer whispered. "Like you said, she made valedictorian. She's starting nursing school in August, and Ma, she's so happy. You'd be so proud of her." She was, even if she couldn't say. "Donovan's still kicking my butt, he hasn't changed too much."

A trail of blood escaped her lips, and before he realized it, a hoarse sob emitted from his.

"Kirsten and I made it," Spencer softly whispered, electing not to tell her about the hospital. They were happy, and that's all Mom needed to know. "Like you said, I just needed to tell her. And I did, and it…"

He shook his head and blinked, trying but failing to make the blurred lines in his vision fade away.

"You were right. Like always, you were right."

Her breathing started to slow, and her hand loosened from his. But she kept her eyes trained on him.

"I'm not gonna mess it up this time, Ma. I promise you."

The color drained her face, leaving her hazel green eyes the only sign of life. They slowly moved around his face, taking in everything as if it was the first time she ever saw him. Sounds escaped her, ones Spencer would have given anything to drown out.

Then, despite how weak she was — despite the pain in her face through every motion — she managed to raise her shaky hand up and run it along his cut-up face. He flinched against the touch, but her hand settled there and Spencer felt the pain dissipate to nothing.

Mom's brow furrowed. And her words were soft, only enough for the two of them to ever know.

"You're hurt."

Spencer softly cuffed his hand over hers. "I'll be okay. You taught me how."

Neither of them spoke as they looked into each other's eyes. Her chest rose and fell, each breath shallow — the agonizing time between made him think she was gone. And one more thing would pop into Spencer's head, he'd think to say it but he'd fail to find the words.

Her chest went down.

And he wanted to tell her he loved her. One more time, even if he had said it so often that the words started to feel like background noise. He kept his eyes on her face, waiting for her to take in one last shallow breath so he could go on to tell her about how—

Her chest didn't come back up again.

But it had to.

He ran his bloodied hands through her hair, shaking as he desperately searched her for something. His mom was reduced to a blurred mess of nothing as the tears pooled back in, refusing to go away no matter how hard he blinked. "Wake up," he cried, the efforts agonizingly and knowingly futile.

But he couldn't help it.

"Wake up!"

All he got in response were the red streams that continued down her face, the maroon blobs serving as the only color against her pale skin. He shook her shoulders, deafening roars emitting from his chest.

He was supposed to fix this.

The nighttime melody roared in his ears, its somber beat taunting him. And he thought about everything he would say to her, how many times he had agonized for this one last time.

Spencer whispered everything, words he couldn't begin to process. How he loved her, how Shelby from history class *did* have a crush on Donovan, that Mom was right — she was always right.

It was over. Spencer couldn't process it; he could only scream, clutching her in his arms. Tears soaked his cheeks, and he thud his head against hers again, watching everything rain down on her.

But she took it, like she always did.

That thought rattled between his ears as his cries carried through, drowning out the melody's finale.

He tearfully whispered, "I love you."

One last time.

Chapter Thirty-Two

Reap

The atmosphere in Spencer's car felt empty. Bare, much like the passenger seat that he kept stealing glances towards.

He'd tell himself he'd stop, but then another moment of weakness would happen, and that'd be that. It was painful how empty the place was — Nikki had just been there. And, even worse, the most optimistic depths of Spencer's brain had truly convinced him that Mom would be there, talking about whatever as he played music they used to love.

But it was silent as he drove to Brett's house, where Kaylee was. He was on his street, but all Spencer could think of was the weight on his chest, how he'd manage to watch her graduation with a smile plastered on his face.

Cops were there. Parked in Brett's driveway.

"No," Spencer weakly cried as he yanked his seatbelt off. He fumbled out, wobbly legs nearly sending him tumbling to the ground. He threw the door closed, not sure if it shut.

The house felt like it was miles away, but he ran to it, still shouting something he couldn't process. Years passed him by, and finally, he made it up the steps.

He raced through the front door. And he screamed at the top of his lungs, "Kaylee!"

There she stood, in the entryway.

Whatever she was frantically talking about came to a halt, and she looked over at him with mascara running down her face. The cops she was talking to silenced, a look of relief washing over their faces.

"Spence!" Kaylee screamed, throwing her arms around him and nearly sending him to the ground. "Oh my gosh, are you okay? After Kirsten, I thought you ran off somewhere. Then Donovan went to see Dad and said you were doing something dumb, and he and Dad went out to look for you, but they couldn't find you anywhere."

"I'm okay," Spencer replied, hugging her shaking body tightly. "You're right, I'm sorry. I shouldn't have left."

"Dad and Donovan thought you went out and got yourself killed." She sniffled. "*I* thought..."

Spencer sighed and buried his chin in the crook of her neck. The cops said something, though Spencer didn't process it too well. Something about how they could call off the missing person's search, but he couldn't leave town in case they had questions. He hadn't called the cops to report what happened to Mom yet, and that was an investigation that he knew he'd have to talk his way through.

In the moment, though, they left Spencer and Kaylee to the shared space between them. It was a comfort that made the two of them break down and unleash anything that they had pent up. Things were muttered; sentences were formed. But everything was a mess of blissful incoherence as they hugged each other so tightly they both struggled to breathe.

"What the hell happened to you?" Kaylee asked, frantically gesturing towards his body, her hand going up and down before wrapping around him again. "You're bleeding — like — everywhere."

Words came to Spencer's mouth, but they dissolved in a heartbeat.

Instead, he simply shook his head. "It's over."

But there, in his baby sister's arms, at least he knew that for one person, he didn't have to be too late. When it mattered the most, there she was.

Spencer drew back and took a shaky breath. "How long until you've gotta be at the school?"

"Four hours," Kaylee said, hesitation lacing her voice. "But if you can't make it, I understand."

"No, it's…" Spencer trailed off, swearing he was seconds away from fainting. But for just a few more moments, he would wear a strong face. For a few more moments, he'd look okay. Then he could figure the rest out later. "I need to shower and sleep a few hours first, okay?"

Kaylee nodded and guided Spencer towards a guest room, one he had seen only once before. Everything was

beige and basic — which, frankly, Spencer appreciated.
Let his mind quiet down, even if for a moment.

"I'll go and get your stuff," she whispered to him.
"Shower, do whatever you need. And damnit Spencer, go
to bed. You look like actual and total crap."

He lightly chuckled and rubbed his eyes.
"Understatement of the year."

"Thank you for everything. I got your voicemail, and I
guess it just really put into perspective how much you've
done. And I thought you might be gone, then…"

But she didn't need to thank him, he hoped she knew
that. It was one of the best things he'd ever done in his
life and one of the few choices he'd never change, even if
he got a do-over. She was there; she was okay.

"Always."

"Wow," Spencer whispered to himself. "Some things
never change."

He was seated amidst a sea of people in fold-up metal
chairs. In the center of the football field, a makeshift
stage was set overtop his view of the graduating class.
Kaylee had three chairs set up near each other — for him,
Brett, and Dad.

Spencer sat in the middle seat, twiddling his thumbs. Of
those three spots, he had never expected only one to be
filled. He had tried to call Dad, but the man never

answered. Then Donovan's phone went straight to voicemail.

Stop worrying, he told himself. For one day, he needed to focus on this. He couldn't make out Kaylee, but he knew she was there. He hadn't decided what he'd tell her, or even if he'd tell her anything.

Kaylee thought Mom was already dead.

What Donovan said echoed in his mind, a sea of truths that Spencer tried and failed to deny. Would it really do anything to tell her this?

But the lies...

He sighed, resigning himself to the simple truth that he'd end up telling her. He'd do it sometime soon, just not yet; this was her day.

Principal Schneider walked up the stage, the sun mirroring off his bald head. He turned and faced the crowd, the same old smile plastered on his face. The same dark-colored suit with a tie that didn't match, the smirk, and the speech was hilariously familiar from the get-go.

Spencer didn't listen much, idly mouthing along as the man referred to the graduating class as the 'most intellectually gifted group of students he had the pleasure of leading.'

Just like Spencer's class, and the one before that. And before that, and before that, and...

There was a buzz in Spencer's back pocket, where his phone was. He turned the ringer off through the fabric.

He *did* zone out for the remainder of Principal Schneider's speech, though, the cookie-cutter ramble serving as background noise. For a moment, he ran through everything in his head, what happened. He didn't know why, maybe he was trying to get his story straight. But just the same, he heard it in the voice.

Fix this

Help her

Come home

I'm sorry

"And now," Principal Schneider bellowed, snapping Spencer out of his thoughts. "Please welcome your Valedictorian, Miss Kaylee Levign!"

And with that, she stood. The crowd erupted with applause, cheers from her friends and her classmates and anyone in between. Spencer found himself clapping so hard his hands hurt, whistling and bouncing in his chair like an idiot.

He cupped his hands over his mouth. "Go Kaylee!"

She got to the stage and dramatically rolled her eyes, unable to hide her chuckles. "Yeah, yeah, that's my dork of a brother."

The people around him chuckled and Spencer sat back down, giving her a thumbs up in the process.

Kaylee's eyes darted between the bleachers and the chairs before resting on Spencer. Then, she smiled. "Most of us really don't have any clue what we're doing. Yeah, there are a select few who already have their lives figured out, but c'mon now, most of us are currently clueless and scared shitless. Am I right?"

Kaylee held her arms out knowingly, and her graduating class laughed along. As did Spencer.

"I, for one, grew up saying I wanted to be an engineer, a teacher, an astronaut, *and* a ballerina. I didn't go through a cowgirl phase though; I was never that cool." The audience clapped again, one person shouting something at her. It must have been an inside joke because Kaylee pointed towards the person and said, "See! You get it!"

Man, she was killing it. She was making him grin so hard his face was cramping.

"Now I'm set to start nursing school, which wasn't even on the list of the seventy-something dream jobs I rotated between when I was a kid." Her face hardened, and she said seriously, "My point is, most of us aren't running off into the sunset towards an absolutely perfect version of what we dreamed of as kids."

Her similarity to their dad was more visible than ever — her crooked smile, the way her dark hair curled. The sun shone off the ridgeback pin that Spencer had given her once upon a time.

"Sooner or later, we'll understand that we can't know how our lives are going to go." She glanced at Spencer. "I know this hasn't played out as I hoped."

Spencer pursed his lips. Her graduation was different than he had hoped, too. At one point, he was so sure she would have the perfect ending to her senior year: he and Brett would be playfully bickering, Dad's lips swelled to a smile as he recorded the ceremony.

But Brett was gone. Dad wasn't answering his calls.

"But this has taught me something." Kaylee smiled at Spencer. "I already have everything I need."

With her same smile, crooked as Dad's and huge as Mom's. The spitting image of both their parents shined towards him, giving way to hope that Spencer could once more hold onto. And he had her to thank — her and her relentless optimism – her gift to see the good in everything.

That is what she got from Spencer.

She shook her head, drawing her attention back to the crowd. "The point is that we don't know where we're going. And we sure as hell do not have any idea what we're doing. But it had been such an honor to have started to figure it out with all of you."

Something about the gleam in her eyes reminded Spencer of Kaylee's friends outside of him and Brett. And he thought about the people she'd meet soon, the places she'd go.

Kaylee would be alright. They both would.

"I am so glad to have gotten the opportunity to meet you."

It took everything in Spencer to not rush the stage right there and give her the biggest bear hug ever.

"Congratulations to you all. I wish you the best of luck."

And with that, she gave the audience one last wave before backing away from the mic. The audience erupted in applause even louder than before. But Spencer was the loudest, getting up out of his seat and jumping up and down. Kaylee blew him a kiss, and he blew one back.

It kept going until Principal Schneider came back up. By the look on Kaylee's face, Spencer could tell that neither of them cared about what the man had to say.

Spencer thought about when he was younger, when he was a little six-year-old who begged his parents for a baby brother or sister. The stories were told countless times. The handwritten letters were kept, the videos saved.

Through The Incident and the ghosts, Kaylee had been Spencer's constant. For so long he had feared he couldn't be enough for her, and maybe a small part of him thought that maybe she'd leave too.

But, clear as day, both those visions — things that he once would have considered prophecies — went unmet.

Kaylee's gaze shifted to him. And it filled Spencer with all the hope and optimism that he could ever need. She mouthed, "I love you."

And in an instant, it was all worth it.

Chapter Thirty-Three

In The End

The ceremony went even better than expected. Principal Schneider's closing speech certainly dragged on, but Spencer and Kaylee made faces at each other long enough to be entertained.

Then, through the ensuing celebration, the weight of the world and all its problems dissipated. For just a bit, Mom wasn't gone. Dad and Donovan weren't out doing, well, whatever they were doing. And Brett was alive, Kirsten wasn't hanging on by a thread.

Everything was blissfully hidden away for a while.

Now, Spencer sat on the bleachers, entranced by the sun's orange hues that cascaded onto the field. Kaylee was off with her friends, leaving him alone with his thoughts. And for the first time in so long, his mind wasn't flooded with visions, equally void of voicemails and ghosts and doubts that he could possibly make things right.

Optimism, hope. It eclipsed everything once again.

Kirsten would love that. Mom, too.

The whisper of the summer breeze captivated him, just like the feeling that this time, his mom really was watching. And thoughts raced to his mind, memories of all the nighttime walks he had spent talking to her. He remembered everything he thought he had told her, and how she never was there at all.

All the chapters of his life that he thought she was aware of: the trivial ones like his classmates' going away present for a retired professor, all the way down to the secrets he had tried to bury. How he wasn't sure if he could be enough for Kaylee, how he missed Kirsten more than words could ever say.

All those truths were told, only to dead air.

Spencer stood, and he did the only thing he could think to do. He started walking.

He made his way along the track, the one that circled around the football field with its rough concrete and faded white lines. Like in school, he stuck to the outside lane. He looked straight ahead and let his muscle memory guide him, knowing he wouldn't falter outside the lines.

All the while, the truths came flooding back. There were things he wished he had told Mom as she laid there in the living room, bringing to life the vision that he had tried to run from. But more than anything, he wished he had assured her that there was no animosity between them. Maybe she realized, maybe she didn't, but he should have told her that he knew she didn't mean it.

He wished he had said that no matter what, it wasn't her fault. And that she was the strongest person he ever knew.

Spencer could only hope that when he lost her, she knew she meant everything to him.

All he knew was that he did.

In response, the cool breeze returned. He closed his eyes, and the loudest truth of all surfaced. He whispered back to it, only for himself and his mom to hear.

"You knew."

He looked towards the center of the football field where Kaylee stood, laughing with a group of friends. She saw him and gave a questioning look, and it screamed 'is everything alright?' He simply smiled in response, sparing her a gentle wave. Kaylee returned it and went back to her conversation.

At the end of that lap, Spencer heard a sound to his right.

And when he looked over, of everything he could see, Donovan was there. He was in the parking lot, separated from Spencer only by a fence and the field.

His mind went to when his phone went off during the ceremony, and he wondered if that's what this was about. But before he could dwell on it, Donovan spotted him and broke into a sprint.

"What the?" Spencer started as he hurried to his friend. They met halfway before Donovan resorted to hopping the fence. "What-Where have you been? I thought you—"

Face red, Donovan doubled over. "Your-your dad and I were looking for you. Then I found out you were okay. The hospital. I went, and I've-I've gotta tell you—" A gasping breath, then he cracked out, "Ari—"

"What? What do you need to tell her?"

"No! I—" He swallowed, Spencer could hear it from where he stood. He looked like it was his first time ever taking a breath. "She told me that..."

Spencer's heart felt like it would explode out of his chest, thinking about the problems that could be happening. Was The Mangled Man out in the parking lot, watching — always watching? Had it not worked?

"Kirsten's awake!"

Spencer's eyes widened.

The words flew right past him.

But the weight of the world dissipated once again, displaced by something else. A feeling so intense and uncharted that he could never describe. Words sprang to Spencer's lips faster than the tears to his eyes, but none surfaced.

None that made any difference.

"Wh-what?" was all he managed.

His friend was crying. And Spencer found himself crying, too; the tickle that ran down his face was enough to tell him.

"Ari was by Kirsten's side, talking to her and holding her hand. Kirsten tightened her grip and opened her eyes, man!" Donovan's face lit up brighter than Spencer had ever seen. "She's awake!"

Why couldn't Spencer move?

Donovan looked like the smile would never leave his face. "Gimme your phone."

"But–"

"Spence, phone."

He felt outside of his own body, but he still grabbed it from his pocket. Donovan took it and didn't need to ask for the password. He scrolled, not taking long to find whatever he was looking for.

Which, Spencer knew what it was. But he couldn't make sense of it.

"Call her," Donovan whispered, the softness not matching how intense his face was.

But he shouldn't be able to call her. "I..."

A tear trickled down his friend's face. He hurriedly wiped it away and held the phone out. "Take it. She's waiting for you."

He shouldn't be able to call her.

"But–"

"She forgives you."

And like that, the puzzle became whole again.

Spencer let out a long gasp of air, spewing open the floodgates. He doubled over and Donovan caught him before he could hit the ground. Spencer placed his hands on his knees, tears pooling out faster than he could blink them away. Kirsten was awake. The grass was clear but swirled in his vision, just like Donovan's hand clasped in his. Kirsten was awake. She was in a hospital room somewhere, lying there, scared because — Kirsten was awake? — she hated medical stuff. Donovan was holding something that would let him hear her voice again, and he'd be able to spend the rest of his life talking to her.

He thought he couldn't, but he could, and she forgave him, even though she shouldn't even have the *chance* to—

Kirsten was awake. Kirsten was awake. *Kirsten was awake.*

The phone was gently placed in Spencer's line of vision, and everything else seemed to vanish. He took it, his hands so shaky that the screen rattled. It was heavy, and it was cold, but Spencer looked up at Donovan. And the tear-filled smile was clearer than anything Spencer had ever seen.

"Kirsten's awake?"

His friend started to nod, but before he could finish, Spencer threw his arms over him.

"Thank you," he whispered between his tears. He tightened his grip on his friend, so much that Donovan grunted. Spencer's voice cracked, "Thank you so much."

His friend returned the embrace, his shaky breaths laced with tears that he tried but failed to hide.

Donovan broke the hug first, and he took a deep breath through his nose. Clear as day, the stress melted off his body. "I'll give you a minute."

And then he left, hands in his pockets as he trod away from Spencer. He made his way to Kaylee, who looked up at him and gave a hug of her own. They talked like two people whose world hadn't gotten turned upside down.

The phone's presence was felt again, only this time, Spencer felt strong enough to look at it. Kirsten's contact was pulled up, ready and waiting for Spencer to make the call that at one point, he feared he'd never be able to make again.

He didn't overthink his words, the things he'd say or the tone he'd use when he said them.

Instead, pressed 'call' and held the phone to his ear, eyes trained ahead as he made his way back to the trail. The motion still felt unnatural, and his two feet could barely manage to hold him up. But he kept moving.

Tears sprang to his eyes when the ringing stopped.

"Spence."

Words eluded him. The ability to stand nearly eluded him.

Because her voice was chiming in his ear, which of course, Spencer had imagined more times than he could count. But its tune was shaky, too. Raspy, weak.

Real.

Was she awake?

"K-Kirs?" was all he could manage.

All he wanted to do was run to her. To hold her in his arms again and tell her that no matter what it took, if she'd have him, he was so ready to spend the rest of his life with her.

'She forgives you.'

Donovan's words rang clear, and deep down, Spencer knew them to be true. He was pretty sure he heard Kirsten echo them, but everything was such a blur that he didn't know for certain.

"Are you okay?" He asked her. "Do me a favor and look at the monitor next to you. What are your stats? Are you still on oxygen? Did they say anything about—"

"Spence," she said firmly. But there was no anger anywhere. "I'm okay."

Kirsten *was* awake.

It was as if the phrase was said just enough times for it to make sense. His face scrunched but he didn't cry — he didn't feel he could anymore. "Can I come see you?"

Because somehow, he had the chance to do that again.

"Please do."

The steps he was idly taking became faster, with more purpose. It was as if he was just feet away from her.

And everything flooded over him. The things he wanted to tell her, how maybe he would have enough time to say them after all. He thought about the letter he had written her all those years ago, its torn edges and its cheesy words. Despite its flaws, he wanted so badly to be able to reread it to her.

Which, somehow, he would be able to do.

"Kirs," he whispered, in awe all over again. "I love you."

"I love you, too."

His face lit up. And he could feel his cheeks flush with giddiness that he hadn't felt since he was just an awkward boy flirting with the shy girl from across the room.

That boy rushed to Spencer's mind again, and for the first time in years, there was a longing. He silently thanked that version of himself, who held the wildest imagination but had no idea how to use it. Life would throw so much at him and he would always keep going.

Spencer wished that he could grab that version of himself by the shoulders and scream to the world that no matter what — no matter how far out of the realm of possibilities it once seemed — everything would work out in the end.

Everything would work out in the end.

The words echoed in his ears: a mantra, much like the ones that had almost ripped him apart. His gaze shifted to the setting sun one last time, lulled by the ever-present glow it emitted on the field. And when he spoke, yes, he talked to his mom and to Kirsten.

But more than anything, he talked to the kid, to himself. And he smiled.

"We did it."